Praise for The Stories We Cannot Tell

"Leslie Rasmussen deftly delves into the heartbreaking world of difficult pregnancies and the tough decisions that need to be made along the way. I can only assume by the heart with which she writes this story, that she has some experience with it. The Stories We Cannot Tell will keep you turning pages just to see if it all works out."—Laurie Gelman, bestselling author of the *Class Mom Series*

"Keenly observed and brimming with empathy for characters who you can't help but root for, The Stories We Cannot Tell explores the complexities of motherhood as well as our ability to choose who to call our family. Leslie Rasmussen brings a fresh and welcome perspective to women's fiction."— Camille Pagán, bestselling author of *Everything Must Go.*

"The Stories We Cannot Tell by Leslie Rasmussen is brilliant, timely. Astonishing. Caught in the middle of a whirlwind of work —her words inspired me, lifted me, awakened me—yes, breathed life into me. She is a writer to be reckoned with. To be taken mighty seriously. She's funny & poignant. A lethal combination. Given the world we're living in, this book is a MUST read. Buy it, share it . . . gift it. Re-read it. I will—buy it, gift it, share it. Re-read it. Brava, Leslie. Brava!"—Amy Ferris, screenwriter, and author of *Marrying George Clooney: Confessions from a Midlife Crisis*

"An incisive look into women's feelings about womanhood, motherhood, relationships and friendship, THE STORIES WE CANNOT TELL is a fast paced, beautifully written tribute to what we can and can't control and who we love in the process. A true delight. This book is GOOD!"—Zibby Owens, author of *Bookends: A Memoir of Love, Loss, and Literature,* and host of *Moms Don't Have Time to Read Books*

"What truly completes a life? Two very different women navigate pregnancy, parenting, love—and the powerful secrets that derail us. Rasmussen proves that the stories we cannot tell are really the ones that we should, and here she does it with aching grace."—Caroline Leavitt, New York Times bestselling author of *With or Without You*

"Leslie Rasmussen's debut, The Stories We Cannot Tell, is a moving tale of family, friendship, and our toughest choices. When Rachel and Katie bond over life-altering decisions, their connection binds them in more ways than one. A timely, emotional read that is sure to touch readers hearts."—Rochelle B. Weinstein, bestselling author of *When We Let Go*

"Rasmussen's talent for scriptwriting shines through in her heartfelt novels. Few authors can effortlessly and expertly tie in heavy subject matter with laugh-out-loud dialogue. Stories We Cannot Tell is a soulful and unexpected journey that will have you smiling through tears by story's end."—Suzanne Simonetti, USA Today bestselling author of *The Sound of Wings*

"Leslie Rasmussen's sophomore novel is not to be missed! It hits home with perfect timing! The Stories We Cannot Tell opens up about stories that needed to be told in a novel that needed to be written. Leslie writes characters that are riveting, compassionate and sincerely likable. I was so moved by the tenderness, honesty and grace shared by each character as their story unfolded."—Annie McDonnell of The Write Review and the author of *Annie's Song*

"Life is the unfolding of many of our dreams, desires, and plans. In Leslie Rasmussen's novel, The Stories We Cannot Tell, she expertly examines what happens when those dreams don't go as planned in a world that makes things more difficult for a woman to make the best choices for herself. Leslie puts a human face to those heart-wrenching decisions that no one ever wishes to make. And in the end, the author invites us to embrace compassion for those stories many are ashamed to tell but shouldn't be. A must-read, especially now."—Meg Nocero, Award-winning author of *The Magical Guide to Bliss, Sparkle & Shine* and *Butterfly Awakens: A Memoir of Transformation Through Grief*

"A powerful story of two women making impossible decisions told with heart and humor. The story moves quickly, and the dialogue is crisp. Leslie Rasmussen is a skilled storyteller and the characters in her second novel "Stories We Cannot Tell" are complex and very relatable."—Mary Camarillo, Award-winning author of *The Lockhart Women*

The
Stories
We
Cannot
Tell

A Novel

Leslie A. Rasmussen

Relax. Read. Repeat.

THE STORIES WE CANNOT TELL
By Leslie A. Rasmussen
Published by TouchPoint Press
Brookland, AR 72417
www.touchpointpress.com

Softcover ISBN: 978-1-956851-60-1

Editor: Gina Denny
Cover Design: David Ter-Avanesyan, Ter33Design
Cover Image: Shutterstock

Connect with the author: www.lesliearasmussen.com

First Edition

Library of Congress Control Number: 2023933349

Printed in the United States of America.

To Bruce, you have been my partner through ups and downs, and I wouldn't have it any other way. We complement each other like coconut and dark chocolate, I love you.

And to all the women who went through the painful decision of ending a pregnancy when it was the last thing you wanted to do. I honor you and the choice you made under the worst possible circumstances. This book is for you.

"What we once enjoyed and deeply loved we can never lose, for all that we love deeply becomes part of us."

—Helen Keller

Chapter One
Rachel

It had been an exceptionally warm February in Los Angeles, but for the last four hours, rain had been drumming on the windows of Rachel's classroom, leaving her no choice but to keep her kindergarten students inside for both recess and lunch. The caged-in five-year-olds were bouncing off the walls like tennis balls from a high-speed launcher someone forgot to turn off.

Rachel worked in an upscale private school, the kind of place where kids would bring sushi for lunch instead of a turkey sandwich. She loved her students, except when they forgot to take their lunchbox home on Fridays.

Only two more pick-ups to go before all the kids are gone and my weekend begins, Rachel thought as she erased the chalkboard and put books back on the bookshelf. She was in a hurry to get home today, knowing what was waiting for her there.

Thirty minutes after the last child was gone, Rachel sat cross-legged on her bathroom floor, holding a small box in her hand. A box with pink and blue and pluses and minuses on it. A box containing something that would decide if she was having a good day or another bad one.

She ripped the cardboard from the middle and pried the stick out. Rachel hated peeing on that thing. Would the stream hit it exactly right? Would she accidentally drop it in the toilet and have to start over?

Every month, that hateful little stick monster would betray her and Brett. Months ago, she stopped feeling a rush of butterflies when her period was late. Like a cruel joke, she'd run out to buy a test, only to get her period the next day. And it didn't help that her cycle was irregular. Some months it was twenty-nine days, some months thirty-two, and some months thirty-six.

Why couldn't she be twenty-eight days like the rest of her friends? The friends who had children already. At this rate, they would have an empty nest before her womb was full.

She pulled down her black pants and her shocking pink panties and sat on the toilet. She held the stick between her legs and felt a rush of warmth. She waited until she was sure nothing else would come out; never knowing if the last drop would be the drop that would tell the stick she was pregnant.

Rachel pulled her clothes back on and put the test on the counter and set a timer for three minutes. She turned her back. She wondered if a watched stick would come up pregnant. She wanted to be pregnant so badly, it was all she could think about for what seemed like forever. She couldn't wait to watch Brett hold his child; she knew that even when they were dating, he'd be a wonderful father. The two of them finally creating the family they've been dreaming about. Please let this test come out positive!

Rachel stopped herself from turning around while the stick was hatching results. She used to use these three minutes to pray to God to help her get pregnant, but she stopped when it didn't work. As a kid, her prayers for a Barbie Dreamhouse (or later, for Steven Parker to ask her out) never materialized either. She decided to try prayer again because now she wondered if God thought she stopped believing. Rachel began speaking Hebrew, or at least the little bit she remembered from her Bat Mitzvah.

She stopped mid-sentence.

What if I'm mispronouncing the words and God doesn't understand me? she thought. What if I've been praying for no baby instead of a baby? Rachel didn't want to make things worse, although she wasn't sure that was possible.

The timer dinged and Rachel caught her breath. She slowly turned, but instead of walking over to the counter, she stayed where she was and squinted. She couldn't see if the test had two lines.

Her legs trembled and wouldn't move. It was as if her heels had grown roots that went through the floor.

This is ridiculous, she thought as she picked her feet up and with both eyes wide open walked over to the stick.

The test had only one prominent line. Rachel crumpled to the floor, the tears that came were as fresh as the ones that flowed each month before.

In the last few years, Rachel had suffered three miscarriages. At least before each pregnancy ended, she had a couple weeks of hope and happiness. When did thirty become too late to start a family?

Was she wrong to want to spend a few years alone with Brett as a couple? *Did I do things in my youth that I'm paying for now?*

How was she to have known it would be this hard to get pregnant? Especially since her mother had told her she'd gotten pregnant with Rachel without even trying.

Rachel had always wanted at least two children, so her kid would have a sibling, so they'd never be as lonely as she was. She was close to her parents, but she wished she had a sister to confide in. A sister who would've kept her company when her parents went out of town. A sister who would've snuck her dessert when she didn't finish her cauliflower. A sister who would cry with her when she miscarried another baby.

Rachel couldn't control the negative thoughts. She blamed herself for not being able to have a baby and wondered if Brett might blame her also if he knew everything.

That feeling of failure had followed her everywhere, even to work. Now she was so lost in her grief that she wasn't the same dynamic, cheerful teacher her previous students had. It didn't help that some of the parents were always on her, complaining about something: "Why isn't my son reading yet?" "Why can't you help my daughter make friends?" Couldn't they just be happy they have kids? *I would give anything to have one, even if they were dim-witted and ate their own hair*, Rachel thought. Those parents don't have to live in my shoes with disappointment and sadness every month. They get to bask in those little arms wrapping around them.

One mother even asked if Rachel wanted to babysit on the weekends. When Rachel declined, the woman was stunned. Rachel loved her students, but it would've hurt even more to see them in their cozy homes, playing with the toys she wished she could get her own child, or seeing them smile when they ate their favorite dessert.

She picked her phone up off the floor and sent a one-word text.

Nope. Even though Brett tried to hide it, Rachel hated seeing the disappointment on his face when he came home. They had been going through the same routine for so long, they were both a little numb. Even the hug he gave her every month now felt robotic. The next text she sent was to her mother. Seconds after the text was sent, her phone rang. Her mother wanted to comfort her, but she couldn't talk to anyone at that moment.

Rachel left the bathroom and walked by the only empty room of the house. Now she wondered if she'd painted those walls and bought a crib, would there already be a baby quietly sleeping in it? These were the thoughts that crashed through her head like a cannonball every minute of every day, especially at night when she couldn't sleep.

Rachel went into the kitchen for a glass of water, but after taking a sip she knew she needed something stronger. It wasn't like she was pregnant. She climbed on a stepstool, reached into an upper cabinet, and grabbed Brett's bottle of Johnnie Walker. She filled a glass halfway, gazed at the orangish liquid, then put her nose in and took a whiff.

How could Brett drink this stuff? she wondered. Well, I'm about to find out. She stuck her tongue in the glass and felt a slight burning sensation, then a weird warmth coated her throat. She couldn't decide if she liked it or not, but she was willing to have more to figure it out.

Rachel took one more sip, then put the bottle back on the counter, and rubbed her aching eyes. She knew they were red from crying, which had become their normal state most of the time. She smoothed her hands over her hair which needed to be cut badly. Her wavy amber mane had gotten so full, she looked like a shrub with eyes. And her skin, with its normal peach undertones, was often blotchy and washed out. Even her gray sweatshirt was drab, in fact, everything about her felt drab.

Brett announced himself with the jangling of keys in the door and the stomping of boots on their front doormat. He did that every time he came home, trying to get the dirt and mud from the construction site off before entering their clean house. She wasn't surprised he would find a reason to come home early.

"Hey," he said gingerly.

"Hey." She tried to smile but felt her lips curling down and her teeth not able to make an appearance; she couldn't even convince her face to pretend she was okay.

"I would say I'll try to cheer you up, but I think that's what Johnny Walker is for."

Rachel couldn't help but let out a small laugh, and then she whacked him gently on the butt. "I don't know how you drink this stuff," she said, swallowing hard.

He took the glass from her. "Like this." He took a gulp, then put the glass down and took her in his arms. She stood on her toes and put her head on his chest. After a moment, he lifted her face to his and kissed her lightly on the lips. She looked into his eyes. No matter how sad Rachel was, looking at him still took her breath away. His face, a golden brown from working outside every day, was decorated with a spattering of freckles like a Jackson

Pollock painting. Rachel noticed a few new frown lines that had emerged between his eyebrows. She wondered if she were the cause of them.

"It's going to be okay," he said. She'd stopped believing him a while back. Two years ago when Rachel first didn't get pregnant, Brett would come home with a dozen roses to cheer her up. She knew he was trying so hard, even though he was disappointed also, he wanted to do anything to make her happier.

"We can adopt if things don't work out," he would say, hoping it would comfort her, but the thought of not ever getting to be pregnant made Rachel twitch with anxiety.

"What do you want to do for dinner?" he asked. Rachel shrugged; she couldn't make any decisions about food at that moment. He kissed her and then ordered from her favorite Italian place down the street.

Brett dropped his jacket over the back of a kitchen chair. His navy and white plaid shirt looked just as clean as it did in the morning when he put it on. Those were the perks of being the boss.

When the food arrived, Brett placed Styrofoam containers of Caesar salad, mushroom risotto, and linguine Bolognese on the table. Rachel grabbed plates, napkins, and silverware. Brett dished out a little of everything on each of their plates.

While Rachel ate a small spoonful of mushroom risotto, Brett took a big bite of linguine. "How was your day?" she asked, trying to swallow the creamy, cheesy substance but the lump in her throat made it difficult.

"Good, I booked a big job in Malibu for next month." Brett had been a general contractor for ten years.

Rachel was happy for him, even if her voice didn't express that. Brett grabbed a beer, while Rachel tried to stab one of the croutons in the Caesar salad, but she kept missing. She gave up and picked it up with her fingers.

"How was your day?" he asked, wiping his mouth with a napkin. "You mean besides finding out that my body still hates me?"

"Yes, besides that," he said facetiously. One of the things Rachel appreciated about him was the way he used humor to try to make her feel better, even when it didn't work.

"I think you should leave me and find someone who can give you a baby. What about Martha from the dry cleaner?" Rachel said, mostly jokingly.

"She's in her sixties."

"She likes you. I've seen her sneaking you coupons."

Brett looked into her eyes. "You will never get rid of me; I love you too much," he said with sincerity. "Besides, if things didn't work out with Martha, I'd have to find another dry cleaner."

"Ha, ha."

Brett took her hand. "I know we'll have the family we both want. We're going through a tough time, but I'm not going anywhere." She forced the corners of her mouth up into a half-smile.

Chapter Two
Katie

Katie's legs ached from kneeling on the sturdy hardwood. She wished God provided cushions for the pews. Why did she need to suffer for the Lord to get his point across? She had discovered The Holy Congregational Church when she moved to Los Angeles from Arizona. As soon as she got settled in her apartment, she searched for a church nearby, a church she could feel at home in. When she saw how the sun filtered through the stained glass at Holy Congregational and made the Virgin Mary's hair shine, it reminded her of how safe she felt when she used to go to church with her dad.

Today Father George was giving a sermon about Saint Dymphna. St. Dymphna was canonized in 1247 as the patron saint of mental disorders. *I didn't realize crazy went back that far in history*, she thought.

As the priest continued to read from the gospel, Katie had a flash of sitting in church with her mother when she was ten years old. Her father was gone by then and the sermon that day was about honoring your parents. She remembered trying to listen while looking at her mother who was slumped over in the next seat, her eyes barely open. Katie was wondering if anyone else could smell the booze emanating from her mother's pores until she saw the look of disgust from the elderly woman on the other side of her mother.

Father George gave communion, then recited the prayer of St. Thomas Aquinas. Lastly, he looked up at the whole congregation.

"Peace be with you," he said.

"And with your spirit," the congregation responded.

Men, women, and bored children of every age stood and filed out. The scampering of feet and the chatter of kids begging to go for pancakes echoed throughout the church.

Katie shuffled her feet slowly as she was stuck behind a flock of people waiting to say goodbye to the priest who was standing at the exit. When it was Katie's turn, Father George greeted her.

"Hello, Katie. I'm pleased you come to church on Sundays. Most young people don't make the time." Father George's white hair and beard matched his collar perfectly.

"Thank you, Father."

"Have you given any more thought to joining our women's group? I think you'd find our community very welcoming."

Katie wondered if Father George felt sorry for her. She was always alone, but at thirty-two and unmarried, she didn't think she'd have anything in common with the women in the group who all seemed to have a gaggle of kids.

Katie fidgeted, crossing her legs, then moved her weight from one leg to the other. She probably looked like she had to pee, but the pressure was getting to her. She also had to pee, but that was beside the point.

Father George had never asked about her family, which was good because Katie would've been too ashamed to talk about them. No one in Los Angeles knew the truth, except her best friend, Sandra.

"I'll think about the group," Katie told Father George. "But work's been kind of busy lately."

When a woman in a Laura Ashley dress that seemed to have forgotten to travel forward through time called to Father George, Katie saw her chance to hit daylight. As she was about to cross the threshold, the priest called out to her, "I hope you'll bake something for the church fair."

"Of course," she said. She was never one to turn down a direct request from the clergy. She wouldn't want to disappoint anyone who might know God better than she did. Then she left alone the same way she came in.

When Katie got home, she was too tired to eat. All that praying and kneeling and promising to be a good person had worn her out. She slipped off her shoes without untying them and fell into her beige chenille couch, reaching under her butt to pull out the TV remote. As she watched twenty-five men vying for the Bachelorette's admiration, she wondered if the show's producers would think at thirty-two she was too old to have that many men competing for her.

Her biggest regret was that she'd wasted years waiting for her college boyfriend to propose. On her twenty-eighth birthday, she was sure he was going to finally get on one knee, but instead, he broke up with her. He'd spent the whole day talking about the future and what he wanted out of life. She hadn't realized he was talking only about his future. Note to self: If a man lets you do his laundry but forgets your anniversary, he's not going to marry you.

After the show's final make-out session, Katie was starving. She pulled out leftover rotisserie chicken. When she'd cooked it, she couldn't remember. She stuck her nose in the container and it smelled fine. She stood in front of the refrigerator with the door open, tearing pieces off it like a lion going to town on an antelope. An advantage to being single was there wasn't anyone judging her; the disadvantage was that Katie had no one to cook for.

After devouring one chicken leg, she uncorked a bottle of sauvignon blanc and took a swig right from the bottle. When she pulled the bottle away from her lips, the wine splashed down the front of her shirt. What Bachelor wouldn't find a hot-chicken-stuffing wino sexy. Katie yanked the shirt over her head, carried it to her room, and threw it in the hamper. She picked up the pajamas that were still on the floor.

As she slipped on her nightshirt with Keith Urban's face on the front, she looked down at herself, wondering what men thought when they saw her. She tried to be objective, but how many people were when it came to themselves?

She was blessed with hazel eyes which could look light brown or shades of green or blue, depending on what she was wearing. Her blonde hair was thick and straight. She was not tall, not short, and slim, but in Los Angeles, there were thousands of women who looked just like her. Katie was not going to give in to getting plastic surgery, even if someday she could afford it. Although, she thought it was funny how men in Los Angeles thought women were pretty when they were less expressive than a mannequin.

When Katie was in her twenties, she was sure by now she would've been married with three kids, but finding a guy who would stick around had not been easy. A psychologist might say that she was attracted to men like her father, but Katie thought she was just a bad luck magnet.

The men she usually fell for were not the healthiest or the nicest. They'd take her to happy hour, order four drinks, then leave her with the bill. Or they'd try to sleep with her after she met them the first time for coffee. No amount of espresso would make that happen. One guy even greeted her with a full-on tongue kiss the first time they met. She didn't require much, but she wanted to get to know the guy before he started licking the inside of her mouth.

The last guy she'd agreed to go out with wanted to do something different. Katie suggested they go axe-throwing.

He thought it was a great idea, but after bragging on the phone for the fifth time that he was going to whip her ass, she canceled, worried that she'd "accidentally" cut parts of him off.

"Katie, you're so beautiful and smart and funny," exclaimed the older women at the fertility clinic where she worked as a medical assistant. They couldn't believe she didn't have men falling all over her. At the same time, they'd claim she was lucky because she didn't have to dote on a husband who lost his phone three times a day or cut her only night out short to pull one of her earrings out of her kid's nose. Whenever they made those comments, Katie would shake her head and think, *Don't you know how lucky you are? You have people who love you and keep you company at night, and I go to bed with a book and a piece of dark chocolate.*

When Katie hadn't been on a date in six months, her best friend Sandra convinced her to set up a profile on a new dating app. The other apps Katie had tried were filled with weirdos, so she jumped on this one, hoping the nutcases hadn't found it yet.

She and Sandra ran around town taking pictures of Katie in different outfits. One minute Katie was dressed in a shimmering navy dress as if she were going to a New Year's Eve Party, the next she was in denim shorts and a canary yellow tank top sitting at the beach. That day was more fun than Katie thought she would have on any of the dates.

Katie had been on the app for a month, but the only messages she'd received were from men who thought her name must've been Ms. Sexy, Ms. Hot, or Ms. I Hope You Have Nice Boobs. How men couldn't understand what a turn-off that was, she didn't understand. Would they be offended if she texted back, *I hope your penis is big*!

One night, Katie found her favorite movie, Pretty Woman, on TV. Now *that* was a love story. She would've gone out with Richard Gere in a second if he weren't married and in his seventies. As the opening credits started, Katie opened her laptop and found she had new messages from men on the dating app.

This should be fun, she thought. She cringed as she scrolled through the men who'd messaged her. "Icky, strange, disgusting, not even on my death bed . . . Where is my Richard Gere?"

She was about to give up when one message caught her eye. A man named Adam had written, *Hi, I'm not big on these dating apps, but you caught my attention. I like your pictures.* He was cute in a slightly geeky way. He had a heart-shaped face, a warm smile, and his hair the color of gingerbread was parted on the side and brushed over one eye. That was the cute part. His black, oval-shaped glasses that were too big for his face were the slightly geeky part. In his next picture, he was hiking with friends without his glasses and Katie saw more of the cute guy and less of the geeky one.

"At least he doesn't look like he'd drag me by my hair into his cave," Katie said to her cat, Mr. Morrison. She picked Mr. Morrison up and put him in her lap, clicked on Adam's profile, and read it out loud to the cat. "So, it says he's not looking for a hook-up; he's only interested in women who want a long-term relationship. What do you think? Would you go out with him if you were gay and a person?" Mr. Morrison purred loudly and nuzzled into her arm. "I'll take that as a yes."

Katie wrote back to Adam. *Hi, I like your pictures too. You have a nice smile.* She hoped she wasn't being too forward, then decided she didn't care. She hit the send button then went into the kitchen for a glass of water. When she got back, she tapped her fingers rhythmically on the side of the glass until she got a message back.

Thanks, I hate putting pictures of myself on there, but it didn't seem right to put up pictures of Brad Pitt. Ha.

Katie breathed a sigh of relief that he didn't call her sexy or babe or tell her he was the one to rock her world. A sense of humor was something she always looked for in a man.

Katie wrote back, *I don't like putting pictures of myself up here, either. I had to take so many shots just to find one I liked.*

"I can't believe I just admitted that to him," she said to Mr. Morrison, who was licking parts of himself he could barely reach.

Adam wrote back, *I love that you're so honest. It's one of my favorite qualities in a woman.*

Katie laid down on the couch with a pillow propped up behind her head. Mr. Morrison had finished bathing himself and curled up on her legs, his warmth wrapping around her like a fleece blanket. She had her laptop on her stomach as she typed out, *I saw on your profile that you like old movies. I'm a huge fan of Hepburn and Tracy. "Desk Set" is a great movie.*

They messaged every few minutes after that until he asked if he could call her, and she agreed to give him her number. He called seconds after her message went through.

They talked for what seemed to Katie like a short while but had been two hours; it was now after midnight, and she had to work early the next morning. When she told him she had to get some sleep, he asked if she'd be up for meeting him that Friday night at eight o'clock at the Formosa Café in West Hollywood.

The Formosa Café was an old Hollywood staple that opened in 1939 and was still trendy with the young, chic crowd. Katie had the looks of someone hip but didn't have the money or the attitude. She thought of herself as a small-town girl, but for the right guy, she could pretend to be cool.

When Katie got to work the next day, she found Sandra in the file room. The room was small, yet every wall had shelves filled with women's stories. Each file could break your heart, but there were so many successful pregnancies, that Katie felt grateful to be a small part of bringing these women joy.

"Sandra, can I borrow an outfit?" Sandra's mom had been a fashion designer and Sandra grew up wearing the latest runway styles before they were out in stores.

16

Sandra's eyes lit up: "Ooh! This is my favorite kind of project. What's the occasion?"

"I'm going on a date with a guy I met online."

"That's great! Is he cute?" Sandra pulled out a file from the wall and scanned it.

"Yes, but not so cute that I'd worry women would be falling all over him."

"Sounds perfect. I knew a great guy would find you." Sandra wrote a note in a file, then handed it to Katie to put back as she grabbed another.

"Yeah, well, I'm going to reserve judgment until I'm sure Adam isn't some sixty-year-old guy using his son's pictures." One of the doctors came into the file room, and Katie, not wanting to look like what she was doing, which was not working, asked if she could help him find something. He gave her a name, she handed the file to him, and he left.

"Where's this guy taking you?" Sandra asked.

"Formosa Café." Katie sat on a step stool that was pushed up to the file cabinet. She shouldn't have worn her new boots to work; the day had just started, and her toes were already rubbing against the leather.

"You have to wear my Dolce and Gabbana dress on your date. It would really compliment your figure."

"He's going to think I'm from wealth. What medical assistant can afford a designer dress unless she's like you and has a mother who shows her love with money?" Sandra put her arms out with her palms open and shrugged as if to say she was okay with it. "Besides, I don't know if I can pull that dress off."

"You could pull off a newspaper hat and a jumpsuit made of

Burger King wrappers. When this guy sees you in that dress, he's going to want to whisk you away to a tropical island."

"I'm just hoping for a second date. I'm not you, I don't have men falling all over themselves to go out with me. And I don't know what to say in every situation, the way you do. Plus, look at you – your face looks like a computer program picked out every feature."

Sandra pushed a honey-brown curl out of her eyes and smacked her full lips, which were as pink as strawberry ice cream. The medical practice had gotten bigger and one of the newer doctors came into the file room; Katie startled and jumped up. She and Sandra made eye contact and the two of them hurried back to their desks situated behind the receptionist. Before they got back to work, they made a plan for Katie to come over to Sandra's house that evening.

Katie lived in Burbank, and the fertility clinic was in Beverly Hills, so after work, Katie went directly to Sandra's condo in a high-rise building on Wilshire Blvd in Westwood. The building had a doorman, a gym, and a convenience store. Sandra's mother wouldn't have let Sandra live any place that wasn't up to her standards. Although Sandra didn't have to pay for the condo, she still wanted to work because her mother had rules for her purse strings.

Katie arrived in the lobby with two plastic food containers. The doorman called Sandra to verify Katie wasn't a burglar even though she'd been there many times before. While the doorman was on the phone, Katie casually touched the burgundy wallpaper with gold flecks. The velvety texture was as soft as a rabbit's ear. Finally, the doorman nodded at her, and she stepped into the elevator, which was nicer than her apartment, and possibly bigger.

Sandra had a bottle of chardonnay and two glasses on the kitchen island when Katie arrived. Katie set the salads down on the granite counter and Sandra handed her money for the food, then poured some wine into Katie's glass.

"I love coming here," Katie said, taking the glass from Sandra happily. "Your place is sophisticated and homey all at the same time." It was shabby chic meets Rodeo Drive. Comfortable, yet every item cost more than a compact car.

Sandra poured wine into her glass, then took the bottle and led Katie into her bedroom where Sandra's walk-in closet door was open. Shelves filled with shoes in every color and purses of all sizes lined the closet. Each article of clothing hung on velvet hangers, arranged by shades of color. Katie reflected on her microscopic closet where her clothing hung on white plastic hangers and stuffed inside indiscriminately.

Sandra pulled five outfits out and laid them out on her king-size bed. She grabbed various accessories to complement each one. She put the Dolce and Gabbana dress front and center.

"You don't have to go to all this trouble," Katie said.

"Are you kidding? I love doing this. It reminds me of how I used to dress up my paper dolls. At least with you, I don't need scissors." Sandra picked up the designer dress and handed it to Katie. It was black and form-fitting with a plunging neckline and back. "Now strip and put this on."

Katie took a big gulp of her wine, then put the glass down on Sandra's dresser. While Katie put on the dress, Sandra refilled her glass.

"I'm not wearing a thong," Katie said. "My butt is going to have lines carved in it."

"Then we'll just look at the front." Sandra zipped up the back of the dress, then scrutinized Katie from every angle. "That looks better on you than it does on me."

Katie rolled her eyes, then assessed her reflection in the full-length mirror. She admired how her legs appeared long and lean in the dress, but since her breasts were a little larger than Sandra's, she had more cleavage showing than she was comfortable with.

"For a first date, this is too risqué," Katie said.

"I don't think so, but if it makes you uncomfortable, let me see what else I have that would be more appropriate." Sandra went back into her closet and pulled out a leopard print tank top and an ultra mini skirt. "How about this?" She winked at Katie as she held them up.

"You're going in the wrong direction; I don't want to look like a truck stop hooker," Katie said, drinking more of her wine.

"Okay, then now you have something for your second date." Sandra snickered and put the outfit back in her closet.

"Why don't I just go naked?" Katie giggled, she was feeling flushed and buzzed.

"That would get his attention." Sandra filled her own glass, then as she started to pour more into Katie's glass, Katie put her hand over it. "If you don't stop pouring me wine, I'm going to pass out right here." Katie slipped down to the floor and sat against the bed.

"You're such a lightweight."

Katie gleefully agreed. Sandra had Katie try on more and more outfits, and Katie nixed them all.

In the end, Katie decided to wear her own white jeans, Sandra's cropped black tank top with a white denim jacket over it, a black belt, and combat boots.

"I wish that top was a little smaller on you." Since Sandra was much taller than Katie, the crop top hit just at the top of her pants, showing Katie's belly only if she lifted her arms.

"It's perfect. It shows just enough of my abs to be sexy, yet still leaves some mystery."

"Then my job here is done." Sandra picked up her glass and clinked it against Katie's.

Chapter Three
Rachel

Rachel woke up to Brett shaking her. "Rachel . . . Rachel, are you okay?" she heard him asking through the haze in her head.

"What? Are we having an earthquake?" she asked groggily. She rubbed her eyes until they were open enough to see Brett on his elbow leaning over her, his brow etched in worry. "Oh God, I was screaming out loud, wasn't I," she said, and he nodded. "I'm sorry I woke you."

"It's fine, I was worried about you."

"It was another bad dream."

Rachel was tangled in the sheets. She threw them off and started fanning herself with her hand. She scrunched up her face and told him what she remembered. She'd overslept her alarm, then realized it was almost time to feed her newborn son. Jumping out of bed, moving quickly to heat his formula; her heart beating out of her pores. Her son had only been born a month ago, but she knew he'd be crying in exactly two minutes. Grabbing the bottle, she tip-toed into his room, the room she'd spent months designing, then redesigning, buying bedding, then returning it until she found exactly the right set. She crept up to his crib and reached beneath the quilt her mother had made with cartoonish ducks happily splayed in pastel glory. When she gazed down at her beautiful son settled in her arms, he suddenly became a vinyl baby doll with unblinking eyes, his soft, powdery baby scent gone, and in its place, the smell of plastic.

"That sounds awful," Brett said, rubbing her back.

"It felt so real." Rachel shuddered at the memory. She felt drained and teary-eyed, so she turned away from him. She didn't want him to always be seeing her like that.

The sun was just beginning to rise, yet it wasn't high enough for it to be considered morning. She glanced over at the clock. "You don't have to be up for another hour. Go back to sleep. I'll be fine."

He pulled her to him, his arms wrapping around her, her chest against his chest. She wished she wanted to have sex right then, it would've taken her mind off the dream. Maybe if he touched her that certain way only he knew how, but after how upset she was, she was sure he wouldn't try. Brett would wait for her signal, the one where she ran her hands along his chest slowly and softly, then after a minute her fingers would find his boxers and travel inside.

Rachel's hands remained still, and she stayed in Brett's embrace until he began to breathe louder and more rhythmically, then she shimmied out from under his arms and gingerly got out of bed. She tried to look at her day's lesson plan, but she couldn't stop the dream from replaying in her head. Tears puddled in her eyes and dropped onto her computer keyboard. How could she keep doing this to herself, and Brett? And what would he think if he found out the only secret she'd ever kept from him?

After she'd had two cups of coffee and felt like she could handle the day, she got ready for work. Brett came into the bathroom as she was spitting mouthwash into the sink.

"Hey," he said.

"Hey."

His eyes narrowed as he looked at her. "How're you doing, honey? I hate seeing dark circles under your eyes."

"That's why I'm putting on extra concealer, but I'm touched you notice my flaws." She smiled up at him.

"I love all your flaws."

"I have more than one?" she asked with mock horror.

"Nope, just the one. I just didn't want you to get a big head." He kissed her on the lips. "Mmm, minty."

"Can't say the same for you," she said, pretending to smell his breath. "I'm going to work; I have some things to do before the kids get there."

Brett turned the water on in the shower and slipped out of his boxers. Rachel couldn't help herself from glancing at his naked butt; his backside could distract her from almost anything. Her nightmare flew right out of her head. She knew that if she didn't leave for work immediately, she was going to jump in the shower with him, and then they'd both be late. Sixteen kindergartners inquiring about the exact reason she wasn't on time forced her libido to cut and run, at least until that night.

After most of the parents had dropped off their kids, Rachel's teaching assistant, Mark, got them settled on the carpet. As Rachel was closing her classroom door, Shawna strolled up with her daughter, Emma, as if they had all the time in the world.

Shawna's bombshell looks, flawlessly applied makeup, and diamond earrings the size of large blueberries made Rachel cringe inside at her ponytail, lightly applied mascara, and clothespin earrings she'd bought off Etsy.

Shawna kissed Emma on the forehead. "Go on in, honey, they're all waiting for you."

Shawna was one of Rachel's least favorite parents, but Emma was one of her most endearing students. Rachel admired the way Emma seemed to already know who she was at only five years old. She'd come to school in a yellow, flouncy dress with ruffles on the bodice, a navy and white Dodgers baseball cap, knee socks, and dirty high-top sneakers. She competed with the boys in sports and played dress-up with the girls on the same day.

"I just need a minute," Shawna said to Rachel haughtily, as if by paying the school, Rachel worked directly for her.

"I'm sorry, I need to start class," Rachel said firmly but nicely.

"Could you send Emma home with more homework? She finishes the assignments in seconds," Shawna went on, ignoring what Rachel said. "She's bored."

Rachel's back tightened; she'd heard this since the beginning of the year from Shawna, who thought Emma should be reading at the second-grade level and memorizing multiplication tables already.

"I'll think about it." Rachel turned away so Shawna couldn't see her rolling her eyes. "Have a nice day."

Shawna didn't move. "Do you have kids?"

Rachel flinched, her right eye twitching. "No," she said.

Shawna nodded. "I get it, having kids is hard work." *As if working with sixteen of these little maniacs every day isn't?* Rachel thought. Shawna continued, "I'm sure you get enough joy from our kids to last you a lifetime."

"I really have to go now." Rachel went into the classroom and closed the door. Mark was leading the kids in a song. Do not cry, do not cry, no crying in the classroom, Rachel repeated over and over to herself. When the song ended, the students began to talk amongst themselves, showing off their new shoes, telling stories about their dogs, or chattering about the new Disney movie.

Rachel walked to the center of the room. "Good morning, everyone."

"Good morning, Mrs. Segal," they responded in unison.

The kids sat on the carpet and Rachel sat in a chair in front of them. Mark picked up the book, *Alexander and the Terrible, Horrible, No Good, Very Bad Day*, and handed it to Rachel. The children crowded around her as she began to read. When Rachel read the part, ". . . I could tell it was going to be a terrible, horrible, no good, very bad day . . ." her eyes filled with tears and her voice cracked. The tears slipped out and fell down her cheeks. *I haven't had a really good day in a very long time.*

Emma, who was sitting right below Rachel, reached out and touched her leg. "Are you okay?" Emma asked, causing Rachel to smile through her tears.

"Mrs. Segal, it's just a story," Samuel yelled out.

"You're right, Samuel," Rachel said. "I'm fine. I just feel bad for Alexander. It's not fun when you have bad days." She wiped the tears away with the back of her hand.

"You okay?" Mark whispered, coming up behind her. "I can take over."

Rachel nodded and handed him the book, stepping outside the classroom.

She leaned against the closed door, which was cold and hard and supporting her weight. She felt like an idiot standing in the hall wallowing in sadness. *What is wrong with me, how can I get set off by a stupid children's book! What if I've become a bad teacher and I can't have kids, then what? Why are things so hard for me when other women just casually remark that they might start trying and wham, they're pregnant?* She cried harder, until she saw the principal, Max Grovner, coming down the hall. Rachel turned around and faced the door, hoping he'd walk on by, but knowing he was going to stop. She wiped her nose on her sleeve and tried to control the tears that still insisted on spilling out onto her shirt.

Max was a young principal and the kids loved him; he was always kind, even if they got sent to his office for bad behavior, he never shamed them.

When Rachel felt Max getting close, she turned around, bent her head foreword, and hoped her full mane of hair hid her eyes. "I'm fine, Max," Rachel said, trying to preempt him from asking her if she was okay.

"You're standing outside your classroom crying; I don't think that counts as fine."

"I just needed a minute. I've been going through a tough time lately."

"I'm sorry to hear that. Maybe you should take a few days off."

"Am I being fired?" Her heart raced. "Can you be fired for

crying?" she stated crying harder. "I can't sit home doing nothing."

"Of course you're not being fired. I just thought you could use a long weekend." Rachel nodded, and he continued, "Do you think you can finish out the day? I can get a sub for tomorrow and Friday."

"Yes, I can do that. Thanks, Max. I appreciate it."

He patted her lightly on the shoulder, then walked away. Rachel went to the bathroom to make sure her mascara hadn't given her two black eyes. That wouldn't sit well if the kids came home saying their teacher got into a fight. Before going back to class she gave herself a pep talk. *You only have to make it through a few more hours.*

When Rachel trudged up to her front porch, her shoulders relaxed as she crossed the threshold. A warm cup of tea and some music would help her get out of this mood. "Siri, play my favorite playlist on shuffle."

The first song that began playing was "Hurt" by Johnny Cash. As he sang in his deep, gravelly voice, Rachel wallowed in his pain hoping it would distract her from hers. When a lump formed in her throat and her eyes started to mist over, she lunged at the phone, to get Johnny to shut up. The next song turned out to be Shawn Mendes,' "It'll Be Okay."

"It might be okay for you, Shawn, but it may not be for me," she said and began sobbing.

By the time Brett got home that evening, she was biting her nails and staring blankly at the TV. He glanced at the screen.

"Uh oh, repeats of 'Full House'? Was your day that bad?" he asked, muting the TV.

Rachel looked up at him. "What if it hurts too much to be around other people's kids and I have to quit my job and do nothing all day? I could become that wacky lady who talks to herself and wanders the neighborhood endlessly. I might even starve to death."

"First of all, I'll always take care of you. Second of all, you're adorable, so if you wander around our block for a long time, some nice neighbor will take you in and feed you . . . like a stray cat."

"It's not funny," Rachel said, but couldn't help a smile from breaking through. "Here's what my day was like. I cried in front of the kids and probably traumatized them, and even worse I cried in front of Max, who then felt sorry for me and gave me two days off."

"Oh cool," he exclaimed.

Rachel glared at him.

"I didn't mean 'cool' that you were crying," he said. "I meant 'cool' that you have two days off. We've been wanting to get away to Santa Barbara, now we have the time."

"Don't you have to work?"

"My next project doesn't start until Monday. We both need a break, and a different environment will be good."

"That does sound nice." Rachel blew her nose loudly.

"And listening to all that mucus coming out of you is already turning me on."

Rachel stuck her tongue out at him.

The next morning, Brett and Rachel took a leisurely drive up the Pacific Coast Highway. Rachel had her window open, feeling the cool air whipping across her face. She immediately felt better leaving Los Angeles behind. It was good to get away, and she was hopeful that she might be able to get a different perspective on everything they were going through.

They checked into the Hilton Hotel directly across the street from the beach. Brett told the front desk clerk they were on a delayed honeymoon, which made Rachel blush. She hated lying, but she loved when Brett was romantic. The clerk promised to send up a bottle of champagne.

The first thing Rachel did when she walked into their room was drop her suitcase on the floor and go out on the balcony. The salty air and roar of the waves instantly made her body relax.

"I feel better already," she said, coming back into the room and wrapping her arms around Brett. "You're the best husband."

"Yes, yes, I am."

A clear, azure sky, seventy-five degrees, and a breeze that whispered across their faces made it a typical day in Santa Barbara. Brett and Rachel decided to take a long walk along the beach across the busy Cabrillo Boulevard. Neither of them wanted to walk to the stoplight on the corner, so they looked both ways and ran across four lanes of traffic. When they were safely on the other side, they cracked up like children who misbehaved and didn't get caught.

They slipped off their shoes and strolled barefoot along the water, holding hands. The cold ocean lapped at their feet, covering their toes in wet sand. When they were approaching the pier, Brett suggested they rent a two-person surrey bike, and Rachel clapped her hands together. They paid for an hour, then, sitting side by side, rode blissfully along the path.

"Look Brett, no feet," Rachel said, giddily kicking up her heels.

"Wait, I'm doing all the work!"

"As it should be!" She giggled and threw her hands up in the air. "Look I'm the queen of the world!" Rachel let herself bask in joy, something she hadn't done in a long time.

Brett looked over at her with a silly grin which told her he was also remembering their life before they had started trying to have a baby.

"That giggle is why I married you."

"And I thought it was because of my toned legs."

"That was an added bonus."

They talked about everything and nothing, and Rachel felt her brain, which normally went a mile a minute, become calm; the fatalistic thoughts disappeared. When the hour was up, they returned the bike and went back to their hotel room and made love.

"We haven't had sex in the afternoon in a long time," Rachel said as she languished in his arms afterward. She enjoyed the afterglow without having to remind herself to keep her legs in the air to increase her chances of conceiving.

He grinned lasciviously. "I didn't hear you complaining."

"Maybe I would've if you ever stopped kissing me."

"You're right I should've been more mindful." Brett put his hand on her breast. "Is this okay?"

"Shouldn't you have asked me that a half hour ago?" She playfully smacked his hand away and got off the bed. Rachel fished through her suitcase for her bathing suit and told Brett they should go to the pool before it got dark. Brett seemed happy to do anything she wanted.

The pool wasn't crowded, so they picked two lounges near the shallow end steps and laid towels down. Brett opened a book while Rachel got into the pool.

She sat on the steps for a few minutes with her face pointed upward, basking in the warmth of the afternoon sun.

After a while, she waded in and swam a few laps back and forth across the pool. When she was out of breath, she grabbed the side to take a break. Across from her were a mother and father with their two kids, a boy around four and an infant girl. The mom held the baby and bounced her in the water, the dad keeping an eye on his son, who floated around wearing water wings. Rachel couldn't take her eyes off them. The boy clumsily moved his arms, splashing his way towards Rachel. He reached out to grab the side of the pool but missed and wrapped his fingers around Rachel's arm. His father swam over to get him and apologized.

"It's fine." Rachel forced a smile. "He's adorable."

The father plodded back through the water to the other side of the pool, carrying his son in his arms. He helped the boy climb out, then moved away from the side, encouraging his son to jump into his outstretched arms. The boy did jump, but not to his father. He bounded off the side in Rachel's direction, then swam over to her as fast as he could with water wings on. It was as if he were drawn to her, like a dieter to a donut.

"He must like you," the father said, smiling at Rachel.

Rachel nodded, then swam back to the steps in the shallow end.

She watched the mom holding her daughter in the water on her back, kissing her all over her belly. When the baby erupted in a high-pitched giggle, Rachel charged out of the water, grabbed her towel from the lounge, and ran off.

Brett called out to her, but she didn't look back. She tried to hold her emotions in but was doing a terrible job. "Are you okay?" an elderly woman asked her as she exited the elevator Rachel was waiting for.

"Yes." Rachel burst into sobs as the elevator doors closed. When she finally got to her floor, she fumbled for her key and dropped it. She got down on her knees and picked it up, then tried to get it to work in the door, but every time the green light flashed, she didn't pull the handle down in time, and the door relocked itself. When Brett finally caught up to her, she was sitting with her back against the door, trying to breathe.

"What happened?" he asked, helping her up and unlocking the door.

She sat on the bed, trying to talk, but everything she said came out in bits and pieces.

"I can't . . . I can't do this . . . I need . . . I need to have a baby."

He sat next to her, putting his arm around her and she laid her head against him. "I hate seeing you like this."

"I'm sorry I'm defective."

"You aren't defective," he stated emphatically.

"Then why can't I have a baby?"

"I don't know." His voice was almost a whisper.

"My gynecologist suggested I see a specialist after the last miscarriage, but I was scared to hear what they might say. What if no one can help me?" She cried.

"What if they can?" he asked.

Rachel stopped crying for a moment. "But what if they can't?" she began sobbing again.

Brett held her for a long time until her sobs turned into quiet crying, then the quiet crying turned into just shallow breathing. When she was spent, she closed her eyes and just sat there. Brett grabbed a tissue and handed it to her.

"I think it's time we got some answers. It could be me for all we know," he said.

"You're just saying that to make me feel better," Rachel gave him a tiny, wry smile.

They both laid back on the bed and drifted off to sleep. When they woke up, Brett let her know how concerned he was about her.

"I feel better." Rachel said, more hopeful than she'd been earlier. "I do want to make an appointment with a specialist when we get back."

"Then that's what we'll do. Now that we have a plan, maybe we can both put it out of our minds for the next couple of days."

"I'll try."

"I might be able to help you." Brett ogled her then pulled her into his arms and slowly peeled off her swimsuit. He got on top of her, and they began kissing. She put her hand on his chest and rubbed it slowly and softly, then nimbly slipped her fingers beneath his bathing trunks.

Chapter Four
Katie

As the sun set, the sky unfolded like a charcoal tablecloth. The waxing crescent moon was supposed to mean good luck, and Katie hoped it was a positive sign for her date.

The Formosa Café, with its fire engine red exterior and black and white awnings, looked a little worn out as if it had witnessed a lot in its time. A gray-haired gentleman in an all-white suit opened the door for Katie. She entered to men's and women's voices, which to her ears sounded like the chatter of a community of chimpanzees. Her eyes darted between the red tasseled Chinese lanterns above the round leather booths and pictures of old movie stars like Frank Sinatra, Dean Martin, and Elvis Presley covering the walls. There was even an old trolley car inside where patrons could sit to have dinner.

Katie stood near the door for a minute, scanning for Adam. When she didn't see him, she moved quickly over to an empty barstool. She didn't want to order a drink, which was a good thing, because the bartender continuously walked past her without even a nod in her direction.

I belong here as much as any of these other women, she thought, assessing the other women around her. One was wearing a micro-mini skirt and a V-neck T-shirt with her oversized breasts sitting so high she could've worn them as earrings. *Well, maybe not every woman.* On Katie's other side was a woman talking to a man at least thirty years her senior. The woman dangled off him like a diamond bracelet.

Katie kept an eye on the entrance as she played Words with Friends with Sandra on her phone. When Adam walked through the door, she let out a sigh of relief that he looked the same as he did in his pictures.

As she stood to wave, the young woman and her much older companion got up to call it a night. It was eight o'clock so definitely past his bedtime.

"It's nice to meet you," Adam said as he approached Katie. "Is it okay if I give you a hug?"

"Sure."

He gave her a quick hug. "Would you like a drink?" he asked.

"I'd love a Mai Tai."

Adam nodded toward the bartender, who came right over. He ordered her a Mai Tai and a Singapore Sling for himself.

Adam and Katie went through the usual first date topics, where they worked, what they liked to do on the weekends, and where they grew up. Katie told him she was originally from Arizona and moved to Los Angeles for college.

"Are you hungry?" Adam asked after they'd been talking for forty-five minutes.

"Actually, I'm starving," she admitted.

"I couldn't get a reservation, but follow me," he said. They walked over to the hostess, who advised them that it would be an hour wait before she'd have a table available. Adam slipped her a twenty, and "somehow" she immediately could seat them inside the red trolley car.

"I can't believe I'm the first person you've gone out with from a dating app," he said.

"I guess I'm picky."

"When was your last relationship?" Adam asked as Katie scanned the menu.

"Several months ago," she said, which technically could be true, if 'several months' could be translated as 'two years.'

The waiter asked if they'd had a chance to look at the menu. Before Katie could answer, Adam said they both wanted orange chicken and pork pot stickers. Katie was tongue-tied; no one had ever ordered for her without finding out what she liked.

The waiter asked if they wanted another drink, even though Katie still had half of hers left.

"Sure," Adam said.

"Thank you, but no. One drink's enough for me," Katie said.

"The lady knows what she wants." Adam ordered himself a martini.

"When was your last relationship?" Katie asked.

"Three weeks ago."

Katie's jaw tightened, and she wrinkled her brow. "That's so—

recent." She took a deep breath and tried to stop herself from making a quick judgment.

A busboy dropped off Adam's drink. Adam held up a finger telling the busboy to wait until he finished his first drink, which he did quickly.

"If you don't mind me asking," Katie said, "Why did your relationship end?"

"We'd gone out on three dates when she told me she didn't have the time for me. Who doesn't have time for a relationship?" Adam began tapping his fingers on the table to the rhythm of the background music.

Katie took a long slow drink from her Mai Tai. There was an awkward silence before Adam stopped tapping and seemed to perk up.

"So, what are you doing this weekend?" he asked.

"Sleeping late and then running errands."

"Do you want company?"

"Uh, thank you, but that's okay, I'm good." *I'm not about to take you with me to buy bras and panties.*

"Well, if you're sure." He pursed his lips together in a pout.

The waiter brought their food. Katie took in the tart odor of sweet and sour and soy sauce. She didn't like orange chicken, but she didn't want to hurt Adam's feelings, so she took a small amount and hoped when she told him how good it was, he wouldn't know she was lying.

"I hope you kept Sunday open for me." He spoke around a mouthful of potstickers. "I'd love for you to come with me to my mom's for lunch. I told her all about you, and she'd like to meet you."

Katie started choking, then dropped her fork on the floor. She pushed it around with her shoe trying to move it closer to her so she could pick it up. She gave up; she still had a salad fork. "That's, that's . . . nice of you, but Sunday won't work for me."

Adam stared at her with indignation. "Really? Well, then I guess I'll just have to disappoint my mom."

Katie could feel that the water in his pot was starting to boil. She shoveled food in her mouth and berated herself for not asking Sandra to call her with a pretend emergency in case she needed an excuse to leave. Katie couldn't wait to be back in her car alone, but for now, she'd try to get Adam back to a simmer.

"So . . . do you like to travel?" Katie asked.

"I love to travel!" Adam brightened. "Hey, do you want to go to Vegas next weekend? I can get us a deal at the Tropicana."

Katie's eyes opened wide, and she ran her fingers along her eyebrows. When she suggested it would be best if they got to know each other better before going on a trip, Adam looked at her as if she had strangled a puppy.

"That's what the last woman I dated said," Adam grumbled. "How come your gender can't be spontaneous without analyzing everything to death?"

Katie put her hand in her purse, trying to feel for her mace. She'd never used it, but she found its plastic case comforting in her hand. Adam continued to rant, getting loud enough that the woman at the table next to them looked at her with pity. Katie nodded at her.

"I know there's nothing wrong with me, so there must be something wrong with you and all the other women your age."

Katie pulled out her phone and pretended she saw a voicemail and had to listen to it. "Oh no, my mom fell, and she can't get ahold of my dad. She needs me to come to her house and help her."

"Should I come with you?" Adam asked.

Katie wanted that like she wanted to be dipped in honey and tossed to a grizzly bear. "I think it's best if I go by myself."

Adam jumped out of the booth as if his pants were on fire, which Katie secretly wished they were. "Fine, be that way."

As the waiter was bringing over the bill, Adam stomped out of the restaurant. Katie thought it was worth the eighty-dollar check not to have him walk her to her car; he probably would've thrown her in the trunk. After putting down her credit card, she opened the dating app on her phone and deleted it.

* * *

"I can't breathe," Katie exhaled loudly as she finished hiking up the first hill at Fryman Canyon.

"Me either," Sandra said, sweat appearing between her breasts in her sports bra.

Julianna and Margarette, their co-workers, and friends strolled easily alongside them as if they were taking a leisurely walk through a shopping mall. A middle-aged man jogged by, his pug keeping up with him.

"What is wrong with this picture?" Katie said, her hamstrings screaming at her.

"At your age, you lose endurance," Julianna said.

"Katie and I are only five years older than you guys," Sandra pointed out.

THE STORIES WE CANNOT TELL

"I was trying to be nice," Margarette said, laughing. "Isn't that better than saying you both are out of shape?"

The morning fog had barely lifted, the tops of the hills still hidden slightly. Katie removed her hoodie, tied it around her waist, and bent over as she took in another big breath. When she stood up, she congratulated herself on being smart enough to buy a fanny pack that could hold a sports bottle. Katie took a big gulp, then offered it to Sandra who showed Katie that she'd brought her own.

"Are you guys hydrated enough to go on?" Julianna asked, seeming impatient.

Katie and Sandra nodded, and the four women continued their trek. Katie was relieved that for now, they were on a straightaway.

"Katie, I can't believe that guy you went out with was so needy," Margarette said.

"I know, it was crazy. We want a man who adores us, not shows up with a minister and the wedding rings he designed himself." Katie pretended to swoon. The women cackled at the absurdity.

"Oh wow, look at that view." Sandra walked off the path toward the edge of the cliff.

"You're making me nervous," Margarette said. "I'm afraid of heights."

"Then don't move and look out from there." Sandra pointed to where Margarette stood. Julianna and Katie walked over to Sandra. Spread out before them was the entire San Fernando Valley. Jutting out from one of the hills sat an overgrown mansion with a rooftop pool, walls entirely made of glass that opened up to a deck with a fire pit, and a dining table with fourteen chairs. It resembled a five-star resort.

"I wouldn't want a house where people like us could stand here and see me in my underwear." Sandra shook her head emphatically.

"I'd be fine with that if I had their money," Katie said. "I'd just buy prettier panties."

"On our salaries, we could only afford camping out on their driveway," Margarette called out from where she stood.

A beautifully chiseled man stopped a few feet away to look at the view. "That guy is gorgeous," Juliette whispered, gesturing with her head. "Which one of us is going to go talk to him?"

"I will," Katie said quietly. "I'll just walk over there, give him a big kiss on the mouth and tell him I'm his."

"I bet he'd appreciate a woman like you." Sandra nudged her with her elbow, eyebrows waggling.

Another man with a model's physique and a face to match walked up to the gorgeous guy, whispered something to him, then wrapped his arms around him and they kissed.

"I guess you waited too long," Sandra said to Katie, and the women broke out in hysterics which ended with Katie snorting.

The two men strolled away holding hands. As the women headed back on the trail, Katie's phone buzzed. She asked them to hold up, unzipped her fanny pack, and glanced at her phone. She'd gotten an alert on Facebook Messenger. She grinned as she read the text.

"What is it?" Julianna asked. A hawk flew above them, looking for its morning meal.

Katie held her phone out. "Read this." The other women huddled around her.

"Who's the guy?" Sandra asked.

"He was my high school crush, but I didn't think he even knew who I was at the time, let alone remember me a decade and a half later." Katie's toes jiggled in her sneakers.

"I bet he came across your profile picture and thought you were adorable," Margarette said. "He's probably kicking himself that he didn't ask you out in high school."

"I doubt it," Katie put her phone away. "He was one of those popular guys who had girls following him everywhere."

"Maybe he's matured, the way men do when they get older and start losing their hair," Julianna said.

"He's my age!" Katie protested.

"Okay, then maybe he has a belly." Julianna mimed a potbelly and Margarette high-fived her as they laughed.

"Next time I tell you about something good that might happen, remind me not to." Katie laughed and started walking again. The women hurried to catch up to her.

"What does he want?" Sandra asked.

"I don't know, he just wrote that he wanted to say hello and catch up."

As they rounded another curve, they jumped out of the way to avoid a couple on bicycles. The woman was in complete control while the man, less steady, slammed his foot down in order not to run into them. They jumped out of the way, and he groaned as if they were the reason he couldn't stay on his bike.

"So . . . are you going to respond?" Sandra asked Katie after the man had safely passed them.

"First I need to figure out what to say," Katie said.

"'Hi' is a good start," Sandra said, and Katie threw a pretend punch at her.

A few hours later, when Katie limped through the door, Mr. Morrison greeted her with loud purring as he stepped all over her feet.

She kicked her sneakers off and picked him up, gave him a gentle hug, then went into the pantry to feed him. She looked at what time Dylan had sent the message and counted out how many hours it had been. Mr. Morrison had scarfed down his food and was already back at her feet.

"What do you think, Mr. Morrison? It's been five hours since he sent the message. Should I respond?" Mr. Morrison nudged her with his cold nose. "Fine, you're as pushy as Sandra." Katie opened her laptop and sent Dylan a message that she'd be happy to catch up with him. She gave him her phone number, figuring talking on the phone would be easier than texting back and forth through Facebook.

Every time Katie got nervous, she craved something sweet. She looked for her stash of chocolate but found only an old wrapper and then remembered she'd eaten all of it the last time she was stressed. She looked at her phone, wondering if she missed his call, but there wasn't anything. She got on her hands and knees and searched every cabinet, even the ones she knew just had cleaning supplies. In the last cabinet she opened, she found a package of diet hot chocolate nestled underneath some tea bags. Her hands trembled as she ripped open the pouch and poured the powder into a mug. Just as she finished adding whipped cream, her phone rang with a number she didn't have programmed in.

"Hello," she answered cheerily, hoping it was Dylan.

"Is this Katie Doherty?"

"It is. Is this Dylan?"

"Yep. It's nice to talk to you. You came up on Facebook as a person I should friend, and when I realized we went to the same high school,

I thought it would be fun to contact you."

Katie took her mug and put it on the coffee table, then settled in on the couch. Mr. Morrison jumped onto her lap, and she stroked his back. His breath smelled like tuna that had been regurgitated. Katie's nose twitched and she turned her face away from his mouth, but the odor wouldn't leave, as if it was being blown into a fan. "How do you like Los Angeles?" Dylan asked.

"It's a lot bigger than Prescott, but I like it."

"I moved to the San Francisco area a few years ago."

"I love northern California; the Redwoods are beautiful." While Katie was trying to decide what to say next, she blew on her hot chocolate and took a sip.

"Did we have any classes together in high school?" Dylan asked. "I can't remember."

Before Katie answered, she realized she had whipped cream all over her lips. "We had a few." She happily licked the white fluff off.

"I'm embarrassed to say I was kind of self-centered back then. I only cared about sports and girls. I hope I wasn't a jerk to you."

"You never spoke to me to be a jerk."

"Really? How could I have missed you . . . unless you weren't as pretty in high school."

"I think I look the same." She felt a flush creep across her face as soon as the words came out of her mouth. She was relieved he couldn't see her. "I mean, thank you."

As they talked, Katie was surprised at how much they had in common. They were both Catholic, both loved museums, and movies, and were huge fans of Green Day. And they both had a thing for cats. She told him how she'd named her cat after their high school English teacher because they shared the same black and white mustache. He thought that was a riot.

As their conversation was winding down, Dylan told her he was flying to Los Angeles the following week for a conference and asked if she'd be free to meet for dinner on Thursday night.

Yes, yes, hell yes!! Katie flipped through a magazine loudly next to the phone as if she were looking at a calendar, then told him she would move a few things around and make it work.

"Cool, email me your address and I'll come by and get you around 7:30," Dylan said.

When Katie hung up, she jumped up and twirled around as if she were a majorette who had lost her baton. She grabbed Mr. Morrison and danced around with him in her arms, then stopped in mid-twirl.

"What if Dylan takes one look at me and is disappointed? He could think my profile picture is better than the real thing." She sat back down on the couch, still holding the cat. "You know I haven't had any luck with men in the last few years . . . or ever for that matter." Mr. Morrison began snoring quietly.

"Then again, what if this is the man I've been waiting for my whole life?" she said loudly, startling Mr. Morrison awake, who then jumped from the couch to his scratching post. "You're right, I'm getting ahead of myself."

Katie picked up her computer, logged onto Facebook, and found Dylan's page, but his account was set to private. They had some friends in common, but few, considering they graduated with three hundred other people. She could see from his profile picture he had dreamy eyes the color of limes right before they were ripe. He was also clean-shaven, which made her happy as she loved rubbing her face against a man's soft cheek. She hoped he hadn't grown a mustache or beard since he'd taken this picture. The photo was only from the neck up, so she'd soon find out if the rest of him looked as good.

* * *

Katie spent the next week grooming as many parts of her as possible to get ready for her date. She got her eyebrows waxed, her hair cut and highlighted. She even sprayed a self-tanner everywhere, forcing her to walk around naked in her apartment for an hour while it dried. She couldn't even sit on the couch for fear the cushions would become the same shade of bronze as her backside.

After work that Thursday, she went to Sephora and had her makeup done and was ready an hour before he was due. She looked around her clean apartment, all the magazines perfectly arranged, her unpaid bills hidden in a drawer, and her kitchen counters sparkling. Now what? She would organize her junk drawer. Nope, too overwhelming. She piled everything back in and shoved it closed. Finally, she called Sandra and talked to her until there was a knock on her door.

Dylan still looked like the guy from high school, but even

cuter, if that was possible. He had on dark-washed jeans, a white T-shirt, and a black casual blazer over it, and was a few inches taller than her, which made them a perfect match.

If he wants to kiss me, I wouldn't have to stand on my toes, and he wouldn't have to bend down, was the first thing Katie thought, her insides buzzing.

"I'm sorry I'm a little early, I just couldn't wait any longer." Dylan came into her apartment without being invited.

He handed her a dozen red roses, a bottle of wine, and a premade plate with cheese and crackers.

"This is so nice, thank you," Katie said.

Dylan made himself comfortable on the couch while she put the flowers in a vase. She joined him, carrying wine glasses, plates, and knives for the cheese and set everything on her coffee table. Dylan opened the wine and poured some into both glasses. He picked up his glass.

"To old friends, becoming new friends." He clinked her glass. "I was an idiot for not noticing you in high school. I hope you'll forgive me."

Katie blushed. "This cheese is really good."

"I couldn't get a dinner reservation until late, and I didn't want you to go hungry." Dylan moved closer to her and poured more wine into her glass.

"I'm kind of a lightweight, I don't normally drink more than one glass." But she took a sip anyway.

They talked about their high school days and caught each other up on who'd already been married twice, who ended up being ultra successful, and who each of them stayed in touch with.

Katie admitted that when she moved to Los Angeles she lost touch with a lot of her old friends.

As she reached down to get a cracker, in her peripheral vision, she saw him staring at her intensely. When she looked up at him, his eyes glazed over. "God, are you beautiful."

As if in slow motion, he moved in to kiss her. She watched it happening and her stomach jumped around as if it were full of butterflies doing the Charleston. At first, the kiss was soft and gentle, and she was sure her heart had stopped beating. When the kiss became more fervent and passionate, her spine collapsed like a bridge in an earthquake. Before she knew it, Dylan picked her up off the couch and carried her in his arms to her bedroom.

Katie had never slept with anyone on the first date, but at that moment, she couldn't think or catch her breath. Besides, she felt safe with him; they had a history together. He laid her down on the bed and ever so slowly peeled off her clothes. She got goosebumps all over her body, her skin reacting to the softness of his hands.

He slipped out of his pants, pulled off his shirt, and then straddled her. When he gazed down at her again, she lost herself completely. As his hands moved down her body, she closed her eyes, hoping this feeling would go on forever. They spent the next hour having intense, romantic sex.

Afterward, as they lay quietly, skin on skin, Katie reflected on how self-conscious she usually felt when she was naked with a man for the first time. But Dylan made her feel comfortable and beautiful.

"I guess we missed our reservations," Dylan said.

"It was worth it," Katie said, and Dylan agreed. "Are you hungry?"

"Very."

"I can make us an omelet." Katie got up and leaned down to pick her clothes up from where they were scattered on the floor.

"Don't put anything on," he said. "I can't get enough of looking at you."

She opened her hands and let her clothes drop back on the floor and the two of them went into the kitchen naked. She made an omelet and toast and after they'd scarfed down the food, they went back to bed.

"I wish I would've found you sooner," Dylan said.

"You were too busy chasing girls," Katie teased.

As he began kissing her neck, he murmured, "But you're not just any girl."

When they finished having sex for the second time, it was after two am. Dylan got up and got dressed.

"I better get going," he said.

Katie would've stayed in bed with him all night—it would have been worth it to be incoherent at work that day. Dylan promised to call after he got back home and for the first time, she was sure a man would keep his word.

Katie got back under the covers, but she wasn't going to be able to sleep. Mr. Morrison crept out from his hiding place under the bed, and jumped up, laying down on the pillow where Dylan had been. He meowed at Katie.

"I know, I know, you don't have to be so judgmental." She rubbed his back. "It's not like I've ever done this before. Maybe he'll be your new dad."

Mr. Morrison closed his eyes and went to sleep. "Sorry if we kept you up." But she wasn't the least bit sorry. She fantasized about what her life would be like with Dylan. Would he move to Los Angeles, or would she move to Northern California and find a job at a fertility clinic there? By morning she had planned their wedding.

At work, Sandra took one look at Katie's glowing face and the bags under her eyes and pulled her into the break room.

"Spill it," Sandra said.

"Let's just say I didn't get any sleep last night."

"OMG, you slut. I love it."

"Nice, real nice."

"So . . . how was it?"

"Do you not see my smile?"

"I'm so happy for you."

"Me, too." Katie didn't get a lot of work done. She kept checking her phone every fifteen minutes to see if Dylan had called.

It wasn't until the day was over and she was walking to her car that her phone finally pinged. Dylan apologized for not texting her sooner, but his plane was delayed on the runway for hours. Her neck relaxed from the tension she'd been holding all day. Katie stood in the parking lot and texted him back.

* * *

During the next few weeks, Katie spent her lunch hour sitting on the steps outside her office building talking to Dylan on the phone. They rarely could talk in the evening because he was always busy with some kind of work event. Sandra wasn't thrilled that she never got to have lunch with Katie anymore, but she was happy Katie had found someone special.

Katie looked forward to waking up in the mornings to a message from Dylan. Once he sent her a picture of his dog, another time a picture of himself eating pizza, and one time he sent a picture of him feeding his dog pizza.

A month after their first date, Katie told Dylan she was going to ask her boss for the next Thursday and Friday off so she could fly to San Francisco and spend a long weekend with him. She thought it would be fun to play tourists together.

"That would've been great," he said, "but I won't be there. I have a lot of business trips coming up. The good news is, I'll be back in Los Angeles soon, and I was hoping to see you . . . and I mean see you in every possible way."

"I'm so excited!" Katie exclaimed. "We can go to Santa Monica and hang out on the beach and the pier and maybe have dinner down there." She was not used to being that forward, but Dylan made her feel more confident, something she never felt with other men, especially after only one date.

"Sounds like fun. I'll be back two weeks from tomorrow."

"Two more weeks feels like a long time," she said, but thought to herself, *How am I going to make it through another two weeks?*

"You'll see, it'll fly by."

Chapter Five
Rachel

Rachel sipped her tea as she paid bills. She closed her computer and pushed it away when she realized she was putting the amount for the mortgage in the place to pay the phone bill. That would be a happy day at AT&T. She took a bite of her bagel and poppy seeds rained down onto the table. Honey, her Great Dane, raised her head and licked them off while Molasses, who with her squat body couldn't reach the table, whined.

Rachel understood what it was like to be at a disadvantage, so she took a piece of her bagel and gave it to Molasses. Then she threw their octopus chew toy across the room and watched the dogs play tug of war.

Brett almost tripped on Molasses as she scampered to the living room to hide the octopus from Honey.

"Those dogs are going to kill me someday," he said as he got himself a cup of coffee.

Rachel tapped her closed laptop. "Then we better make sure your life insurance is paid."

"Did you get any sleep last night?" he asked, kissing her. "You still have bags under your eyes."

"There's my sweet-talking husband."

"You know how much I love to give compliments."

She reached across the table and kissed him back. "I'm worried about the appointment with that infertility specialist this morning. I don't know what she's going to say."

"I'm confident she'll be able to help us."

Rachel shrugged. "I guess that could happen." She frowned.

"Your optimism is overwhelming. I'm blinded by the lightness being radiated off you."

"You're right, I need to be more hopeful, being negative isn't getting me anywhere. And I assume she's good; it took a month to get an appointment."

"I know you said not to, but I'd like to come with you."

"There's no need, she's only going to talk to me and order some tests, but you can be there for all the other fun stuff."

"Good."

Rachel sat in the waiting room with four other women. Three were staring at their phones, not talking to anyone, while one with a small yet distinctly extended belly sat next to her husband who smiled at her as if she were carrying the only baby ever to be gestating. Rachel found herself putting her hand on her flat stomach, hoping that would be her and Brett someday.

Rachel heard her name being called. Her hands shook holding the clipboard and pen with her paperwork.

"Hi Rachel, I'm Katie. I'll be taking you back to an exam

room." Rachel dropped the pen and Katie reached down to pick it up.

"You have the prettiest hair," Rachel said. "My mom's hair is the same color. In college, I almost dyed my hair the same shade, then I chickened out because I was sure my hair would fall out—I figured brown hair was better than having bald spots." Rachel couldn't stop herself from blabbering on.

"I think your hair is pretty, I love natural waves," Katie said, motioning for Rachel to go into room number four. As Katie was walking in after Rachel, she tripped over her untied shoelace. She put her hand on the wall to avoid falling. "I'm such a klutz." She cracked up and let out a little snort. "Sorry."

"I snort after I laugh, too. My husband loves to tease me about it, he thinks it's weird but cute."

"Then I guess we're both weird . . . and cute," Katie said.

Katie wrote Rachel's name and birth date on a sterilized cup and asked her to provide a urine sample.

Rachel did what she was told, and when she got back to the exam room, she put on the gown that was waiting for her on a chair. She hated those stiff gowns and couldn't get comfortable on the exam table. Her body was moving around so much; she hoped she wasn't tearing the crinkly paper beneath her. Why couldn't she have remembered to bring a book. She opened her purse and looked for what, she didn't know. Her phone wasn't an option; she just kept doing internet searches for infertility horror stories. She looked at a brochure for some new medication, then put it back because she was actually starting to feel the side effects as she read each one.

Why do doctors make you wait so long? she thought. *By the time they finally come in, I've diagnosed myself and I'm ready to go home.*

Rachel got off the table and walked to a bulletin board. It was covered in photographs of adorable babies and heartfelt thank you notes to Dr. Marley. *I hope someday my baby's picture will be up there.* The thought brought a smile to her face. Maybe Dr. Marley could help her dream finally come true.

On the countertop near the sink sat a 3D model of a pelvis with a uterus and a baby inside. Rachel couldn't help but touch it and when she did the model of the baby fell onto the sink. *Oh, no!* She was trying to push the baby back inside the womb when her phone rang. As she hurried back to the exam table to check her phone, she hoped the doctor wouldn't notice the baby's butt was sticking out of the womb. "Hi, Mom."

"Hi, Honey, how are you? Your dad and I barely hear from you anymore."

"I haven't felt like talking much, but I'm okay. I'm waiting for the fertility doctor right now to hopefully find out what's going on with me."

"Good, let me know what happens."

"I will. I better go, she should be in any minute." "Okay. I love you, and I'm praying for a grandchild." "Seriously, Mom," Rachel said, not hiding her frustration.

"I'm sorry, honey, but I'm sure it's going to happen. I feel it down to my bones."

"I gotta go."

"Okay, good luck," her mom said, and Rachel hung up. *Like I'm not under enough pressure as it is.* She put her hands up to her throat and fiddled with the Jewish star she wore on a gold chain around her neck.

After a light knock on the door, Dr. Marley came into the room. She was in her late forties, wearing a white lab coat, skinny jeans, and a bright purple shirt. She had on long, dangling earrings with penguins on them. Dr. Marley's gentle smile made Rachel feel as if she were in good hands.

"Hi, Rachel, what can I do for you today?"

"I want to have a baby, which I assume you've figured out because why else would I be here. I've had three miscarriages and now I can't even get pregnant – I'm only thirty – and I'm hoping you can help me." She felt her eyes mist over, but she restrained herself from crying.

"I don't know why it's so difficult."

Dr. Marley pulled a chair up next to the exam table. "I understand. I know how hard this can be, and I'm going to try to find some answers for you."

When Rachel heard even that tiny reassurance from a professional, the tension left her neck. "Thank you."

"Let me take a moment to look over your paperwork." Dr. Marley slowly read through the forms Rachel had filled out.

Rachel's eyes darted around the room. She coughed, then cleared her throat, then coughed again. "Umm . . . Is possible that an abortion

I had eight years ago could be causing my problems?"

Dr. Marley looked up. "I don't see an abortion on your paperwork."

"I left it off."

Dr. Marley nodded.

Rachel's hands went to her heart, and she bent her head down. "I've never told anyone, not even my husband."

"I'll need to add it to your file, but your husband will never see it." Rachel wondered if Dr. Marley thought she was a horrible person for keeping something so important from him. "It's not likely that the termination did any damage, but just to make sure, I'll do an ultrasound and look for scarring. I'll also do a hysterosalpingogram to look at your fallopian tubes and the inside walls of your uterus. After we get those results, we'll know more, and we can go from there."

Rachel was hoping to do all the tests that day, but the radiologist was already booked, so Dr. Marley promised she'd get her in within a week.

"What if all these tests don't show anything and I still can't get pregnant?"

"Then we'll explore other options. There are medications like Clomid that make sure you ovulate, and procedures like intrauterine insemination, IVF, and GIFT, but let's not get ahead of ourselves. After the tests, I'll sit down with you and your husband, and we'll make a plan together."

"Thank you," Rachel said, feeling lighter than when she got there. "The nurse will come in and take blood, and I'll look at your hormones and your thyroid and where you are in your cycle." Dr. Marley stood. "Don't hesitate to email me or call me if you have any questions. The women at the front desk will give you my email when you check out."

Rachel drove home in silence, her back rigid against her seat as if she were balancing a book on her head. The only sound was the engine changing gears. She wore the quiet like a shawl wrapped around her on a cool summer night.

The thought of all the tests Dr. Marley described ricocheted through her mind. *Why am I putting myself through all this? I'm going to end up having to do IVF anyway. I've already been waiting over two years.* Rachel sank deep into the leather car seat, trying desperately not to get ahead of herself, but she was losing that fight. I don't want to wait any longer.

Instead of going home, she drove to the grocery store and bought filet mignon, potatoes, asparagus, and all the ingredients for chocolate chip cookies.

Brett got home that evening to the scent of oatmeal and chocolate. "Whoever is baking those cookies, I'll have to leave my wife for," he called out before he walked into the kitchen.

Rachel was wearing his apron that read in big letters, 'MR. GOOD LOOKIN' IS COOKIN.' "You've been promising you'd leave your wife for me for years," Rachel murmured flirtatiously, pulling the cookies out of the oven, and putting them on the stovetop to cool. "I was beginning to think you never would."

Brett stuck his nose almost on the cookies.

"None for you until after dinner," Rachel said, picking up his face and kissing him.

"Filet mignon, asparagus, potatoes, and cookies. I'm going to assume the doctor's appointment went well," Brett turned the steaks over in the marinade.

"I liked her."

"Good."

"I think we should do IVF."

"What? Did the doctor say that?"

"She's going to start with some tests, but if we skip the tests and just do IVF, we'll get to what we want faster."

"Doing the tests first makes sense, what if the issue is something easily fixed? IVF is more involved and really expensive. We have a mortgage payment."

"Are you saying that our house is more important than starting a family?" Rachel's jaw got tight.

"Of course not, I want a baby as much as you do, but jumping to IVF doesn't make sense. Besides, it doesn't even work all the time."

"Why are you being negative?"

"I'm just trying to be realistic. Your mother keeps bringing up grandchildren, is that part of this?"

"No."

Brett took the steaks out of the marinade and put them on their indoor grill. "You just went to the doctor today; let's at least give her a chance to see what she can find."

Rachel felt her face turning red. I've gone through three miscarriages; I think I've been incredibly patient. I don't think you understand what it's been like for me."

"Okay." He took a breath and moved over to where she stood. "Honey, why are we fighting about this right now?"

"Because having a baby is the only thing that's important, and I'm wondering if you really want that."

"That's not fair, I've been in the trenches with you."

"We're definitely not in the same trenches." Rachel took off her apron and tossed it on the counter. "I'm going to my parent's house."

"What about dinner?"

"I'm not hungry anymore." Rachel grabbed her purse and marched out the door.

It was late before she headed home. Her parents had spent time calming her down and helping her realize she needed to at least do the tests before making any decisions. Her father told her that if it came down to her having to do IVF, he and her mother could help pay for it. Rachel was grateful for their support.

The dogs came charging, their toenails clicking on the wood floor when Rachel closed the front door. She gave them each a treat and sent them back to bed. She sighed with relief when she heard Brett's snoring echoing from the bedroom. She didn't feel like rehashing their conversation from earlier.

She put on her pajamas and crawled under the covers. The warmth of his body radiated over to her side of the bed and even if he was a pain, she was comforted that he was her pain. The whole day had worn Rachel out, and within minutes, she fell asleep.

Rachel woke to the sound of water running in the shower. She wondered if Brett was trying to get to work before she was up, to avoid having to talk about her doctor's appointment again. Rachel picked her phone up off the nightstand and saw there was a voicemail from Dr. Marley asking her to call the office.

She pressed her hands against her mouth.

Oh my god, they must've found something in my blood work. Why else would she call me so early in the morning? Her hands were shaking so much that she couldn't find the doctor's number in her contacts. Then she remembered she hadn't put it in, so she googled her. The first Dr. Marley was a podiatrist and the second one she found was a psychiatrist. Even though she could use one right then, that wasn't the right one either. Finally, she put in the name with Los Angeles next to it and came up with the right number.

She called, only to hear a recording that the office wasn't open yet and if it was an emergency to call 911.

I wonder if not being able to wait is considered an emergency. Rachel was now even more freaked out, wondering why the doctor would call from home instead of waiting until the office was open. *Maybe I could use one of those search engines to find her home number. Now, that wouldn't be too weird,* she thought.

Rachel wouldn't be able to call from work, so she phoned her assistant, Mark, and told him she was going to be late. She glanced at the clock again, only five minutes had gone by. Picking up a book off the nightstand, she read the same two pages four times, she still didn't know what was happening in the plot. Tossing the book toward the foot of the bed, she turned on the TV, but Savannah Guthrie's perky voice stressed her out.

Rachel called the office again, hoping someone had come in early, but she got the same recording. She wrapped her arms across her chest as if she were giving herself a hug, then closed her eyes and tried to meditate, but couldn't get her mind off the fact that she was sure she was dying. When she opened her eyes all she heard was the excruciatingly loud ticking of the clock. She pulled the pillow out from behind her head and placed it over the clock, but she couldn't stop herself from lifting the corner of the pillow every few minutes to see what time it was.

When she tried the office again, someone finally answered.

Rachel's voice cracked as she gave her name and said the doctor had left her a message to call. The receptionist told her to hold while she went to see if the doctor was available. While Rachel waited, she picked at a mosquito bite on her leg. When it started bleeding, she held her fingers on it with one hand and held the phone with the other. Even if she was dying, she didn't want to get blood on her new sheets.

"Hello, Rachel, this is Dr. Marley."

"Hi," Rachel wondered if the doctor could tell her blood pressure was through the roof.

"I thought you'd want to know that you're pregnant." Rachel was silent.

"Rachel, are you there?"

"Could you repeat that?" Rachel hit the speaker button so she could hear the doctor loud and clear.

"You're pregnant."

"I don't think that's possible," Rachel said, crinkling her forehead.

"Well, it must be, because you are."

"You're sure?"

"Yes, we checked both your urine and your blood. Looking at your levels, you're about five weeks along."

"Could you be confusing me with someone else?"

"I know it's a surprise, but we're positive. Congratulations."

Rachel's lips curled into a smile so big it almost made her cheeks hurt.

"I called in a prescription to your pharmacy for progesterone," Dr. Marley said. "I want you to get on it as soon as possible, it'll help support the pregnancy."

"I'd say I love you, but we just met."

Dr. Marley laughed. "I'm happy to give you such good news.

Since you're higher risk, you'll see me until the first trimester is over, then you can go back to your regular OB. One of our schedulers will call you later today to set up your first ultrasound."

"Great, have a nice night – I mean morning – I mean . . . Bye." Rachel hit the end call button. She sat in bed staring straight ahead; she couldn't stop grinning.

Brett walked into the room; a towel wrapped around his lower half. "Hey," Brett said tentatively as if he was walking on something that looked soft but might have spikes.

"Hey."

He ran his fingers through his wet hair. "You don't look like you're still mad at me."

"So, what do I look like?"

He stared at her a moment. "Happier?"

"Do I look . . . pregnant?" She put her hands on her belly and rubbed.

Brett's eyes narrowed. "What are you talking about?"

"I'm pregnant!" Rachel jumped out of the bed and ran over to hug him.

Brett stared at her. "I know you want a baby, but you're scaring me. You haven't snapped or something, right?"

"It's true, the doctor just called."

"You were only there yesterday, how could you be pregnant?"

"I don't know, but I am. I made the doctor repeat it twice."

Brett sat on the edge of the bed. Rachel registered the look of shock on his face that she assumed she'd been wearing mere minutes ago.

"Are you excited?" Rachel asked.

"Of course I am, I just need a second to absorb it." Brett lay back on the bed, looking up at the ceiling.

Rachel danced around the room. "I'm pregnant! I'm pregnant!" She returned to the bed and climbed on top of Brett. "All that sex we had in Santa Barbara must have done the trick."

"Glad I could be of service." Brett grabbed and tickled her.

"I'm sorry about last night," Rachel said after she snorted from laughing so hard. "I thought my irritability and exhaustion were depression, but now I know it was hormones. And I plan to blame everything on hormones during the next nine months."

"Thanks for the heads up. So . . . I'll be moving out until you go into labor."

"Then who'll get me ice cream in the middle of the night?"

"We have dogs."

Rachel catapulted off the bed as if somebody shoved her. "I need to get to the pharmacy. The doctor wants me to get on progesterone as soon as possible." She grabbed a pair of sweats and a hoodie out of a drawer. After she'd put on one sock, she froze and dropped the other one. "What if I miscarry this one, too?"

"One step at a time." Brett stood up. "Let's enjoy this for the day, then you can worry." Rachel nodded happily. "Give me a second and I'll drive you to the pharmacy."

Rachel reached over and yanked Brett's towel off him, leaving him naked. "I can't believe you aren't dressed yet."

Chapter Six
Katie

Katie left work early, exhausted, and not feeling well. When she got home, she fell into a deep sleep, missing Dylan's phone call for the first time. She woke up to rumbling in her stomach that sounded like Barry White singing inside her. The room was completely dark, the only light coming from the lamppost outside her apartment building. Katie was disoriented as she made her way into the kitchen to make a grilled cheese sandwich. Her calendar, stuck to the fridge by a Mickey Mouse magnet, caught her attention. Katie always put a star on the day she got her period so she could know exactly when to expect it. Her period was always twenty-eight days like clockwork, but when she scanned the month, she couldn't find a star. Katie turned the page back to the month before and counted the weeks. Her teeth chattered even though she wasn't cold.

I've only had sex twice in the last year and that was on the same night, Katie thought. *We used condoms; I can't be pregnant.*

She sat and went through a checklist. Her stomach had been bothering her for over a week, every day after work she'd fallen asleep for at least an hour, and she was too anal to have screwed up the date on her calendar. To top it off, she wanted another grilled cheese, and she hadn't started eating the first one.

Katie felt nauseous and her body stiffened. She frantically looked for her keys but couldn't find them. She gave up and looked for her spare keys. Those were missing, too. Why weren't either of them in the bowl on the table at the front door? She started digging through purses in her closet, throwing them one by one onto her bed. Finally, she found both sets of keys under her comforter. At the drug store, as she looked for the correct aisle, she couldn't stop blinking to the point that her eyes were drying out. She grabbed eye drops and two pregnancy tests, just to be sure. She all but jogged to her car, tearing the box open and reading the instructions, wanting to be ready as soon as she got home. Unfortunately, when she did, her bladder wouldn't cooperate. It didn't want to know the answer either.

Completing the test wasn't hard but waiting for the results was torturous. To distract herself, she went to feed Mr. Morrison. While the cat chowed down, Katie continuously repeated, "I am not pregnant, I am not pregnant, I am definitely not pregnant."

Then she went back to the bathroom to look at the stick.

"I am pregnant, oh shit, I'm pregnant."

The panic attack she'd tried to hold off was on top of her.

She took the second pregnancy test, just to make sure, and unfortunately, that too came out positive.

Katie sat on the closed toilet seat; afraid she might pass out. Mr. Morrison sauntered into the bathroom.

"This can't be happening, Mr. Morrison, I was only kidding when I said Dylan could be your new dad." She tried to slow down her breathing but couldn't. "I have to relax. If I pass out, there's no one here to revive me, and I doubt you know CPR, Mr. Morrison." Katie picked up the phone and called Sandra.

"Hey, are you feeling better?" Sandra asked.

Katie began to cry hysterically. "I'm pregnant."

"Oh my god, what can I do? Do you want me to come over?"

"Thanks, but no, I'm kind of a mess."

"Have you told Dylan?"

"He's coming here next week; I'll tell him then. Sandra, what have I done?" Katie sobbed harder.

Sandra tried to reassure her that she and Dylan would figure it out, but no amount of reassurance was making Katie feel better.

For the rest of the week, Katie avoided Dylan's calls. She told him she had meetings during lunch; she didn't think she could talk to him on the phone and pretend she was fine. Instead of going to the lunchroom, Sandra and Katie ate at Katie's desk, which had files scattered all over it; the tornado that was her life had entered her job. Sandra piled the files on the floor, leaving the only thing on the desk a wind-up robot Katie's grandmother had given her.

Katie was happy to talk about anything and everything except the pregnancy. As she took a bite of her sandwich and described the crazy ending of the book she'd just finished, Sandra wound up the toy robot over and over, staring at it as it wobbled around the desk.

After the tenth time it made its way toward her food, Katie grabbed the robot. "What is wrong with you, Sandra?" Katie asked. "I'm the one whose life is falling apart and you're the one who's acting crazy."

"I can't take it anymore, what're you doing?" Sandra blurted.

"What do you mean?" Katie asked, her mouth full.

"Monday, you brought tuna, which is filled with mercury, Tuesday it was sushi from the market, and today, deli meat and soft cheese. You can't eat any of that when you're pregnant."

"Oh, geez, of course I know that. What's wrong with me?"

"I've been trying not to judge you, but pretending you aren't pregnant doesn't make it go away." Sandra's voice softened.

Katie tossed her sandwich into the garbage. "Then I guess you would think it was a bad time to take up helicopter skiing?" Katie said, trying to lighten the mood.

Sandra shook her head, then handed Katie the rest of her salad. After that, every time Katie reached for something to eat or drink, she heard Sandra's voice in her head: Pretending not to be pregnant didn't make it go away.

* * *

Katie's neck ached from tossing and turning all night. The torrential rain pelting her windows matched perfectly with what she felt inside. She grabbed her raincoat and umbrella and headed off to work. Even though it was a busy day, and she barely had time to sit, she couldn't stop fidgeting. She must've looked to the patients like the anxious mess that she was.

When Dylan knocked on her door that evening, she would've

given anything not to have to tell him she was pregnant. He came in like a foam ball shot out of a Nerf gun and before Katie could get the word hello out, he grabbed her.

"I've missed you," he said as he ran his hands over her body. "I've especially missed all these parts."

Darn, he looks even cuter than he did last time, she thought. He wore a sage green sweater that made his eyes sparkle, and his hair was just slightly messed up in the best possible way. He carried in a bottle of merlot, and she wanted to grab it and down the whole thing but knew the baby and Sandra would not look kindly on that.

"I've missed you, too," she said. His now-familiar scent of musk and citrus made her lightheaded.

I want to rip that sweater off him. Would it really hurt to have sex with him before I tell him? she thought, but knew it was better to get it over with. She took his hand and led him to the couch.

As soon as they sat, Dylan lifted her onto him, so she was straddling his lap. When she got off, he frowned.

"What's wrong?"

"I'm pregnant."

Dylan jumped up. "What're you talking about? That's impossible,

I used a condom."

"I guess it didn't work. I'm definitely pregnant."

"Are you sure it's mine?"

Katie jerked back as if he'd slapped her. "Of course, I'm sure."

Dylan was almost vibrating. "It'll be okay, we'll figure it out." Katie thought he would be the one making her feel better.

"I can't have a baby with you. I'm married and I already have two kids."

Katie shot out of her seat. She gasped and began to shake. "Wait what? You never said you were married."

"I didn't think it was relevant. You seemed as into me as I was into you."

"I was, but I didn't know you were having an affair." Katie paced around the room; she couldn't have gotten her legs to stop even if she'd wanted to.

"If you cared about my marital status, you could've asked," he said matter-of-factly.

"You asked me on a date, and you don't wear a wedding ring. I never would've slept with you if I'd known the truth!"

Dylan raked his fingers through his hair. "I can't believe I flew out here for nothing," he muttered.

"Did you really just say that?" Katie said slowly and deliberately, her heart hardening.

"What do you want from me?"

"To help me figure out what to do."

"You should have an abortion," Dylan said, as if it was the most obvious choice.

"What if I don't want to have one?" Katie's fingers reached up and fiddled with the cross around her neck.

"I'm not messing up my marriage and family for some little mistake."

"Little? Mistake?" Katie felt her mouth hanging open.

"Yes. I'll give you money for the abortion, but if you decide to keep it, that's on you."

Katie yanked the front door open. "Get out!"

He looked at her and shook his head as if she were in the wrong. Katie held her hands down at her sides so she wouldn't hit him. After he stepped out, she slammed the door with gusto, then grabbed her phone.

"Sandra . . ." she sobbed, "I need you."

"I'm on my way."

* * *

Katie's head rested on Sandra's shoulder, a box of tissues on the coffee table.

"No more dating," Katie sobbed. "I wonder if my church could use a pregnant nun."

"I can't believe what a jerk that guy is." Sandra pulled a wad of tissues from the box and handed them to Katie.

"I should've known better than to sleep with someone I barely knew. I told myself that since we went to high school together, I could trust him." Katie blew her nose using all the tissues. "What a fool I was."

"You couldn't have known he was married."

"No, but I knew that condoms weren't one hundred percent effective." Katie put the used tissues in her pocket and Sandra handed her a few more.

"I'm so sorry," Sandra said.

"I thought that since we were in our thirties, we could've made it work." Katie scratched her nails up and down her arm, the pain a distraction from the real pain she was feeling. "What am I going to do?" She picked her head up off Sandra's shoulder.

"You only have a few choices."

72

"Is one of those choices to turn back the clock?"

"This may not be the way you thought things would go, but what if this had been an immaculate conception? What would you do?" Katie stared at her. "Humor me a minute. What would you do?" Sandra asked.

Katie wrinkled her forehead and put her hand on her chest and was silent as she contemplated Sandra's question. "I would have the baby," she said releasing her jaw, a small smile growing on her face.

* * *

Katie bounded through the door of The Cheesecake Factory, her hair falling out of her ponytail and whipping across her face. The back of her neck was wet with sweat even though it was sixty-five degrees out and the restaurant had the air on. The jacket in her hand trailed along the floor behind her as she made her way through the crowd.

Sandra sat at a table having a glass of wine and eating a piece of bread. As Katie approached, she knocked over a glass of water on another table. The liquid spilled all over the table and a woman jumped up, grabbing her purse before the water hit it.

"Oh, I'm so sorry," Katie said to the woman then pulled out the chair across from Sandra and sat. She grabbed her napkin and wiped her clammy neck. A waiter picked up her jacket from the floor and draped it over the back of her seat. Katie hadn't realized she'd dropped it.

"You're kind of a mess." Sandra looked her over.

Katie's eyes misted. "You can't say that to a pregnant woman who's emotionally on the edge."

"I'm sorry, that's not what I meant. Well, it is what I meant, but I shouldn't have said it out loud. Are you okay?"

"No. I have no idea how I'm going to be a good mother. I'm anxious and I can't sleep."

"I think not sleeping makes you a great mother," Sandra said, obviously trying to lighten the mood. "From what I hear, it's a requirement until your kid goes to college, then you give it up to a higher power . . . or track their phone."

"What do I know about taking care of a child?"

"What did you know about cooking a chicken? You'll figure it out."

"Sometimes I undercook a chicken. Sometimes I overcook a chicken. Oh, no, what if I ruin this kid?" Katie gestured wildly and knocked her jacket off her chair again. This time it remained on the floor.

"Don't worry, your kid's going to come out fully cooked," Sandra reassured her.

The waiter asked if Katie wanted a glass of wine.

"Really?" she asked him incredulously. "I can't drink wine anymore," she burst out and slumped in her seat. "And I love wine." The waiter narrowed his eyes at her and walked away.

"One sip won't hurt." Sandra slid her glass toward Katie.

"I'm not sure I can do this," Katie said.

"Of course you can, just put the glass to your lips and drink."

"I meant; will I be able to handle the responsibility for someone else's life?" Katie took a tiny sip and handed the glass back.

"You definitely can. You're caring and patient – most of the time," Sandra winked.

Katie's jaw clenched and she wondered if Sandra could hear her grinding her teeth.

"If you're this freaked out, you can always consider placing the baby for adoption."

"I couldn't do that either. Every time I saw some random kid around the same age, I'd have to find a way to yank a hair from their head so I could get it tested for their DNA, and that would leave a lot of bald kids out there."

"Not to mention you'd be in jail."

Sandra ordered a salad with oil and vinegar on the side, and Katie ordered a cheeseburger with extra cheese and fries, extra crispy. Then Katie took two pieces of bread from the basket and put them on her plate.

"Here, you can have my bread, too," Sandra said.

"Thank you. I've decided if I'm going to get fat anyway, I will enjoy it." Katie smothered the bread with butter.

"I know you're overwhelmed right now; it's going to take time for you to get used to all these changes."

"I just thought my life would change with a husband and he'd show me how to be a mother. I mean . . . well, you know what I mean."

"Scarily enough I do."

"Children can have all sorts of problems," Katie said. "Like what if my daughter can't stand up for herself and she gets bullied? Or worse what if she's the bully? What if she's an idiot, or all the other kids hate her, or she steals my credit card and destroys my credit?"

"If you put your purse on the counter, your baby isn't going to come out of the womb tall enough to reach it."

"Ha ha!"

"You keep calling the baby a girl, what if it's a boy?" Sandra asked.

"I can't raise a boy; I can't even get a boyfriend." Katie started to tear up. "Oh no, he or she is doomed, and I'll be the cause of their therapy bills, and I can't afford those either."

"Your baby isn't even born yet, and you've decided it's a stupid criminal who bullies people. Do you think you're going to be giving birth to Al Capone?"

"I'm sure Al Capone's mother didn't think that either."

Katie eyed Sandra intensely as Sandra took another sip of wine. Sandra finished her last gulp and handed the glass to a busboy who was walking by. Katie couldn't believe how hungry she was, so when the waiter brought their food, she took a big bite of the cheeseburger and savored the taste. As she started to tell Sandra a story about one of the new doctors, Sandra took her own napkin and reached across the table to wipe a dab of mustard that had dripped onto Katie's face.

"See, you'd make a better mother than I would," Katie said after she swallowed. "You're so caring."

"Not really, I couldn't pay attention to anything you were saying, I just kept staring at the yellow blob."

Katie giggled, which then turned into a boisterous guffaw. She was so tired, and her emotions were all over the place that she didn't care how loud and out of control she felt. When she had almost exhausted herself, she snorted.

"I think you just entertained the whole restaurant," Sandra

said. "Except maybe that table." She gestured to where a woman at the next table was shaking her head and whispering to her friend. "If she comes over here, I'll protect you."

"You're so maternal. Hey, do you want to raise my kid?"

* * *

A week later, Katie had spent most of the morning sitting at her desk and almost didn't notice when Dr. Marley pulled up a chair next to her.

"Katie, you haven't moved from here for the last hour and Sandra's doing all the scheduling."

"I'm so sorry." Katie stood quickly.

"It's just not like you. Is everything okay?"

Katie picked up a pen and clicked it open and closed repeatedly. Thoughts ran through her mind in a jumble. Should she tell her boss what was going on? Would Dr. Marley think badly of her? Would she be unhappy that Katie was going to have to take maternity leave?

Finally, Katie said, "I'm pregnant."

"I'm gathering that this wasn't planned."

"It wasn't, but I've decided to keep it, and raise it alone."

Dr. Marley nodded and Katie waited for her to ask more questions, but when she didn't Katie continued, "I'm thirty-two and work in an infertility clinic and got pregnant by accident. I'm so embarrassed, what will everyone here think of me?"

"We're not just people you work with, we're your friends. Have you talked to your parents?"

"Sandra's the only person who knows right now."

"Have you seen your OB/GYN?" Katie shook her head. "You should make an appointment and in the meantime, go downstairs to the drug store and pick up some prenatal vitamins."

Katie almost wanted to smack herself. She was eight weeks pregnant and knew exactly what to do. How could she not get on prenatals when she told women all the time to get on them?

Katie made sure Dr. Marley knew that she didn't want anyone else in the office to know her circumstances right now.

"You tell the staff when you're ready, although, I think eventually they're going figure it out for themselves." Dr. Marley patted her arm and headed back toward her office.

I better get back to work, my kid's going to need a lot of diapers, Katie thought, then moved over to the receptionist's desk to look at the schedule. She breathed a sigh of relief when there weren't any patients in the waiting room.

Sandra headed toward Katie, trying to comfort a crying woman. "I can't believe this round of IVF didn't work either," the woman said, trying to make eye contact with Katie, who averted her eyes.

Katie picked up a file off the receptionist's desk and held it in front of her midsection, even though there was nothing to hide. *I hope she can't tell I got pregnant without even trying,* Katie thought.

Sandra escorted the woman out, then locked the door so they wouldn't be disturbed during lunch.

"Thank you for taking over for me this morning, I promise I won't make it a habit." Katie kicked off her shoes and balanced her feet on her desk.

"You can lean on me any time . . . unless you have to throw up," Sandra said, sitting next to her.

"You just said I could lean on you anytime?" Katie smirked.

Later that afternoon as Katie pulled the church door open, it creaked loudly. The echo pierced through the nave. When her eyes adjusted, she saw that she was all alone. She hadn't been to a service in weeks; it felt sacrilegious to go, knowing she was pregnant with a married man's baby. She walked down the aisle and sat in the pew closest to the altar. She wanted the best seat as if she were at a concert.

God, please take care of me and my baby and help me be a good mother. You know I didn't grow up with great role models, so go easy on me when I make mistakes. She basked in her thoughts and the silence for a little longer then made her way to the exit. When she opened the door, she almost knocked Father George down as he came in.

"Hi, Katie!" He looked slightly startled. "It's nice to see you."

Katie wondered if Father George had some kind of spiritual ability to be able to tell she was pregnant, and if so did he wonder why she wasn't wearing a wedding ring. "I'm sorry, I haven't been coming to services for a while." Katie bit her lip, feeling the priest's eyes boring into her.

"Is everything okay?" he asked gently. When she couldn't come up with a response, Father George continued, "Sit with me." He led Katie to a pew, and they sat next to each other.

She waited for him to start, then realized he was waiting for her. She knew he'd wait for hours if she didn't say something. "I, uh, got myself into a mess."

"What kind of mess?"

Katie unconsciously touched her belly. "I'm pregnant."

"Oh." She wished she could know what he was thinking, but

his face was void of any expression.

"I'm sorry," she said absentmindedly.

"You don't need to apologize."

"I thought I'd be married before I had a child, but the father isn't the man I thought he was, so he's not going to be in the picture."

"It is best to be married, but sometimes life throws us curveballs and we need to be able to hit them. Sorry for the baseball metaphor, I was watching the Dodgers earlier."

Katie smiled through the tears that were beginning to pool in the corner of her eyes.

"You may not be having this baby under the circumstances you wanted but bringing a new life into the world is a blessing. Do you have family to help you?"

"No, just a good friend."

"Then our congregation will be your family. Say the word and I'll let our parishioners know you're in need."

"Thank you, Father, but I'm not ready to tell people yet."

"I understand." Father George stood. "I'm here anytime you need me. And have faith in yourself, I do."

"I appreciate you talking to me."

Father George left, and Katie kneeled down in the pew, figuring that praying one more time wouldn't hurt.

Dear Lord, please help me get through this pregnancy and love this baby growing within me. Please forgive me for my sins of not getting married first, and for sleeping with someone I barely knew. I've made mistakes in my life, but I don't want this baby to think of itself as a mistake. I don't want it to have a childhood like I had. Amen.

Chapter Seven
Rachel

8 weeks pregnant

Rachel finished setting four places at the dining room table. At the center, she put a vase of hydrangeas she'd cut from her garden that morning and lit the scented candles she kept for special occasions. She admired her work, then stuck her nose right up to one of the candles and luxuriated in the sweet aroma of vanilla and lavender, her two favorite scents.

Rachel hadn't had her parents over for a Friday night dinner in a long time, but since she'd found out she was pregnant, she had a burning desire to cook and nest with family.

The dogs suddenly scampered to the front door, their tails wagging expectantly. They knew the sound of Brett's car from a half-block away. Rachel grabbed a Corona from the refrigerator, popped the top off, and met Brett at the door, the dogs at her heels.

He thanked her then took the bottle from her. "Not that I'm complaining, but having my gorgeous wife greet me with a beer, makes me wonder if she's buttering me up for something?" Brett took a sip.

"I just love you a lot."

He glanced at the table. "You're using our best china; I don't think it's love you're buttering me up for."

Rachel checked the timer on the oven. "I invited my parents over for Shabbat dinner. I want to see their faces when we tell them I'm pregnant."

"I thought we agreed to wait until you pass the first trimester," Brett said.

"I know, but I've been pregnant for three weeks, and not telling the most important people, besides you, of course, makes me feel like I'm lying to them every time they ask me how I am." Rachel put a challah on the table.

"The mailman asks you how you are, are you going to tell him, too?" Brett laughed and Rachel screwed up her face at him. "I'm not sure it's a good idea to get your parents so excited this early. Especially your mom."

Brett put his beer down and helped her put one of their good crystal glasses at each place setting. They'd gotten them as wedding presents, but Rachel was always afraid to use them, as they were expensive, and she was worried they'd break. Tonight she couldn't care less.

"It's not going to feel real to me until I tell them."

"We don't need to tell anyone for it to be real."

"Then I'm scared these feelings I have that something's wrong won't go away. Last night, I had a dream that the doctor's office switched blood samples and they called to tell me I wasn't pregnant." Rachel stirred the pot on the stove so vigorously that grains of rice became airborne, like tiny caterpillars taking flight.

"We saw the heartbeat," he stated.

"We heard it, but it could've been any baby's heartbeat."

"So somebody else's baby is inside you, or the baby inside the woman in the next room is so loud we're hearing it on your ultrasound?" Rachel laughed at the absurdity.

"Sweetheart, you are pregnant," he said.

"I know, but is it weird that I haven't been nauseous, . . . and my breasts haven't gotten bigger." She put his hands on her breasts.

"Your breasts couldn't be more perfect," he said. "I know you're scared, but you have to start believing."

"What if I've convinced myself I was pregnant, and my body went along with it? Haven't you heard of a hysterical pregnancy?"

"I've heard of a hysterical wife."

Rachel whacked him playfully with a dish towel. "Okay, I get it, you're too funny."

"Honey, you can't keep going from excited to distraught," Brett said. "You're making me and the dogs anxious."

One of the dogs was chasing its tail, the other was eating a dust bunny.

"I think I'll feel better after I tell my parents."

"Then tell them, I only want you to be happy, but keep in mind when your mom finds out she's going to go nutty, you might feel even more pressure. Remember when you told her we got engaged? You came home to a banner across your entire apartment complex."

"Yeah, and it was embarrassing watching the other tenants have to crawl under it to get up the stairs." Rachel tasted a piece of broccoli to make sure it was ready, then turned the flame down to simmer.

She kissed him as the doorbell rang. "They're here!"

"I'm going to go change my clothes . . ." He headed toward their bedroom, then turned back around and picked up the Corona. ". . . and finish this beer."

Rachel opened the door.

"Hi, sweetheart," her dad said, enveloping her in a hug.

"Hi, Dad." Rachel kissed her mom on the cheek. "Come on in, Brett's changing his clothes." The dogs bounded toward her parents who showered them with affection as if they were grandchildren.

Rachel looked much more like her father than her mother. Her mother had thick, straight blonde hair, light eyes, and was a few inches taller than Rachel. Rachel had inherited her Dad's wavy brown hair; except now he was going gray at his temples. However, she was grateful that she'd gotten her mom's thin build, and like her mom, she was able to eat a lot of food without gaining weight. Rachel wondered if that would change after she had the baby, but she'd take fifty extra pounds if it meant she'd have a baby in her arms.

"The table looks lovely, honey." Her mom ran her hand across the lace and linen tablecloth that Rachel's grandmother brought with her when she immigrated from Poland.

"And it smells wonderful in here, too. What're you cooking?"

her dad asked.

"Well, actually, I'm cooking something big, but it might take a while." Rachel smiled.

"That's okay, we can wait; we ate a late lunch," her mom said.

"Can you wait nine months?" Rachel said.

"Nine months?" her mother asked, squinting at Rachel.

"You're pregnant?" Her parents spoke over each other as they grabbed her in a three-way hug, bursting with excitement.

Brett had barely walked into the room when Leah was on him, hugging him tightly. "We couldn't be happier for you guys!"

"Thanks, we're excited too," Brett said, looking at Rachel, who shrugged.

"We should celebrate!" Ezra clapped his hands once.

"We aren't quite at that point yet, Rachel's only at eight weeks." Brett put his hands up in a stalling gesture. "But we are excited, and doesn't she look beautiful? Not that she doesn't always look beautiful."

Rachel put her arm around him and nuzzled his neck. "Brett's going to be such a great father, he's fun and sweet and thoughtful and this baby's going to be lucky to have him."

"The baby will be lucky to have us both," he said. They gave each other a kiss.

Rachel's mother looked as if she were going to do handsprings across the floor. "I can't believe we're going to have our first grandchild. All my friends have three or four apiece, and they're always jamming pictures in my face. I can't wait until I have pictures to shove at them."

"Rachel, is dinner ready? I'm starving," Brett said.

"I can't wait to take him or her to the zoo," her mom said.

"And to the children's museum, and to Rachel's grandmother who'll want to show the baby off in the nursing home."

Rachel asked her parents to have a seat at the table, and she and Brett went into the kitchen to get the food. She picked up the salad and the rice. Brett got the brisket and broccoli.

Brett gave the Shabbat blessing over the challah before passing the food around the table.

"This looks great, Rachel." Her dad dished food onto his plate. "Your child will be fortunate to have a mom who's a great cook. Just like your mother." Ezra looked at Leah with admiration and Leah beamed up at him. For a moment it was as if it was only the two of them in the room. When Rachel was little, she thought it was embarrassing how openly affectionate her parents were with each other, but as she got older she saw it differently and was happy she found the same thing with Brett.

"Hopefully, the doctor is right and I'm pregnant." Rachel passed the rice to her mother.

"I'm confused, Brett just said you were eight weeks along." Her mom began to tear her napkin into pieces.

"Rachel *is* pregnant," Brett said. "She's having a tough time accepting that it's real."

"Oh, you scared me." Leah breathed a heavy sigh of obvious relief. "That's not nice to do to a woman with a heart condition." Her mom reached for another napkin.

"You have a heart condition? When did that start?" Rachel asked, her voice rising an octave.

"Your mother doesn't have a heart condition." Her dad shook his head.

"You don't know, I could," Leah protested. "I haven't been to a doctor in a while."

"Mom, you're giving me a heart attack," Rachel said.

Her mother reached across the table and put a big spoonful on Rachel's plate. "You need to eat more broccoli. A baby needs lots of vegetables to grow up big and strong."

Rachel nodded and took a bite. "Please, don't tell anyone yet that I'm pregnant," Rachel said to her parents after she swallowed. "I'll let you know when I feel comfortable."

"We'll wait," her dad said.

The four of them ate the rest of dinner with Leah talking nonstop about the baby shower she wanted to plan and what colors she hoped the nursery would be because she was going to knit a blanket and she already had some yarn. Rachel and Brett rolled their eyes at each other behind their napkins, then stifled a laugh.

* * *

When Rachel was almost at the end of her first trimester, she was slowly beginning to feel more relaxed. Over the last two years, she'd come to understand how an anxiety disorder could come on quickly and change an entire personality.

Rachel moved throughout the classroom helping the students as they worked on an assignment. She took pride in how much the kids had learned and matured over the year, but just when she got them where they needed to be, they moved up to first grade. *I wonder what my baby will be like when he or she is this age? I can't wait to find out. Will they be smart, or have a great sense of humor like Brett?*

The one thing she hoped was that her child wouldn't divulge things about her that she wouldn't want their teachers to know. One boy in Rachel's class told her that his mom's job consisted of getting her nails done and talking on the phone. Another girl told her that her dad is a superhero and is always trying to rescue young women and her mother isn't happy about it.

As each child was busy writing and illustrating a memory from their lives, Rachel asked Mark to watch the class for a minute while she ran to the bathroom.

When she pulled down her pants, she noticed a small bit of blood on her panties. She shook her head repeatedly and felt her legs weaken beneath her.

I knew as soon as I let myself be happy about being pregnant, I was bound to miscarry again. Someone must hate me for making me go through this over and over, especially when I'm almost in my second trimester, longer than I've gone without miscarrying.

She rushed back to her classroom, her legs shaking so much she thought she might fall.

"I need to leave right now; can you take over?" she whispered to Mark.

"Of course. Are you okay?"

"I just have to go." Rachel pulled her purse out of her desk drawer and raced out.

On her way to her car, she called the doctor's office. When she told the nurse about the blood, the nurse told her to come right over. Then she called Brett and as soon as he answered she said bluntly, "I'm miscarrying."

"Are you sure?"

"Yes. I'm going to the doctor's office; can you meet me there?"

"I'm on my way."

As soon as Rachel arrived at Dr. Marley's office, Katie greeted her and led her into an exam room. Rachel laid back on the table, looking up at the ceiling, her stomach twisted into a knot.

The door opened and Brett rushed in. Rachel grabbed his hand.

"I'm so sorry," she said. "I can't believe I'm losing this baby, too."

"We don't know anything yet."

"I got to ten weeks this time." Her breathing was quick and shallow.

Brett put his arm around her, and after a minute, her breathing slowed.

"Rachel, what's going on?" Dr. Marley asked as soon as she entered the room.

"I'm bleeding, I'm sure I'm having another miscarriage."

Dr. Marley introduced herself to Brett, then explained that bleeding during pregnancy is often normal, as well as some cramping, especially in the first trimester. The doctor left while Rachel took her clothes off from the waist down.

While a nurse put all of Rachel's information into the machine, Dr. Marley explained to Rachel how a transvaginal ultrasound worked and that she'd be able to assess clearly if there were any issues.

Rachel squeezed Brett's hand and closed her eyes tight when Dr. Marley inserted the probe, then she opened her eyes and stared at the screen even though she had no idea what she was looking at.

"I don't see anything that looks like a baby," Rachel said, shaking her head slowly back and forth. *The baby is already gone.*

"Well, I do," Dr. Marley said.

Rachel studied the doctor, but all she could detect was her calm demeanor. She looked back at the screen, to where the doctor was pointing. She didn't understand the image, but Dr. Marley seemed sure. Her heart lifted. Dr. Marley turned a knob on the machine to allow Brett and Rachel to hear the baby's heartbeat. The thump was strong and rhythmic.

"I've looked at your uterus, the placenta, and your baby and everything looks good."

Rachel put her palm on her heart. "My baby's okay?"

"Yes. Twenty to thirty percent of women bleed a little, so unless it's a lot, you don't have to worry. You can go back to your regular gynecologist now; I think you're out of the woods."

Rachel sighed. Dr. Marley told them if they needed anything they could call, but she was sure Rachel would be fine.

"I'm sorry I scared you," Rachel said to Brett after the doctor and nurse had left the room. "I saw the blood and panicked."

"It's fine."

"I promise to be more relaxed after the first trimester," she told him.

"That's only a week away."

"Oh, right. Then, it might be after the second trimester." Brett and Rachel walked out of the office hand in hand.

* * *

Six weeks flew by, and Rachel was now well into her second trimester. She was sound asleep on the couch when Brett came home one evening.

"Rachel," he whispered into her ear.

She opened her eyes slowly and looked at him for a moment as if he had come from another galaxy. "Hi," she said in a raspy voice when she was fully awake. "What time is it?"

"Six-thirty."

"I've been asleep for three hours?"

"I guess so."

"Do you want me to make dinner, or do you want to go out?" she asked.

"Let's go out, we can celebrate the beginning of your summer vacation."

Rachel went to the bathroom to clean up. After reaching for a washcloth to dry her face, she felt what she thought was a strange twitch in her pelvic region. She rubbed her hands over it, and it stopped. She sprayed dry shampoo in her hair, then brushed it out. As she turned to leave the bathroom, she bent over as she felt another twitch along her side. Frozen in place, she felt sweat forming under her shirt. She yelled out to Brett, who came charging into the bathroom.

"What's wrong?" he asked.

"I don't know. I feel kind of crampy, and I'm burning up." She lifted the bottom of her shirt to fan herself. "I think I should call my doctor." Brett put cold water on a washcloth and brought it to her forehead. Rachel sat on the edge of the tub.

"What do the cramps feel like?" he asked.

"They're gone now, but like a quick spasm."

"Could it just be you twisted something?"

"I don't know, I guess, maybe."

"You said they stopped, so maybe it's nothing." "I'm scared," she said.

"I know, I am, too, but Dr. Marley said you might have a little cramping, and that would be normal."

"I think I just need a lot of reassurance right now."

"I've been trying, but my reassurance doesn't seem to be working. Why don't you call Caitlin and Gabby, they both have kids, so they'll understand what you're feeling better than I could."

"Then it's okay if I tell them I'm pregnant?"

"You haven't told your best friends? It's fine, you're in your second trimester."

"Good, because I told them a month ago." Rachel smiled sheepishly.

* * *

Caitlin and Gabby shared a pitcher of strawberry margaritas while Rachel nursed a lemonade. They were at Casa Vega, a Mexican restaurant in Sherman Oaks they'd been going to since their freshman year of high school. They had their favorite booth and their favorite waitress, Isabella. Before they were twenty-one, they couldn't even use their fake IDs because all the waiters and bartenders had watched them grow up. Gabby swayed a little to the mariachi playing in the background.

Rachel wanted to dive into the chips and guacamole.

"My baby's so hungry and loves avocado." Rachel crunched loudly.

"Then it's definitely one of us," Gabby said.

"It certainly is, although right now it's the size of a turnip," Caitlin said.

"A hungry turnip," Rachel said.

"Caitlin, remember what we were like pregnant?" Gabby asked.

Caitlin pushed the basket of chips closer to Rachel. "Oh, yeah, I almost bit my husband's hand off once when he opened a bag of barbeque potato chips."

"My poison was a Western Bacon Cheeseburger from Carl's Jr. I think I kept them in business during my pregnancies," Gabby said.

Isabella came over to take their order. Gabby and Caitlin ordered a chopped taco salad, light on the cheese, and Rachel, who usually ordered the same, ordered a combination plate with two tacos, a tamale, rice and beans, and extra guacamole on the side.

"So, I've heard that someone needs a pregnancy pep talk," Gabby said.

"Are you talking to my husband behind my back, or are you psychic?" Rachel asked.

"Neither. Brett mentioned to David that he was hoping you would either get less nutty or nutty enough to have you put away," Gabby joked. "And before you go thinking you married an impatient Neanderthal; I can tell you David felt the same way when I was pregnant with all three of our kids."

"I know I've been making Brett a little crazy, but I can't get my head around the fact that things are going to work out."

"You're in your second trimester, enjoy it now, before that

turnip gets big enough to tap-dance on your intestines." Gabby refilled her and Caitlin's glasses.

"No offense," Caitlin said, "But I'm glad I'm not going to go through that again. Once you have twins trampolining on your bladder, you get your tubes tied. By the end of my pregnancy, Donnie was sleeping in the guest room because he got tired of me getting up ten times a night to pee."

"We don't have a guestroom, so Brett will have to sleep in the crib," Rachel said. "I guess we better buy one soon."

The busboy picked up the empty basket of chips and dropped off more. Rachel thanked him as if he'd brought her the Cullinan diamond.

"You guys have known me for sixteen years, so you know I've always been easy-going. Since I started trying to have a baby, I've become a neurotic stress cadet, and now that I'm pregnant, I'm worse, if there even is something worse than a neurotic stress cadet."

"If it helps, I can tell you that there'll be lots more stress once the baby comes," Gabby said in a half-joking tone.

"That doesn't help," Rachel said.

"Rachel, may you be as exhausted and sex deprived as we are," Caitlin said. Gabby and Caitlin picked up their glasses.

"To Rachel and her little root vegetable!" Caitlin toasted.

"We celebrate you!" Gabby's words were slightly slurred.

"You two have had a better time 'celebrating' than I have."

"Just pretend your lemonade is a Lemon Drop." Caitlin waved a hand at her dismissively.

"We will enjoy the next many months watching your belly grow and then pushing a fifteen-pound baby out of your tiny body," Gabby said. Rachel stuck her tongue out at her, then they all clinked glasses.

When Rachel got home, Brett was at the kitchen table with a large white sheet of paper stretched across it. He was sketching out a design for a new two-story home he had been hired to build. "How was dinner?" he asked.

"Good." She got a glass of water. "You were right, Gabby and Caitlin convinced me that I need to mellow out and enjoy being pregnant."

"You just made my night." He stood and hugged her. "We should do something fun!"

"How about we take a bath," she said, sticking her chest out and arching her back a little.

"Oooh, I like how you think."

"You first." She put her fingers in her glass and flicked water at him. She giggled uncontrollably but didn't stop. He started laughing and tried to grab the glass from her.

Rachel stopped flicking water and held the glass away from him as best as she could. "Be careful, I'm pregnant."

"How could I forget? You keep bringing it up." He playfully grabbed her butt.

"Well, father of my child, you better have all the sex with me that you can, because when my belly gets so big that I can no longer see my private parts, the party's over."

"I'll still be able to see your private parts," he said.

Rachel laughed so hard that she let out her little snort.

"You did that on purpose," he said. "You know I can't resist you when you snort." Brett wrapped himself around her and Rachel happily sunk into his big, strong arms.

Chapter Eight
Katie

18 weeks pregnant

The wonderful aroma of greasy, cheesy pepperoni pizza seeped under the door of the breakroom.

Pregnancy had heightened Katie's senses dramatically. Recently, she'd gotten a whiff of Old Spice cologne when her UPS man drove his truck by her apartment building. She remembered how her late grandfather wore that scent and she had almost cried, although lately she cried at everything.

As Katie opened the door, her stomach growled as if there was a grizzly bear inside her who'd just spotted a deer. Sandra, Julianna, and Margarette were already eating lunch.

"Have a seat, oh pregnant one," Julianna said. She playfully bowed to Katie, then pulled a chair far away from the table for Katie to take a seat.

Katie looked at the distance from the chair to the table. "How much room do you think I need? Are you trying to imply that I'm getting fat?"

"Hardly, you look better than I do after I've had pasta for dinner." Julianna chuckled.

Katie put last night's leftover chicken and zucchini in the microwave, then sat and scooted her chair in as far as it would go, her belly touching the table.

When the microwave dinged, "I'll get it!" Margarette said, jumping up.

Katie put a hand out to stop her. "I may be pregnant, but my legs still work."

"Hey, when do you get to find out the sex of your little bundle?" Margarette asked, taking a bite of her pizza.

"Hopefully at the ultrasound I have next week."

"And I get to go with her," Sandra said. "I'm her birthing partner." She puffed out her chest as if she'd won the grand prize.

"Well, if you need me, I'm available," Margarette said. "I've always wanted to watch a baby kick its way out of someone."

Julianna popped a piece of a spicy tuna roll into her mouth. Katie tried to forget how much she missed eating raw fish.

"Not me," Julianna said. "I don't want to be there when my own kids are born. I'm having a planned C-section. That way I can pick my kid's birthday and have a tummy tuck at the same time."

"Can anyone spell 'control freak'?" Sandra said.

"Babies may be cute, but they mess up your body," Julianna said.

"You guys should do a motivational speech for pregnant women." Katie reached over to Sandra's plate and took a crouton out of her salad.

"Have you heard from that guy who knocked you up?" Margarette asked.

Sandra glared at Margarette. "He shall remain in the hell I hope he's in forever and we need never to speak of him again."

"My little bulldog." Katie gave Sandra a knowing grin, then turned to Margarette. "No, and I doubt I ever will. I can't imagine he'll even show up at our next high school reunion. I'm probably not the first woman he's gotten in touch with to impregnate. There were a hundred and fifty girls in my graduating class." Katie took a bite of her food.

"You could form a club, then have all the half-siblings show up on his doorstep to meet his wife," Julianna said.

Katie started laughing, then she snorted and accidentally spat out a piece of zucchini, which landed on the table. Sandra took her fork out of her salad, closed the Styrofoam container, and pushed it away. "Well, my appetite's gone."

"If that grossed you out, good luck in the delivery room," Margarette said.

* * *

While Katie and Sandra waited for the ultrasound technician to come in, Sandra flipped through a copy of Vogue she'd taken from the waiting room.

There were pages and pages of beautiful women in elegant outfits and Sandra pointed most of them out to Katie as clothes she thought Katie would look pretty in.

"I can't believe you're torturing me this way," Katie said, turning her head away. "It's bad enough seeing you looking that sexy."

Sandra was wearing tight jeans and a black cropped T-shirt and black wedges.

"What's next, you're going to make me look at bridal magazines?"

A woman in scrubs came in and greeted Katie, who introduced Sandra. "I'm Michelle, I'll be doing your ultrasound today. How's your pregnancy been going?"

"Good, although I have nothing to compare it to."

Katie handed her purse to Sandra and got up on the exam table. Michelle pulled the ultrasound machine over to the table and typed in Katie's information. Katie pulled up her T-shirt and pushed her leggings down a little so her whole belly was showing.

"This might be a little cold," Michelle said as she squeezed the thick goo on Katie's belly.

"You must say that a hundred times a day," Katie said, and Michelle nodded.

"If I'm able to tell, did you want to know the sex of the baby today?" Michelle asked.

"Yes." Katie was vibrating with excitement.

"You sure you don't want to be surprised?" Sandra asked.

"The fact that I'm pregnant is all the surprise I can handle."

"Okay, I'll do my best," Michelle said. "Hopefully, your little one cooperates and isn't crossing his or her legs."

Michelle placed the probe on Katie's abdomen and moved it around. Katie's body temperature had been extra hot the last few months, so the gel felt like a cool massage. "Your placenta looks good, and your uterus looks healthy. Michelle moved the probe around then stopped. "She has ten fingers and ten toes . . ."

"Did you say she?" Katie asked.

"You're having a girl."

"We're having a girl!" Sandra shrieked, grabbing Katie's hand. Katie grinned. "Oh my god, I secretly wanted a daughter."

"Was it really a secret? I think you might've mentioned it a few hundred times," Sandra grinned at her.

Katie picked her head up off the table. "Are you positive?"

"Yes, she flashed me pretty well."

"Then she's your daughter," Sandra said. Katie pretended to scowl at her but was so excited she couldn't hold the scowl for long.

"The arms and legs are measuring where they should be, her spine looks good . . ." Michelle's voice took a sudden downturn, and quickly faded to silence as if it had been on a speeding train that fell off a cliff.

Katie's senses became amplified. The soap in the dispenser made her sinuses twitch, and the *whoosh* of air coming through the vent grated on her nerves.

"Give me a minute, I'll be right back." Michelle walked out of the room.

"That was weird. Don't you think that was weird?" Katie put her hands on the gold chain she wore around her neck and grasped onto the cross that hung from it. "Do you think something's wrong?"

"Maybe she ate something bad for lunch," Sandra said, but Katie could tell Sandra didn't believe it.

"What could she have seen that made her have to leave? And where did she go?"

Sandra walked over to the ultrasound machine and stared at the frozen image of Katie's baby. "I don't know," she said quietly.

"I've had ultrasounds before, the technician doesn't just walk out." Katie was holding the cross so hard, she almost yanked it off the chain. "Is she coming back? She better come back; she has to know that walking out without saying anything is not okay."

Sandra remained silent, which made Katie even more freaked out.

A man in a white coat walked in. He introduced himself as Dr. Prost, the head radiologist. He said he was going to take over.

"Why? Where did Michelle go?" Katie asked putting her hands above her belly as if protecting her unborn baby. Katie whispered to Sandra, "I liked Michelle."

"It's fine, Michelle asked me to step in."

"That doesn't sound good, tell me what's wrong with my daughter." Katie's voice quivered.

"It might be nothing," Dr. Prost said.

"Your face doesn't say it's nothing." Katie sat up so fast she felt dizzy.

"It's okay, just lie back, so I can take a look and I promise I'll let you know what I see." He picked up the probe and Katie moved her hands to her sides. He spent the next few minutes checking one thing over and over.

Katie's eyes bored into him, willing him to say anything. Well, not anything; all she wanted to hear was her baby was fine.

"Tell me, please. What are you looking for?" Katie begged; she was sure she could hear her blood moving through her body.

Dr. Prost picked up the probe and put it back on the ultrasound machine. "Your baby has a thickened nuchal fold and the fluid behind her neck is measuring at a higher amount than we like to see."

"What does that mean, in human speak?" Katie barked, not caring if she was being rude.

"A nuchal fold measuring greater than six millimeters in the second trimester could possibly mean the baby has Down's syndrome. Your baby is measuring at barely under that," he said in a professional, yet calming voice, but no matter what his tone conveyed, Katie wasn't calm.

"Oh, my god." Katie's voice came out almost in a whisper, as her shoulders hunched, and her body began to cave in on itself.

"You said 'possibly'," Sandra said. "What are the chances the baby has Down's?"

"I'd say one in three."

Katie tried to talk, but her words were coming in fits and starts and weren't comprehensible through her sobbing. Sandra put her arm around Katie.

"How can you be so sure it's one in three?" Sandra asked.

"Because there have been studies done when a baby is at the top of the scale."

"Can you measure again? Maybe you made a mistake?" Now that Katie was finally able to speak, her voice was crackling and hoarse.

"Michelle measured three times, and I just measured twice,

and we both came up with the same number." Dr. Prost turned off the ultrasound machine.

"My baby can't have Down's syndrome, I'm not even thirty-five," Katie said.

"Babies with Down's can be born to women of any age. There's a blood test we can do, but I need to tell you that it sometimes comes up as a false positive. An amniocentesis will give you more accurate results. I'll send a report to your doctor, and you can decide what you want to do. I'm so sorry to have to give you this kind of news," Dr. Prost said and quietly left the room.

Katie turned to Sandra. "I'm going to throw up."

Sandra stayed with Katie that night. They sat on the couch, with a blanket across their legs, while Katie cried, then stared off in the distance, then cried again. There was an almost empty box of tissues on the couch and a bunch of used tissues on the ground below Katie's feet.

"When I first found out I was pregnant, the last thing I wanted was a baby. I secretly hoped I'd miscarry. Now that I'm totally in love with her . . ." Katie's voice trailed off as she sobbed.

"I'm so sorry. I wish I knew what to say." Sandra picked up a sandwich from the coffee table and handed it to Katie. "You need to eat something."

Katie shook her head, but Sandra insisted, so she took a small bite, then handed the sandwich back to Sandra. "I was worried that I'd be a bad mother to a kid without special needs, I have no clue how to take care of a child who has Down's syndrome."

"If she does, and that's a big if, there are professionals who can help."

"But they won't be living with me twenty-four hours a day." Katie blew her nose and let another tissue fall onto the ground.

Sandra got the trash can from the kitchen, got on her hands and knees, lifted Katie's feet, and picked up the tissues that were scattered around the floor. "If you have the blood test and the amnio then you'll know for sure, and you can decide what to do."

"What do you mean, decide what to do?" Katie asked, so startled she stopped crying.

"Whether you want to terminate the pregnancy. It's still an option in California."

"Not for me, I'm Catholic."

"These are extenuating circumstances."

"God doesn't look at it that way."

"*Catholicism* may not look at it that way, but I think *God* would recognize this is a difficult situation." Sandra handed Katie a glass of water and urged her to drink.

Katie took a sip, but swallowing wasn't easy with the huge lump in her throat. She sat a moment and contemplated what Sandra said. "I don't know if I could do that." Katie pushed the blanket off her and gazed down at her burgeoning belly. "With every day that goes by, this baby feels more a part of who I am, to think about ending it is. . ." Katie started crying again, her eyes ached, and she could barely open them. She took the last tissue out of the box. Sandra went into the bathroom and brought back a new box.

"This is an impossible situation, but no one would judge you."

"Of course they will. I'd have to tell people I miscarried."

"Then that's what you'd do. Besides, it's no one's business." The sun was beginning to peek through her closed blinds.

"You've been here all night," Katie said.

"I wasn't going to leave you."

"I feel terrible that you have to go to work after not getting any sleep."

"It's nothing a double espresso won't take care of."

Katie wanted to get under her covers and not face the day. Her bones felt like they were cracked or broken, and she had nothing to keep her upright. "I am grateful for you, more than I can say, but I need to be alone to think and you need to go to work."

"I understand." Sandra stood and hugged Katie. "Call me if you need anything. You're sure you'll be okay alone?"

Katie nodded, then Sandra picked up her purse and left. Katie wrapped the blanket around herself and headed to her bedroom. She got under her covers and prayed for sleep, but her brain was on overdrive. Today had been more traumatizing than the worst day of her childhood. She flashed back to 1999 when she was nine years old.

On a ninety-degree summer day in Prescott, Arizona, her father had the trunk of his Toyota Camry open. He was putting one large suitcase and five tightly taped boxes in the car. Katie asked him where he was going, and all he said was he couldn't be around her mom another day. Katie begged him not to go, but he said it had nothing to do with her, that he loved her very much.

She asked him to wait, and ran inside, putting on the T-shirt with the dancing bear he had bought her at the county fair the year before. She had been convinced that if he thought about the good time they had that day, he wouldn't want to leave her.

The screen door clanked behind her as she sprinted back to his car. Her father was sitting behind the wheel with the engine running. He didn't say anything about her shirt, just rolled down his window, leaned out, and kissed her on the head. He promised to send for her after he got settled. She never heard from him again.

Katie watched her father drive away, his arm out the window and his hand waving goodbye. Katie, not caring if she was naked from the waist up, took off the T-shirt and threw it in the mud and stomped on it. When she went back into the house, she found her mother drinking vodka straight from the bottle.

The next morning, her mother woke her up and told her to pack a few things in her backpack, and she drove them to Katie's friend Celeste's house. When she dropped Katie off, she said she'd pick her up in a little while. When Katie turned to say goodbye, her mother said, "I don't know why I wanted you."

Katie's mom didn't call or come back for five days, and when she did, her car was pulling a U-Haul behind it. They drove to Reno, where Katie was left alone during the day at a Motel 6 while her mother looked for work. When her mother finally got a waitressing job, they moved into a shabby one-bedroom duplex, where the two of them had to share a bed and Katie learned to stay away from the old man across the street. Katie went to school during the day and her mother worked nights. Eight months later, her mother up and moved them back to Prescott, Arizona, where Katie stayed until she left for college.

Katie used to wish her mother had never given birth to her. And now she wondered, if her baby did have Down's syndrome, would she someday be upset that Katie chose to have her, knowing her life wouldn't be easy. Katie's daughter might never go on a date or get married or even go to a regular school.

"I wish you could tell me what would be best for you," Katie said, looking at her belly. "That's all that matters." Mr. Morrison jumped up on the bed, snuggling into her belly. He seemed to like the extra weight she'd put on. As he purred, Katie put her face against his fur and closed her eyes. She hoped that this horrible nightmare would soon be over, but she knew it was just beginning.

Hours later, Katie woke up with a start in a dark room. As she laid there, the whole previous day came back to her. She opened her nightstand dresser and pulled out her Bible. It had been a while since she'd read it. She was hoping to find a passage that stated whether abortion was or was not a sin. The closest thing she found was the sixth commandment: Thou shalt not kill. She then found the Mosaic law in Exodus 21:22-25, which stated that an embryo or fetus is not a human being.

How am I supposed to make this decision if even the Bible can't figure it out? She thought, then put the book back in the drawer.

Her stomach growled, and although she knew it was hunger, she hoped it was her baby trying to tell her something. What, she didn't know. Katie pulled herself out of bed and went into the kitchen. A picture of her and Sandra on vacation in Palm Springs was held up on the refrigerator by a magnet that read, Cleverly Disguised as a Responsible Adult. Katie let out a big laugh; she felt like she hadn't laughed like that in forever.

Dr. Marley had said she'd be happy to go over Katie's ultrasound and offer a second opinion. Katie was terrified of what she'd say, she felt like a seventy-five-pound weight was sitting on her heart. Or more like a six-ounce baby.

Mr. Morrison looked up at her, purring loudly.

"I forgot to feed you, didn't I?" she said as she got out his food. "If I can't even remember to feed my cat, how am I ever going to decide something as important as my daughter's life?"

Chapter Nine
Rachel

18 weeks pregnant

"With this many choices, how're we going to figure out what we're supposed to need?" Brett asked. The shelves at Babies 'R' Us were filled with pacifiers in every color of the rainbow, and bottles with too many types of nipples to count. Angled, petite, full-sized, some made of latex and others made of silicone. Brett picked up a bottle and read the label which stated it was for colicky babies. "How do we know if our baby is colicky before it's even born? Why can't there just be a bottle that says: 'your baby won't know the difference'?"

"Because then they couldn't get you to buy more than one," Rachel said. "You're not supposed to figure it out until you have the second kid." She pulled a onesie off the shelf. Written across the front was, 'Sorry Ladies, My Daddy's Taken.' "I'm buying this." She put an arm around Brett possessively. "That's right, ladies, he's mine, too."

Brett looked deep into her eyes, and she puckered up for a kiss. He reached down and wiped something in the corner of her eye. "Sleep boogers."

"Whoever said romance is dead hasn't met you."

"I'm one in a million." He kissed her.

When they turned down the next aisle, Brett picked up a plastic apparatus with two suction cups attached to it. "What's this for?"

"It's a breast pump. Those go on your nipples," Rachel said matter-of-factly.

"I'm not putting anything on my nipples."

"Then it's good you won't be feeding our baby."

Brett studied the breast pump, looking at it from all angles. "It looks like some kind of sex thing."

"Don't get any ideas. It's a contraption that will milk me like a cow."

"I've never been so glad to be male." He picked up the black plastic case the pump came in. "And when you're through milking yourself, you get a new purse," he said, as if he was being serious.

Rachel tossed her head back and shook her head at him. They continued through the store picking up teething toys, bibs, and blankets.

"I'm having so much fun," Rachel said.

"You know what would be more fun?"

"We're not having sex in a Babies R' Us."

"I meant we should come up with some baby names."

"We don't know if it's a boy or a girl yet." Rachel picked up a pair of yellow pajamas.

"But we will after your ultrasound today," Brett said.

"I hope so. I wonder if we'll be able to tell which one of us the baby looks like."

"It better not look like our Sparkletts delivery man, although he is pretty good-looking."

"If our baby takes after me, it's not going to find your jokes amusing."

"We'll see." They continued down another aisle, and Rachel pointed out the bassinet she wanted. She liked that it had a white eyelet skirt with ruffles and a hood over it to protect the baby from monsters. or germs, or monsters with germs. She liked that it had wheels because when the baby napped, she planned to bring it with her to every room in the house.

"So, here are the names I've come up with for our child," Brett said in a lilting, teasing voice. "If it's a girl, we name her Sushi, and if it's a boy we name him Gizzard."

"Neither of those sound very Jewish." Rachel winked at him.

"I think Gizzard sounds extremely masculine; he'd have a leg up in life right away."

"He would have both legs in the air because the other kids would be holding him upside down to stick his head in the toilet. We're not naming our child after food."

"Fine, be boring. What names have you come up with?"

"Hannah if it's a girl and Noah for a boy."

"How about Natalie for a girl?" Brett asked.

"We're not naming her after Natalie Portman, even if she is your hall pass."

Rachel thought she felt something strange. As it was her first real pregnancy, she wasn't sure what it was supposed to feel like when the baby moved. She grabbed Brett's hand and placed it on her belly. "Oh my god, I think it just kicked."

Brett waited patiently, then said, "I don't feel anything."

"I felt something, or maybe I'm just hungry."

"Or maybe it likes the name Natalie." Then talking into her belly, "Right, Natalie?"

They turned the corner and stopped at the Baby Bjorn carriers. Brett picked up the sample and tried to put it on but got all twisted up in it. A woman holding a baby girl in her arms walked down the aisle. She had four other young boys who were holding hands in a human chain. She watched Brett wrestling with the Baby Bjorn.

"Can I help?" the woman asked. Her T-shirt had a large stain of what looked like spit-up near her shoulder.

"It's our first kid," Rachel said excitedly, bouncing on her toes like one of her students.

"I never would've guessed," the woman laughed. Brett handed her the Baby Bjorn and she untwisted it and showed him how to use it. Brett thanked her. One of her kids let go of the human chain to pick his nose and the oldest boy chastised him. The mom looked at her son, whose pinky finger was so far up his nose he appeared to only have four fingers, but she only sighed. "I remember being that excited. Five kids ago."

"Are these baby carriers worth the price?" Brett asked the woman, looking at the tag.

"If you want to get anything done they are," the woman said.

"I'm planning to wear my baby most of the day," Rachel said. "While I exercise, put on makeup, and cook gourmet meals."

The woman chuckled. "Good luck with that." She grabbed the hand of the child next to her and the human chain linked back up.

Brett looked down at his phone. "We better hurry, or we're going to be late for your ultrasound."

"I can't leave without this onesie," she said, holding it up as if it were a delicate piece of art.

"Then we need to get in line."

"As soon as I find pants to go with it. What would the neighbors think if our kid is pants-less?"

"That it's a baby?"

"You're lucky I love you." Rachel turned and headed back toward the section of infant clothes, Brett trailing after her.

* * *

When Rachel and Brett were led into an exam room, Brett sat on a chair next to the exam table and Rachel laid down with her head on a pillow.

"You didn't even notice my new top." She sat up.

"It's cute."

"I wore it especially for today."

"I'm sure the baby is impressed."

Rachel laid back down and lifted her top exposing her midsection.

"We could be waiting a while; the baby could get cold," he said.

"You're right." She yanked her shirt down, crossing her arms across her belly to provide warmth.

"I'm kidding."

"I know."

The radiologist came in. "Hi, I'm Dr. Morales, I'm sorry to keep you waiting. I'll be doing your ultrasound today."

"I'm Rachel and this is my husband, Brett. We're so excited, we'd love to find out the sex of our baby. It's our first," Rachel exclaimed.

"Well, let me see if I can tell," Dr. Morales said.

When the machine was all set up, Rachel pulled up her shirt and he applied the gel to her belly and began the scan. Rachel was so impatient; she vibrated like a guitar string that had been plucked.

"Try to hold still so I can get a good picture," Dr. Morales said.

Rachel held her breath and froze while Dr. Morales moved the probe around her belly. She concentrated on all the clicking of the mouse.

"Your placenta looks good, and you have enough amniotic fluid." Dr. Morales continued moving the probe around.

"Did you hear that, Brett? My placenta and fluid are perfect," Rachel bragged. Brett had a wide smile.

"The baby is measuring at the right amount for your due date." He clicked some more. "Its kidneys and liver look good . . ." More clicking. "It's stomach and heart are healthy, and . . ." He paused for a minute and stared at the image. "It looks like you're having a girl."

"A girl?" Rachel said.

"Wow, a little girl," Brett said. "A little Rachel."

Rachel turned her head to beam at Brett but tried to keep the rest of her body still.

Dr. Morales kept clicking but stopped talking. After what felt like many minutes, Rachel realized he hadn't moved the probe off of one spot. The sound of the mouse clicking overpowered the room, like a malfunctioning water heater.

Rachel's excitement turned into something else that caused her skin to feel like it was shedding from her body. She cleared her throat. "Everything good?" she asked.

Dr. Morales didn't say anything, he just kept looking at the image on the screen. It seemed as if he'd forgotten there was a person attached to the body. Rachel's stomach hurt. "Dr. Morales, is something . . . wrong?"

"Has your obstetrician done an Alpha Fetal Protein test?"

"I don't know, I was supposed to get some blood drawn at my next appointment. Why? What're you seeing?" Rachel's voice went up an octave and she held her breath.

"There seem to be some abnormalities in the brain," Dr. Morales said.

"Wait, there's a problem with our baby's brain?" Rachel almost screamed.

Brett stood and began pacing. "What're you talking about?" Brett asked.

"I'm so sorry, I know this is hard, but the baby might have what's called anencephaly."

Rachel put her hand over her mouth. "What is that?"

"It's a defect in the closure of the neural tube, which means that major portions of the brain and skull don't develop." Dr. Morales continued to scan for another minute, then stopped.

"Wait, keep going, you must've misread it," Rachel cried out when he took the probe off her.

He pulled a chair up next to her. "Do either of you have a family history of birth defects?" Dr. Morales asked. Rachel and Brett both said 'no,' and he nodded.

"Oh my god!" Rachel said, blinking rapidly, trying to push away the horrific images that were forming in her head.

"You said the baby 'might' have anencephaly, so you can't be positive," Brett said.

"It's still a little early to be sure, so I suggest you go to your obstetrician as soon as possible and have an AFP test."

"If . . . and that's a big if, the baby has it, she could have surgery or something, right?" Brett asked. "I mean, this can be fixed?"

"Let's not jump to conclusions, get the AFP test first, then you can talk to your obstetrician."

Dr. Morales stood up. "I know this is a shock, but nothing is definite yet. I wish you both the best." Dr. Morales shook Brett's hand and left.

Rachel trembled uncontrollably. "This can't be happening. He's wrong, our daughter's fine. That man is just overworked and tired and doesn't know what he's seeing." Rachel tried to stand up, but she felt like she might faint.

Brett's face had turned ashen. "I--I—" He didn't finish his sentence.

The next afternoon, Rachel and Brett were sitting in the office of Rachel's obstetrician, Dr. Weissman, going over the results of her bloodwork and her ultrasound.

"I feel awful having to tell you both this; especially after all you've been through, but I have to confirm the radiologist's findings. I'm so sorry."

"But at the last ultrasound, the baby was fine." Rachel couldn't grasp what he was saying.

"It was too early in the pregnancy to see how the baby's brain was developing," Dr. Weissman said. "Anencephaly is detected accurately as early as twelve weeks, and your previous ultrasound was at ten weeks when you feared a miscarriage."

Brett tried to wipe away his tears with his shirt sleeve, but no matter how much he wiped his eyes, more tears kept coming. Dr. Weissman handed him a box of tissues.

"I don't understand how this could happen," Brett said.

"It's a complex condition and there can be many factors involved. It can occur due to an interaction of multiple genes or environmental factors, or sometimes it's just a random gene that mutates. There are other maternal risk factors, but Rachel, you don't have any of those. It's a rare condition, but unfortunately, we can't know for sure what took place."

"So, it's possible we could've caused it?" Rachel said through heaving sobs.

"Please, don't blame yourselves. You didn't do anything wrong. In this case, it's likely a gene defect."

Rachel couldn't speak and Brett put his arm around her. "What'll happen when she's born?" Brett asked.

"Babies with anencephaly don't have a functioning cerebrum, so the baby would be blind, deaf, and wouldn't ever gain consciousness. Most of these babies die at birth, some live for a few days, a week or two at most. Many more are stillborn."

"Are you saying our daughter doesn't have a chance?" Brett asked. "Unfortunately, not." Dr. Weissman sounded sad.

"What're we supposed to do?" Rachel asked, pulling her legs up onto her chair and curling into herself. She shuddered as the reality became excruciating. Tears continued to pour out.

"Even with the Supreme Court decision, living in California, you still have the option of terminating the pregnancy now. Otherwise, you can choose to carry to term and let nature take its course," Dr. Weissman said.

"How're we supposed to make a decision like that?" Rachel moaned.

"I wish I could answer that. I know this is painful and a decision that feels overwhelming. Nothing I can say will make it better, just make a decision that feels right to both of you," Dr. Weissman said, putting his hand on Rachel's shoulder.

Rachel and Brett were speechless.

"I know how much you both wanted this baby. I'm so sorry." He pulled a piece of paper from a pad and wrote something down. "Here's my cell phone number, call or text me if you have any questions, or you just need to talk. I don't want to put any pressure on you, but it might be best if you decide soon if you plan to terminate."

Brett stood and put his arm around Rachel. Dr. Weissman reached into a small bowl on his desk that held business cards. He pulled one out. "There's a psychologist I know who runs a support group for women going through this kind of thing. The group has helped some of my patients who've been where you are."

Brett took the card from Dr. Weissman when Rachel didn't move to take it.

Rachel leaned into Brett, closing her eyes, and wishing she could make this all go away.

Later that night, Rachel was lying in bed with both dogs next to her. She had her mother on speaker phone.

"Oh Rachel, I just feel so badly– I'm so sorry you are going through this." Her voice cracked.

"Mom, please don't cry," Rachel said.

"You know how much we love you, honey," her mom said.

Rachel started sobbing so hard that she dropped the phone on the floor.

Brett walked into the room and heard Leah's voice.

"Rachel . . . Rachel . . . are you okay?" Leah called out.

"Leah, can she call you later?" Brett said, picking up the phone.

Rachel tried to say something, but her words were garbled.

"Of course, is she okay? Are you okay?"

"No," Brett said. "Talk to you later." He hit the end call button and put the phone on the nightstand. He pushed the dogs to the foot of the bed, got in, and wrapped his arms around Rachel. Tears were streaming down both their cheeks. He reached for a box of tissues, taking one for himself and handing one to Rachel.

"Could I have done something to hurt our baby?"

"No."

"What if it's the wine I drank when we were in Santa Barbara?"

"You weren't even pregnant yet." Brett raised his hands,

rubbing his temples. "Why are you doing this to yourself? The doctor said it was probably some freak gene mutation."

"But if I can figure out why it happened, then maybe there's something we can do."

"Dr. Weisman said there's not anything we can do."

Rachel couldn't stand the sight of her baby bump anymore. She yanked the pillow out from behind her head and covered her belly. "What if all the doctors are wrong?" she asked.

"As much as I wish they were, the tests were all positive. We're going to have to decide what to do."

"I don't want to decide," Rachel said.

"I don't either." Brett got off the bed.

"I want my little girl."

"So do I." Brett walked over to the corner of the room where laying across the chair, was the onesie they had bought the day before. He stared at it for a moment, then picked it up and carried it to their closet. He opened the door and tossed it up on the top shelf as if it were an old rag doll. Then he closed the door so hard the walls rattled.

Chapter Ten
Katie

18 weeks pregnant

My baby's fine, my baby's fine, Katie told herself over and over like a mantra. She crushed a tissue in one hand and tapped her fingers on the desk with her other hand while Dr. Marley reviewed her ultrasound results. Katie looked at all the diplomas on the wall behind the desk. *Dr. Marley will see things differently, that radiologist made a big mistake.*

After what seemed like an interminable amount of time, Dr. Marley looked up. "I wish I could disagree with the radiologist, but I can't. Your baby does have a higher chance of having Down's syndrome."

Katie's shoulders fell. "Why is this happening to me?"

Dr. Marley came around her desk and sat in the chair next to

Katie. She put her hand on Katie's shoulder. "Crappy things sometimes happen. I've seen women who've tried for years to get pregnant, done multiple rounds of IVF, and finally got pregnant, only to have the baby die in utero in their eighth month."

Katie rocked back and forth in her chair. She'd cried so much since yesterday; she didn't think her eyes had anything left. "So, what am I supposed to do?"

"I can't answer that."

"Neither can I. One minute I'm thinking about how I'm going to make ends meet for this baby, the next I'm forced to consider ending a pregnancy that shouldn't have happened to begin with." Katie opened the tissue she was crushing and blew her nose.

"You just found all this out; give yourself a little time. Your obstetrician can set up the diagnostic blood test for you, and then an amnio if you need more confirmation."

"I haven't decided about the blood test yet. I understand that there's a chance of a false positive, so I still wouldn't know for sure. And if I decide to have her, I don't want to have an amino and risk a miscarriage."

"You know how small that risk is."

"I do, but I'm thirty-two without even a boyfriend. What if this is the only chance I get to have a child?"

Dr. Marley nodded. "The ultrasound you had isn't a diagnosis, the baby may not have Down's."

"I'm praying she doesn't, but if I decide to have her, what should I know about Down's syndrome?"

"Well, every child born with it will be a little different, but in general, most of the babies will have flat facial features, small heads and ears, and poor muscle tone. They'll likely also have developmental delays and a lower mental capacity."

Katie felt as if she were Raggedy Ann being carried in a dog's mouth.

"I assume my daughter would need a lot of help, how am I going to afford that?"

"Social services will provide all kinds of free services, but I think you're getting ahead of yourself. There's plenty of time to figure it all out if the baby is born with Down's."

Katie pushed on her forehead as if she were back in high school trying to cram the Pythagorean theorem into her brain. "If you were me, what would you do?"

"What I would do doesn't matter, and if you ask someone, they'll likely tell you they know exactly what they'd do in your situation, but they can't know unless and until they have to face something like this. People will often do exactly the thing they swore they never would." Dr. Marley stood and went back to the chair behind her desk. Katie twisted her hair around and around her finger.

"Katie, why don't you take a few days off and think about what you want to do."

"I appreciate that and thank you for all your help." Katie went to leave.

"Before you go . . ." Dr. Marley said, holding her hand out as if to stop a moving car. As the doctor rummaged around in her desk drawer, Katie rubbed her hands together so briskly she could've started a fire. Dr. Marley unwound a rubber band from a stack of business cards and pulled one out. She reached out to hand it to Katie. "One of my colleagues is a psychologist who runs a support group for women who have or may have children with special needs. I think you'd find comfort talking to other women in a similar situation."

Katie took the card from her but barely looked at it before shoving it into her pocket. "I'll think about it."

When Katie got home that afternoon, she dropped the business card on the coffee table and turned the air conditioner on high. Before she was pregnant she was always cold when everyone else was hot, but now her clothes stuck to her, even after she'd just showered.

Katie went to the kitchen and got a pint of ice cream, a canister of whipped cream, and a giant spoon.

"This may not be the healthiest snack, but you'll enjoy it as much as I will," she told the baby.

She retreated to her couch and turned on the TV to *Project Runway*. Instead of licking the ice cream like she would a cone, she took a bite, then sprayed whipped cream straight into her mouth. She hummed as she savored the flavors of mint and chocolate chips and looked forward to the much-needed sugar high. As she scooped out more, the doorbell rang.

"I'm glad you called," Sandra said.

"I didn't want to be alone. And Mr. Morrison was more interested in his cat nip than me." Katie said with a somber smile.

"It's freezing in here." Sandra crossed her arms over her chest and sat. She motioned to the tub of ice cream and whipped cream. "Mind if I join you?"

Katie got another spoon and Sandra dug in, losing herself with each bite she took. When Katie passed over the whipped cream, Sandra declined.

"Eating ice cream straight from a tub is bad enough, but whipped cream would mean I'm completely out of control."

The sound of crunching chocolate chips competed with the volume of the TV.

Sandra stopped eating and when she put her spoon down on the coffee table, she noticed the psychologist's business card. What's this?" she asked, picking it up.

"Dr. Marley gave it to me. It's for a support group for women who are having similar stuff as me."

"Are you going to go?"

Katie wrinkled her nose as if smelling sour milk. "I don't want to talk to a bunch of strangers about something so personal."

"I think you should go."

"You do?" Katie cocked her head in surprise.

"I went to therapy when I was in my early twenties, and it helped a lot. I think you could use more support than I can give you."

"I've never been someone who opens up easily."

"All the more reason to go, it's okay to be vulnerable and ask for help." Sandra handed Katie the business card. "Call her."

"I'll see."

"Promise me you will."

"Fine, but right now I need to stuff my face. Don't make me imbibe alone," Katie said, handing Sandra's spoon back to her.

Sandra nodded, took the spoon, and they enjoyed the dessert that had become their dinner. Katie turned the volume up on the TV and the two of them went back to watching *Project Runway*.

"Do you think Heidi Klum has ever tasted ice cream?" Katie asked.

"If she has, it was probably that healthy vegan stuff."

"Right. Dairy-free, sugar-free, and taste free."

"Ben and Jerry would roll over in their freezers," Sandra said.

Katie held up the whipped cream canister. "I wouldn't give this up even to have a body like Heidi's." Her words were distorted by the glob of whipped cream she'd squirted into her mouth.

"I bet you would if Heidi's money was part of the deal."

Katie nodded. "For that, I'd give up anything, including sex. Oh wait, I've already given that up, so where's my money?"

* * *

Katie pulled up to the address the psychologist gave her over the phone. It was a two-story Spanish-style house on a tree-lined block behind Sunset Blvd in West Hollywood. Katie had to enter through the side and go to an office through the backyard.

When she opened the gate, the door to the office stood open, and three women were inside.

I don't want to be here. Katie wrung her hands. She thought about running back to her car, but one of the women looked toward the backyard and acknowledged Katie with what seemed to be a knowing nod. *Ugh, I've been spotted.* Katie took a breath and walked into the office. The women in the room smiled warmly at her but continued their conversation.

The room's creamy beige walls contrasting with the dark mahogany hardwood floors created a warm space. On the red, blue, and taupe tapestry rug that partially covered the floor sat eight chairs placed in a U-shape. Katie noticed a bathroom on the side of the room and thought about hiding in there like a cocaine addict at a Hollywood party.

Now, where should I sit? Katie pondered. The decision alone made her want to run again. If she sat next to the three women, would they think she was eavesdropping on their conversation? Or if she sat by herself at the end of the U, would they think she was antisocial? Lately, even the smallest decisions were overwhelming. Instead, she went to the back of the room, to a table that had a platter of snickerdoodles. She picked one up, but before taking a bite, she wondered if the other women would think she was insensitive for eating a cookie while they were all dealing with so much sadness. Katie put the cookie back on the platter and hoped no one had seen her. Instead, she settled for a cup of water; who would judge her for hydrating herself?

While she ever so slowly sipped the water, a woman approached her.

"Hi, I'm Nicole." Nicole looked to be in her forties, which was younger than Katie had expected from her deep voice on the phone. Katie had no idea what a psychologist should look like, but it wasn't one with curly red hair, wearing chestnut colored Ugg boots and feather earrings.

"I'm Katie."

Nicole touched Katie lightly on her arm. "I'm so glad you decided to come today, welcome."

Katie smiled and thanked her. A few more women had come in. "Ladies find a seat; we're going to get started in just a minute," Nicole announced as she walked towards the front of the room.

Katie scanned the remaining empty chairs and spotted a woman sitting in the last chair closest to the door, looking down, her face obscured by her hair. Katie wasn't in the mood for small talk and this woman looked like she was hiding from the paparazzi, so Katie sat next to her.

When the woman looked up, Katie recognized her.

"Excuse me," Katie said, "Aren't you a patient of Dr. Marley's?"

"Uh, yes." She met Katie's eyes, and Katie saw recognition dawn there. "You work in her office, right?"

"Yeah, I'm Katie."

"I'm Rachel." Rachel's eyes widened. "I didn't realize you were pregnant."

"Yeah, scrubs hide everything," Katie said.

"It's my first time here." Rachel looked like she was trying hard not to frown.

"Me, too. It's nice to see someone familiar." Nicole took a seat at the top of the U.

"For those of you who are new here, I'm Nicole and I'm a licensed clinical psychologist. I've been running this group for the last five years. When I was eighteen weeks pregnant, my baby was diagnosed with spina bifida, and I was devastated, and none of my friends or family understood what I was going through. I started this group so women who were experiencing this kind of trauma could not only vent their feelings but meet other people who they could commiserate with. This room is a safe, no judgment zone. Anything shared, stays here. Is there anyone that would like to start today?" Nicole looked at each woman with compassion.

A woman cleared her throat. "Yesterday, my husband and I told our three-year-old son, that the baby boy I'm carrying isn't going to be the playmate he was hoping for." She took her glasses off her face, fiddling with them in her hands. "He wanted a brother so badly and it broke my heart when he brought out his push-and-ride fire engine and his toy lawn mower to give to the baby. He couldn't understand that his brother may never walk or sit up by himself." She blinked rapidly, then stopped talking and put her glasses back on.

Katie's bottom lip jutted out as she held back tears. She felt so sorry for this woman. *At least I wouldn't have to explain anything to my other children,* she thought.

It was quiet for only a split second, then another woman began talking. "I feel you, Jada. The siblings get cheated in so many ways. My two-year-old son has severe autism, and his older sister says we spend all our time taking care of her brother, and we're too tired to do much with her, and she's right. I'm trying to make one day a week all about her but dealing with my son takes all my energy. I'm worried that we're screwing her up."

Jada spoke again. "That scares me, too. Lately, I've been thinking a lot about ending it, but I don't know how to explain that to my son.

Do I say this baby isn't perfect, so we decided not to have it?"

Katie noticed Jada said ending 'it;' she didn't say ending 'the baby's life.' *If I stop referring to her as a baby,* Katie thought, *I might not get attached and it might be easier to make a decision.*

The woman two seats over from Katie coughed, then cleared her throat and uttered quietly. "Last week, I ended my pregnancy. My husband didn't even want to consider having her and he wanted it over quickly. I mostly agreed with the decision, but it was the hardest thing I ever had to do and now I don't want to look at him. He doesn't show his emotions, so it seems like he doesn't care, and I haven't been out of bed except to come here."

"I'm glad you're here with us today, Callie." Nicole's voice was soothing.

The woman next to Callie jumped in. "It's hard not to be mad at your husband if you aren't exactly on the same page, or even if you are. I heard that divorce is high amongst couples going through what we're going through."

"Everyone grieves differently," Nicole added. "It's important that you try to make time to nurture yourself and your marriage."

Katie remembered that at Rachel's last appointment with Dr. Marley, her husband came with her. Katie watched Rachel out of the corner of her eye as Rachel rested her hands on her belly, then shifted in her seat, then scratched her ear. Katie wondered if Rachel were about to bolt from the room, or just had an itch.

"Rachel, did you want to say something?" Nicole asked.

Katie saw Rachel's eyes darting around the room. No one jumped in. It was as if they would wait hours if Rachel wanted to speak. Rachel nodded, then shook her head, then shrugged. "My baby was diagnosed with anencephaly," Rachel blurted, her voice cracking at the end of the sentence. "It means her brain won't function. Now I'm supposed to decide whether to terminate my pregnancy or wait and go into labor knowing that my daughter is going to die anyway."

The women nodded, their faces showing genuine empathy.

"I've wanted a baby for so long," she continued, "and it's killing me to have to decide how and when her life will end."

Callie nodded in agreement; tears running down her cheeks.

Rachel bowed her head and Katie couldn't tell if she was also crying or just exhausted from sharing.

This isn't helping me, Katie thought, rubbing her temples. *I'm only getting more scared and confused.*

The rest of the hour, every woman shared except Katie.

When the meeting was over, Nicole thanked them for coming and said she hoped to see everyone next week. Some of the women hugged each other, others left quickly alone. Grief in many forms hung in the air like dust particles that float from one place to another yet never quite land.

Katie got up and waited for Rachel, who stood up so quickly that she knocked her purse onto the floor. Rachel's wallet, sunglasses, two hair ties, and a handful of red and green M&M's rolled across the floor.

"Let me help you," Katie said, bending down.

"Thank you." Rachel joined Katie on the floor, but instead of picking up her things, she put her hands over her eyes. "I'm such a mess."

"Join the club." Katie put all of Rachel's belongings back in her purse, except the M&M's, which she tossed in a trash can. "It was brave of you to share your story. I couldn't bring myself to say anything."

"It wasn't bravery," Rachel said. "I'm a people pleaser, so when Nicole asked me to, I didn't feel like I had a choice. I'm kind of glad it's out there though. I was kind of hoping that someone would speak up and give me advice."

"I tried to get Dr. Marley to tell me what to do, but she wouldn't," Katie said. "It royally sucks that we're the ones who have to decide our baby's fate."

Rachel began trembling.

"Are you okay?" Katie asked, moving closer to her. Katie had worked with many women going through multiple failed IVF cycles.

Part of her job was to try to comfort them when they found out it didn't work. She'd always been able to keep her emotions in check, but for some reason, she felt Rachel's pain as well as her own.

"It's just all too much," Rachel said.

Katie held her hand out to Rachel to help her off the floor. "I'll get you some water."

When she brought the water to Rachel, she found Rachel staring off in the distance. Katie tapped Rachel lightly and handed her the water and one of the two cookies she snagged from the platter.

"Thanks." Rachel took a sip of the water, then a bite of the cookie. "I'm sorry you had to see me fall apart, especially when you're in the same boat. Can I ask you what's wrong with your baby?"

"My daughter has a one in three chance of having Down's syndrome." Katie hadn't said those words to anyone except Sandra and her doctor, so when she said them out loud to Rachel, the reality of her situation hit her, and she started to tear up.

"You're having a girl?" Rachel asked.

"Yes."

"My baby's a girl also," Rachel said. "I'm sorry that you have to go through this, too."

"Do you want to get out of here and take a walk?" Katie asked, surprising herself with how much she hoped Rachel would say yes.

Rachel nodded and the two of them crossed through Nicole's backyard, out the gate, and strolled slowly down the sidewalk on her street. They talked about their jobs and how each of them admired the other one for choosing careers where they helped people. They bonded over how they don't readily admit that they love reality TV. They both liked to read, and their favorite author was Harlan Coben. They talked about so much, but very little about their pregnancies.

It was an exceptionally hot summer day, so even though Katie was wearing a light sundress, little puddles were forming under her bra. Rachel wiped the perspiration off her forehead with the back of her hand. "I feel like I'm always a wet mess. If it's not coming out of my eyes, it's coming out of my pores."

"Who said pregnancy was beautiful and magical?" Katie said.

"An obstetrician with a beach house in Malibu." They started laughing, and as they were still so emotional, their amusement took on a life of its own. When they stopped, they both snorted at the same time.

"Oh my god, you snorted," Katie said.

"So, did you," Rachel said defensively.

"I didn't mean that as an insult. I remembered when I met you, you said your husband makes fun of you for snorting. I'm happy I'm not the only one who does that."

Katie stopped walking. Rachel, who was a step ahead of her, realized and turned around.

"Something must be wrong with us," Katie said. "How can we be laughing when we're living through hell?"

"Humor has always saved me, and it's better than crying all the time."

"I've done a lot of that, too."

After walking a few more blocks, the heat got to them, and they decided to head back to their air-conditioned cars.

"Thank you for being so nice to me," Rachel said as she unlocked her car.

"Are you kidding? I'm grateful I found someone to talk to who understands . . . and snorts."

They said goodbye and Rachel got in her car. As Katie walked toward her own car, Rachel rolled down her window and called after her.

"Wait. Can we exchange phone numbers?"

Katie returned to Rachel's car, and they traded contact information. "Maybe we can meet for coffee soon," Rachel said.

"I'd love that. Too bad we can't do shots of tequila."

Chapter Eleven
Rachel

19 weeks pregnant

Rachel reclined on a lounge in her backyard, Molasses curled up with her paws hanging off the end. Rachel kept trying to read, but every bird that squawked, every bush that rattled, and every bee that buzzed distracted her. She laid the book down on her chest.

A ladybug found a place to land on her knuckle and seemed perfectly happy to take a trip along her hand. "Ladybug, ladybug, fly away home, my house is on fire, my child is gone." She began to cry. "Don't stay here," Rachel said, staring at her hand. "I'll end up hurting you, too." She waved her hand, but the bug didn't move, so she lightly flicked it with her finger, and it flew away.

Rachel wiped the tears from her eyes and picked up her book. A squirrel shimmied through the leaves of the eucalyptus tree behind her and let out a high squeak, teasing the dogs. Molasses leaped off the lounge, her back paw hitting Honey in the face, waking her up from a sound sleep. The dogs took off chasing the squirrel, who mocked them from a low branch, and Honey kept barking in her loud, deep bellow.

Brett handed Honey a treat to quiet her when he came into the backyard. "How can you read with all that barking?" he asked Rachel, plopping down on the end of her lounge.

"I couldn't concentrate even if I were at a monk's retreat." Rachel dropped the book to the ground. She gave Brett a kiss and smelled sweat mixed with paint from a long day of working on other peoples' houses. "How was your day?"

"The usual." He pulled off the long-sleeved shirt he was wearing over a T-shirt and draped it over the arm of the other lounge. "How was the support group?"

She scrunched her feet close to her butt, so he had more room, but he had her stretch her legs out, laying her feet in his lap. "It was ok. It didn't help me make a decision, though."

"That wasn't the point of it. Did it make you feel less alone?" He rubbed her bare feet.

"A little. One of the women there works at Dr. Marley's office. You met her the last time we were there. Her name's Katie. She's really nice. We're going to get together for coffee."

"I'm glad. It seems like you haven't seen any of your friends lately," Brett said. "When was the last time you saw Caitlin or Gabby?"

"When we went to dinner. They've called to check in, but it's hard to talk to them. It just reminds me that other people have had healthy kids." Brett nodded, a sorrowful look on his face.

Rachel picked up the book and used it to fan herself as the humidity and oppressive heat of the late afternoon hunkered down on her skin. Brett took off his T-shirt and wiped his damp chest with the fabric. He and Rachel corralled the dogs and headed inside to cool off.

"What I wouldn't give for a glass of wine right now," Rachel said as Brett opened a bottle of chardonnay.

"At this point, I don't think it's going to hurt anything." Without meeting Rachel's eyes, Brett poured wine into a glass and handed it to her.

She took a sip then put the glass on the sink. "I can't drink this. Even if the baby is doomed, it still doesn't feel right."

Brett poured the rest of her wine into his glass. "I think it's time we made a decision. I know you haven't wanted to talk about it, but you're coming up on twenty weeks."

Rachel raised one eyebrow and shook her head. "As if I don't know that," she said, her lips curling.

Brett visibly recoiled from her sharp tone.

"Sorry." She sighed. "I just meant that it's not like I'm not constantly reminded every time I shower or get dressed or eat anything. How can I miss that my belly grows bigger every day, with a baby that's going to die."

"I'm not trying to upset you," he said.

Rachel headed to the bedroom, put on her pajamas, got in bed, and put a pillow over her head. Brett slipped off his shoes and laid down next to her. She turned her back to him, keeping the pillow on her face.

"I just want us to work through this together," he said.

"I don't think we can. You aren't going to go through it the same way I am." Rachel's words were muffled by the pillow. Brett gently took the pillow off her face, she turned toward him.

"I'm going to be losing her, too."

"I know, but you won't be in that room if we terminate, and if we go the nine months, I'll be the one pushing her out of my body only to watch her die." Rachel flinched at those words. She couldn't believe this was her life.

"She's my daughter, too. Can't you see that's going to kill me?" Brett's eyes filled with tears.

"Yes, but I don't think it's the same." Rachel looked at him, a sinking feeling enveloping her as if she were falling through the ground.

"That's not fair," he said, his tears now falling onto the bed.

"You're right, but it's still how I feel." Rachel picked up her phone.

"Who're you calling?" he asked raising his eyebrows.

"Katie."

"We're in the middle of something, and you're calling a friend over talking to me?" When Rachel didn't answer, he dried his tears, got off the bed, and put his shoes on. "You obviously don't need me."

"Where are you going?" she asked.

"I don't know." Rachel heard the front door close. She got back under the covers, then dialed Katie to see if they could meet the next morning.

* * *

Rachel was a few minutes early when she got to The Aroma Café in Studio City. The place had a cozy ambiance and felt like the home of an aging hippy. A hippy who adored statues, hanging fountains, potted plants, and crystal chandeliers. Best of all, there was a bookstore inside, which kept Rachel busy whenever she was early, and she was always early.

Katie was exactly on time and Rachel noted another thing they had in common: they were both punctual. While they waited in a long line to order, Rachel's mouth watered at the scones, muffins, and croissants that teased her taste buds from the glass case. She inhaled the scent of vanilla, blueberries, and warm, nutty coffee.

As they approached the counter, Katie's eyes widened as she pointed out eggs benedict and brioche French toast topped with strawberries being carried to a table. "That food looks so good," Katie said. "If I hadn't had a big breakfast this morning, I'd get that French toast for sure."

"We could split an order," Rachel offered. "Then neither of us will feel guilty."

"I like the way you think."

When it was their turn to order, the woman behind the counter grinned at them. "You two are so cute," she said. "When are you due?"

Rachel's relaxed posture stiffened, and she took a step backward. For an awkward moment, they both just stood there.

Finally Katie said, "We're almost five months along."

The waitress clapped her hands together, "That is so—"

"Two chamomile teas, please," Rachel interrupted her.

Katie ordered the French toast and added a side of bacon.

"Oh, no, did I just insult you?" she asked Rachel as their order was being tallied up.

"What do you mean?"

"You're Jewish and I ordered us bacon."

"I'm reformed, and I love pork, bacon's one of my favorite food groups. But don't tell my parents, they don't know I've been eating pork since I moved out."

"Your secret is safe with me." The women looked for an empty table. They found one on the patio under a red umbrella. "It's so nice that your parents are still together. Are you close to them?" Katie asked.

"Yes. I'm an only child, so it's always been just them and me." Two oversized mugs with hot water and chamomile tea bags and slices of lemon were served. "How about you, do you have a good relationship with your parents?"

Katie winced. "I'm also an only child, but my father left when I was nine and my mother's a drunk, so I don't talk to her much."

Rachel could see the crimson glow of embarrassment creep up Katie's face. "At least I have good memories from before my father left and my mom started drinking. It makes me sad to think about those times."

"That must've been terrible," Rachel said sincerely.

"It was. It still hurts."

"I feel like *I'm* the one who's hurting my parents. They're supportive of me no matter what, but all I do is disappoint them. My mom has wanted me to have a baby for so long, and now she may never get to be a grandmother." Rachel was about to cry but bit her lip instead.

"I'm sure your mom just wishes she could protect you from all this pain," Katie said.

"I guess, she's been protective of me my whole life." Rachel told Katie about when she was four years old, and she and her mom were about to cross a busy street to get to her preschool. Her mother let go of her hand for a second to push the walk button at the signal. Rachel saw a girl about her age on the other side of the street carrying the exact American Girl doll she'd wanted. Rachel took off running, not realizing that a car could hit her. Her mom screamed and ran after her. When her mom caught up to Rachel, she grabbed her and carried her across the street, sobbing the rest of the way to the school.

"I wish I could protect my daughter," Rachel said. "She'll never know how much I loved and wanted her."

"But you'll know, and that means something." Katie took a sip of tea.

"I noticed you aren't wearing a wedding ring. Is the father going to help you with the baby?"

"No. I got pregnant by accident, and then I found out the guy was married and had kids. What a fool I was."

"You can't blame yourself that he's a jerk," Rachel said, sneering. She hoped Katie could tell she was on her side. "Give me his address and I'll go beat him up. I'm stronger than I look."

The server brought over their French toast and bacon but didn't leave after giving them an extra plate and asking if they needed anything else. She hovered as Katie dished half the food onto the empty plate and handed it to Rachel.

"I can't believe you two are sharing one meal." The server said gesturing between them. "When I was pregnant, I wouldn't have let anyone touch my food."

Rachel picked up her fork and knife hoping it would be a hint for her to leave.

"My daughter's two now," the server said, "and she's just like me. She eats everything in sight."

I hope she's not like you and knows when to walk away, Rachel thought.

"Are these your first babies?" the server asked.

Katie looked at Rachel, who shrugged, then nodded and said, "Yes."

"We wouldn't want to keep you from all your other tables," Katie prodded.

"I'm talking to two pregnant women; they'll have to wait."

Is this woman going to grab a chair and join us? Rachel thought. *Go away, go away go away.*

Katie looked directly at the server. "I think we're good now."

The server looked at Rachel who was nodding her head ferociously. She finally took the hint and left.

"Why does a pregnant belly make everyone your best friend? I have enough friends," Rachel said, drenching her half of the French toast in syrup. She put a piece of bacon on top and took a bite. She loved the way the flavors melded in her mouth, savoring the mixture of the crispiness of the bacon, the sweetness of maple and brown sugar, and the richness of the egg-soaked bread.

"This food is like crack, and probably about as healthy." Katie laughed after taking her first bite.

Rachel thought about all the personal things Katie had been sharing. They had such different backgrounds, religions, and childhoods, yet Rachel couldn't get over feeling like she'd just met her new best friend. In such a short time, Rachel knew she could tell Katie anything and Katie would understand.

Katie blew on her tea and the steam rose into her face. Rachel clasped her hands together and stared at her wedding ring.

"I had an abortion in college," she said quietly. "I never told Brett because I was ashamed. I never told my parents or friends either. I don't know why I'm telling you, except that I somehow knew I needed to."

Katie put her mug down and leaned across the table toward Rachel.

"I'm honored that I'm the person you chose to share that with. Thank you for trusting me."

Rachel felt a warm almost cozy feeling come over her and she knew she'd made the right decision in confiding in Katie. Katie's face relayed empathy and concern and nothing else.

"Thank you for not judging me because I've been judging myself for years," Rachel said. "I can't get out of my head that the abortion is the reason I keep miscarrying."

"First of all, I'd never judge you. Second of all, I don't believe that the abortion caused any of your issues. At the office, we've seen a number of women who've had abortions and went on to have healthy pregnancies."

Rachel felt one of the many rain clouds that had been hovering over her body disintegrate. "As hard as it was to go through with it, I knew it was the right thing for me at that time. Even though I'm prochoice, this pregnancy feels different. I'm almost five months along, even if my daughter's going to die anyway."

"I'm Catholic and I've always thought that terminating a pregnancy is wrong. Now that I'm in this situation, I'm no longer sure what's right or wrong, which makes me doubt who I am. I mean, how could I do that and still be a Catholic?" Katie covered her eyes with her hands. "I'm not sure I would be able to come to terms with it and still go to church."

"I think God forgives us if we do things for the right reasons," Rachel said. "And your child's quality of life should mean something."

"Do you think it's selfish to give birth to a child knowing that they'd have major challenges in life?" Katie asked, peeling the last of her cherry red nail polish off one of her fingers.

Rachel narrowed her eyes; she'd been wondering the same thing.

"I'm thirty-two," Katie continued, "and I don't have a good track record with men sticking around. This could be my only chance to have a baby, but I don't want to put my desires ahead of a child's quality of life." Katie took her napkin off her lap and wiped the syrup off her lips.

"You can't know what the future will bring, and I can't believe there isn't a man out there who'd be lucky to find you."

"That's sweet of you to say, but I'm not so sure anymore. You're lucky you have Brett."

"It's not all wine and roses, though, we have our issues. Right now, everything he says agitates me. Whenever he brings up that we have to make a decision about the baby, it makes me hate him." Rachel looked at Katie to see if she had a reaction, but Katie's face was devoid of judgment. "I didn't really mean that, but you know what I mean."

"I do. I'm sure Brett feels helpless. It would be understandable if he just wants to get past all this quickly. It's hard for the man also," Katie said.

Rachel couldn't hold back her tears any longer and they slid down her cheeks.

A busboy headed over but before he cleared their dishes away, he locked eyes with Rachel. He turned around, retreating toward the kitchen, leaving the dishes on the table. "It must've been too much for him to see a pregnant woman crying," Rachel said.

"He better get used to it; we pregnant women cry all the time."

All the tables around them were now full, and a few groups of people were staring daggers at Rachel and Katie as they waited for them to finish and leave.

"Maybe we should get going," Rachel said.

"Yeah, they're bound to be sitting in our laps if we stay much longer."

As Rachel pushed away from the table, two elderly women raced over, practically knocking two young men out of the way.

"I bet those women would kick our asses in a fight."

Katie chuckled. "I'm glad we did this."

"Me, too."

When they got outside, Katie looked both ways, then jaywalked across Tujunga Boulevard; Rachel followed quickly behind her.

"Is it weird that we just met, and I feel closer to you than friends that I've known for years," Rachel said.

"I was thinking the same thing. My best friend, Sandra, is so supportive, but she can't possibly understand what I'm going through."

"I think you've seen me cry more than anyone else."

"Would it be okay if I hugged you?" Katie asked. Rachel didn't say a word, she just stepped into Katie's open arms.

Chapter Twelve
Katie

19 weeks pregnant

Katie woke up to the sun tapping on her eyelids as it crept through the side of her window blinds. She yawned, pushed the comforter off her, sat up, and stretched her arms above her head, then twisted her core from side to side. Her ever-expanding belly got in the way; she was sure it was growing another inch every day.

While she continued to wake the rest of her body up, she gave herself a pep talk.

"Be grateful for the things in your life that have made you stronger." She repeated the phrase three times. Katie had been giving herself positive affirmations every day since she found out she was pregnant, even when she felt stupid doing it. She hoped at some point she would believe every word.

She rolled herself out of bed, longing for the double espresso she used to have as soon as her feet hit the floor. Now she settled for peppermint tea, although it didn't have the kick she needed.

"Siri, play my favorite Billy Joel songs," she said to her phone, which connected automatically to a speaker in the living room. "She's Always A Woman" came on. Katie sang as if she were onstage, and a director had told her to project her voice to the back of the room. She swayed her body back and forth and danced even though she was still sitting in her chair. Billy Joel was the first concert she'd ever been to; on the first date she was ever asked out on. She enjoyed the concert, although from her seat he looked like a piano-playing microbe.

When the song ended, "Just the Way You Are" started. Katie grabbed the Los Angeles Times from outside her front door and turned to the entertainment section. She spotted an ad for the once-a-month Sunday swap meet at the Rose Bowl, which reminded Katie it was another weekend that she hadn't been planning on attending church.

What kind of Catholic am I? she thought, then answered her own question. *The kind that's an embarrassment to the entire religion.* She looked up, "If you still think it's okay for me to go to church, give me a sign." She waited a moment, but nothing happened. Mr. Morrison purred loudly at her feet. "I'm guessing that wasn't your sign. It would be pretty silly to use a hungry cat to make your point." As Katie scooped food into the cat's bowl, "Keeping the Faith" began playing.

She looked up again. "Okay, you don't have to hit me over the head." In the church parking lot, Katie sat in her car until right before mass was to start. She wanted to sneak in the back, hoping she could avoid Father George. She hadn't decided what to do about her pregnancy, and she didn't know how she could tell him what she was considering.

The church choir was singing a hymn as she moved steadily toward a back pew, keeping her head lowered. The elderly couple she sat next to smiled at her and nodded and she felt welcomed and connected, two of the things she most loved about church.

Father George began his sermon about how miracles don't have to be something huge, like Jesus walking on water. A miracle could be when your pet makes it through surgery, or when you win a tennis match against a more accomplished opponent. Katie found herself nodding in agreement.

Or when you make a really tough decision that could affect the rest of your life, she thought, her eyes stinging with salty tears.

When Father George got to the part of the mass where he offered communion, Katie followed the elderly couple out of the pew and walked a few feet, then stopped. She turned around and walked back to her pew. She didn't feel worthy; how could she partake in such a holy sacrament when she was considering ending her pregnancy? Her shoulders drooped. Would she ever be able to accept communion again? She wiped her damp eyes when she saw the elderly couple coming back. She was relieved they didn't say anything about her emotional state.

When the service was over, she was determined to get to the exit as fast as she could, and she'd almost made it when she heard Father George's deep, solemn voice. "Katie?"

Katie turned around. "Hi Father, it's nice to see you, but I'm in kind of a rush today." She felt like she was tripping over her words.

Father George looked at her, concern etched into his face. "Katie, please wait, I would like to talk to you where we can have a little privacy."

Katie nodded, but the sides of her mouth quivered as she tried to hold back a frown and she knew her mascara was smudged from her earlier tears.

She moved away from the door and stood against a wall in the back of the church. She watched families thank the priest as they headed out to enjoy the rest of their Sunday. She wished she could forget her life for a while. Other people were having fun, they had no idea what she was going through. They went to work, and out with friends, and enjoyed themselves. She was jealous of people she didn't even know.

After all the congregants had left, Father George led Katie to his office. Katie had never been in his office before. The first thing she noticed was a cherry wood desk with a tall bookcase behind filled with religious books and icons he had collected. Father George directed her to sit in the chair opposite him. A large crucifix adorned the wall next to Katie. She thought Jesus must be disappointed in her; sins like hers weren't the kind he sacrificed himself for.

"I can tell something's wrong," Father George said. "The last time I saw you, I thought your situation had improved."

Katie dropped her arms on his desk, almost knocking over a candle of Saint Jude, the patron saint of hopeless causes. "It had, until I found out my daughter might be born with Down's syndrome. I've been wrestling with what to do because I'm not sure I'm equipped to raise a baby with that issue." Katie exhaled loudly.

"I'm sorry to hear that. That is a lot, and I can understand how you might struggle with it." The priest seemed genuinely concerned for her. "You don't have family that can help you, is that right?"

Katie crossed and uncrossed her arms as if she were trying to prevent her heart from falling out of her chest. She realized she hadn't answered him. "Uh . . . no, I don't have anyone."

She figured priests, like psychologists, learned not to pry if someone didn't want to talk about something. *I wonder if he knew about my parents if he'd think I was just a chip off the old block of losers?*

Katie imagined her mother, her voice soaked with vodka, yelling at her for even thinking about terminating the pregnancy. Her mother would not have seen how hypocritical it was to think that ending a pregnancy would be worse than abandoning a child for alcohol.

"Questioning your situation is understandable, not everyone is cut out for that kind of challenge."

Katie bit down on her lip and closed her eyes for a moment. Then she opened them and breathed a heavy sigh. "Father . . ." she stopped and took another breath. "What do you think about ending a pregnancy when the baby might not have the best quality of life?" Katie's eyes darted everywhere but at him. She also made sure she avoided looking at the crucifix.

Father George's expression was soft, but she felt his gaze on her. "Every human being has things that they have to deal with, and it's up to us to figure out how to accept our hardships and move through them. When we're loved and have faith, we can have a quality of life that might not be perfect but can still be meaningful," he said.

Katie bowed her head and blinked back tears. *What was I thinking, bringing up the idea of abortion to a priest?* She wondered what he thought, but he didn't look horrified that she'd asked the question. She knew, though, if she made that decision, she'd be on her own.

Katie put her hand on her mouth and tapped on her lips with one finger; she felt that Father George was waiting for her to say something when they were interrupted by a knock on his office door. He called out for the person to enter. A young man poked his head in. He had forest-green eyes the same shade as the rain boots Katie had bought last year.

"I'm so sorry, Father," he said when he saw Katie. "I didn't know you were in here with someone."

Katie felt as if she were caught in the principal's office for cussing in class. She rooted around in her purse pretending to look for something.

Father George got up from his desk and walked toward the door. "That's okay, Daniel, what do you need?"

"Do you know if the boxes for tonight's group were delivered?" Daniel asked.

"Yes, they're in the corner of the supply room."

"Great, thanks." Daniel smiled at Katie, then closed the door.

"Sorry, about that. Daniel's our new youth director, and he's still getting the hang of things."

Katie nodded. "It's fine, Father." She was happy for the interruption.

Father George sat back down. "Katie, if you decide that you

don't want to raise the baby, I can help you find a loving family to adopt her. And if you decide to raise her yourself, our women's group will offer to cook and babysit and be there for whatever you might need."

Katie had taken care of herself most of her life, but if she kept this baby she would need to accept all the help she could get.

"That's nice of you, father, thank you. I'll let you know." She headed for the door. She hadn't figured out what she was going to do, but she felt grateful that the church was a place she could go for help if she needed it.

* * *

When Katie's alarm on her phone went off, she felt as if she were trudging through sludge as she shoved the covers aside and reached over to turn it off. She went into the bathroom to pee for the tenth time since she went to sleep the previous night. Her bladder and her daughter were always fighting over who would wake her up the most.

Katie normally applied bronzer and blush to brighten up her fair complexion, but even if she put on all the makeup from the MAC counter in the mall, it wouldn't take away how pasty she looked.

Today would be her first day back at work after her time off. She wasn't ready, but if she decided to keep the baby, she needed this job to support them.

Katie was the first to arrive at the office. After filling up her thirty-two-ounce sports bottle with water, she laid her head down on her desk. *I'm already exhausted, how am I going to get through this whole day?*

"Good morning, Katie," Dr. Marley said, startling her. "It's good to have you back."

"Thank you." Katie sank with relief.

"Did the time off help you come to a decision?"

"No, but I'm getting there."

"Did you go to the support group I told you about?"

"I did."

"Good, I hope it helped." Even though Katie wasn't sure yet, she appreciated that Dr. Marley cared. "I know you'll figure this out," Dr. Marley said and turned, bumping into Sandra, who'd come up behind her.

Sandra scooted her desk chair next to Katie and took a handful of M&Ms out of the jar on Katie's desk. "When you didn't return my calls yesterday, I got worried. If you didn't come in today, I was going to break your apartment door down. I wasn't even going to knock first."

Katie hugged Sandra. "I didn't mean to ignore you; I just didn't feel like talking yesterday."

Sandra drummed her fingers on the desk. "I've been thinking about you a lot." She leaned across the desk as if she had a secret. "Catholic or not, I'd end the pregnancy if I was in your shoes. I couldn't deal with a baby by myself, especially one that I knew might have problems."

Katie didn't say anything right away; she wanted to get her words right.

"I think it's easy for you to say that. You aren't religious or dealing with it."

"I'm sorry, I should've kept my big mouth closed."

"I know I asked you once, but I realized that I needed to make my own decision without anyone's input, even my best friend's."

"You're right, I overstepped." Sandra rolled her chair back over to her desk.

"It's okay, I know you only want to be helpful." Katie picked up a pen and chewed the end of it. "Does everyone here know what's going on?"

"I don't think so," Sandra said. "They think you took time off because you weren't feeling well."

Sandra and Katie stood when they saw Dr. Marley, accompanied by a patient, coming toward them. The woman was beaming from ear to ear and Katie knew that look; it was the look of a woman who'd just found out she was pregnant after a war on the fertility battlefield.

Dr. Marley handed the patient and her file to Katie, who took the woman to the front desk.

"Does a month from today work for your next appointment?" Katie asked, opening the file.

"I guess . . . I mean, yes." The patient began to cry. "I'm not usually this emotional. It's just I've wanted to be pregnant for so long, and now I'm terrified that something could go wrong."

"Something could go wrong with any pregnancy, you never know what might happen," Katie said. A horrified look crossed the woman's face. Katie wanted to slap herself. "Oh, that's not . . . I mean . . . I meant to say, it's doubtful that something would go wrong."

"So, should I be worried or not? Is there something in that file that I don't know?"

Sandra joined Katie at the front desk, having apparently overheard the exchange. "Of course not," Sandra jumped in. "Your baby's fine. We'll see you next month."

The woman left looking like she'd been run over by a pregnant woman with a big mouth.

"Maybe I shouldn't be dealing with patients right now," Katie said.

Sandra put her arm around Katie. "It's fine, I'll take over."

"Thanks." Katie made her way to the file room, closing the door behind her.

Hopefully, I won't say something stupid to the files and make them freak out. Katie spent the rest of the day filing and processing data. She didn't trust herself around anything that could understand her if she spoke.

* * *

At the support group that week, Callie and a few other women from the last meeting were milling around. There were also some new, somber faces. Katie wanted to make sure she saved a seat for Rachel, so even though she knew it was rude, she put her purse on the seat next to her.

Rachel scurried in at the last minute, out of breath. If Katie hadn't grabbed her purse, Rachel would've accidentally sat on it. "I was worried you'd changed your mind about coming," Katie said.

"No, I was late because none of my clothes fit," Rachel said. "I don't want to buy any new maternity clothes now, but the elastic on my sweats is so stretched out that they literally fell off me as I was leaving. I hadn't done laundry, so I grabbed one of Brett's shirts." Katie looked down; Rachel had on a black skirt with a large shirt hanging over it that read, THIS BEER TASTES LIKE I'M NOT GOING TO WORK TOMORROW.

Rachel looked sheepish. "I didn't read what it said until I was halfway here."

Katie's shoulders relaxed; she hadn't realized how tense she was, worrying that Rachel wasn't going to show up.

"I'm glad you're here; I wouldn't have wanted to stay if you hadn't come." Katie was finding herself more and more bonded with Rachel. A woman sitting alone at the end of their row with her lips pursed together, continuously crossed, then uncrossed her legs. Katie nudged Rachel and discreetly pointed out the woman. Rachel seemed to know exactly what Katie was thinking.

"Excuse me, is this your first time here?" Rachel asked the woman.

"Yes," the woman answered, barely making eye contact.

"Do you want to come sit with us?" Katie asked.

The woman nodded and moved over to the seat on Katie's other side. "Thank you, I'm Roberta."

Katie and Rachel introduced themselves.

Nicole repeated the rules of the group.

"Before we start," Nicole said, "some of you may have noticed that Jada isn't here today. She asked me to let you know that she suffered a miscarriage a few days ago."

The women in the room were noticeably quiet.

"Why don't we start today with what feelings that news brings up for you," Nicole said.

"Even though my miscarriages were traumatic," one of the

women volunteered, "I'd consider it a blessing to have this pregnancy miscarry so I wouldn't have to decide if I should terminate it."

"I agree," Callie said. "If I wouldn't have had to go through ending mine, I wouldn't have all this guilt."

"Guilt means you did something wrong; do you feel that way, Callie?" Nicole asked.

"It depends on the day. I know I did it for the right reasons, but I'm not sure I think of it as *right*—if that makes sense. I told almost everyone that I miscarried; I couldn't tell them the truth." Katie nodded vigorously in agreement.

"You don't owe anyone an explanation." Nicole's voice was gentle. Rachel's lower lip trembled, then she blurted out, "My daughter's going to die no matter what. I can't believe I'm being forced to decide exactly when that'll happen."

Katie put her hand on Rachel's shoulder as the other women chimed in with their sympathy.

"And I'm mad as hell!" Rachel's voice broke. "I should be welcoming my daughter into the world, instead I'll be saying goodbye to her."

"You have every right to be angry," Nicole said. "This is the perfect place to express it."

The room got so quiet again that Katie could hear a dog barking from somewhere on the block. Katie wasn't sure she was ready to open up, but she felt almost guilty listening to everyone else's stories and not sharing hers. Why was she coming if she wasn't willing to speak?

She licked her lips and forced the words out. "I got pregnant by accident by a guy who doesn't care about me or the baby, and then I found out that the baby has a one in three chance of having Down's syndrome."

"A one in three chance is not that high," Callie said.

"Would you jump out of a plane if you had a one in three chance of dying?" another woman asked.

Callie's remark made Katie's blood boil and she puffed out her chest. She refused to be judged by some woman who didn't even know her.

"Ladies, remember this is a safe place where we all need to feel comfortable expressing ourselves," Nicole stated, Callie and the other woman nodded at each other. "Katie, let's try something," Nicole said. "Close your eyes and pretend you're in the delivery room." Katie closed her eyes tight. "Now imagine you're seeing your baby for the first time. How do you feel?"

With her eyes still closed, Katie put her hands on her belly and tried to go deep into her soul. "I feel happy and excited, I can see her tiny hands and feet." Katie opened her eyes and could feel herself smiling.

"Now close your eyes again and picture yourself seeing your daughter for the first time . . . and she has Down's syndrome."

Katie closed her eyes again and sat with the feelings. After a moment, she felt her breath seeping out of her chest, she didn't realize she'd been holding it. "I feel happy, and that I want to protect her," Katie said, surprising herself. "I think I'm already in love with whoever she is." Rachel nodded and smiled at Katie, and Katie smiled back.

"Maybe that's your answer," Nicole said, and Katie felt the stress escape her body as if it were a balloon a child had let go of. She put her hands on her belly and willed her daughter to move.

As if the baby could hear her, she kicked, making Katie jump. *Oh my God, she's listening. She knows I want her,* Katie thought.

"I'm thinking of giving my baby up for adoption," Roberta said. "I don't think I'm the kind of person who has the patience to raise a child with muscular dystrophy. I saw what my parents went through with my brother, who has cerebral palsy. I don't see myself being able to do that."

"Knowing who you are and what you can handle is important and placing your baby with a family who truly wants that child is a loving thing to do," Nicole said.

When the meeting came to a close, Nicole approached Rachel.

"I wanted to check in with you and see how you were doing?"

"I've been crying so much, I didn't realize until today how truly angry I am," Rachel said.

"Yell, scream, cry, it's all okay. Just don't bottle it up inside." Nicole patted Rachel's shoulder, then walked over to Callie.

"I wish there was something I could say to help you," Katie said. "It somehow feels wrong that I'm going to keep my baby and you don't get that choice."

"Please don't feel bad. I want you to be happy, even if I'm not."

"I want you to be happy, too."

"Well, you can't have everything." Rachel gave her a small smile. The women walked out of the room together, with Rachel so close to Katie that she was almost leaning on her.

Chapter Thirteen
Rachel

20 weeks pregnant

Rachel pulled up in front of her parent's house, a house she had no childhood memories from. As soon as she moved out on her own, her parents downsized and sold the home she'd loved as a kid. She missed the colonial with the navy-blue shutters and the sycamore tree she used to climb when she wanted to show boys how tough she was. She missed the white picket fence that made her feel protected and safe from the outside world.

Before Rachel had a chance to knock, her mother opened the door. Rachel knew that the moment she'd called her parents and said she was on the way, her mother had been watching through the front window. Her mom's eyes were red and swollen and Rachel had the burden of knowing she was the cause.

Her mom pulled her into the foyer and enveloped Rachel in a hug so tight her breath caught in her throat. When Rachel pulled away, her father took over and hugged her tighter, if that was possible. Feeling her parents' love being showered upon her, Rachel's heart was both full and also breaking. When her father pulled away, Rachel backed up, for fear that they might start the process all over again, and she'd completely fall apart.

The three of them went into the living room and sat. Rachel found a loose string on the hem of her shirt and twisted it around and around her finger.

Her mother opened and closed her mouth as if she wanted to say something but wasn't sure what, then jumped up from the couch. "Do you want some water? Or are you hungry? I just bought a pound cake—"

"I'm fine, Mom," Rachel said. "I'm not hungry or thirsty."

"I'll get you some water, just in case."

Rachel's father put his arm around her. "We were so glad you called; we've been worried about you. We haven't seen you in weeks."

"I'm just trying to get through, a day at a time, Dad," Rachel said.

"Are you okay?" he asked, then sighed and shook his head. "What a stupid question, of course you aren't okay."

Rachel had never felt uncomfortable around her parents, but their anxiety was causing her palms to sweat. She didn't have the energy to deal with their feelings, too.

When her mom came back in, she was holding an extra tall glass of water that she put down on the coffee table directly in front of Rachel, then sat on the other side of Rachel, sandwiching her daughter between herself and Ezra.

"Did you and Brett decide about the baby?" she asked delicately.

Rachel wedged herself off the couch and moved to the chair across from them. "I know you guys mean well, but I don't want to talk about it."

"We just want to be here for you," her father said.

"I know."

"We've all been through traumas in life, and eventually you learn how to move on." Her mother reached for her father's hand. Rachel noticed his expression and wondered what kind of trauma her mom could be referring to, but her thoughts were interrupted by her father.

"What did the doctor say will happen if you go through the whole nine months?" he asked.

"That the baby would likely die within a few hours, or a few days." Rachel's voice was thick with emotion. Her mother picked up the glass of water and pushed it, so it was directly in front of Rachel again. She took a sip even though she wasn't thirsty.

"That's awful." Her mother began to softly cry.

"Wouldn't it be easier to end the pregnancy now?" her father asked.

"Maybe . . . I don't know." Rachel was trying hard not to get emotional, but she was losing the battle.

Her mother pulled a tissue out of her sleeve and handed it to Rachel, who took it and blew her nose then wiped her eyes. At that moment Rachel didn't care where that tissue had been.

"What does Brett think?" Leah asked.

"I'm not sure."

"Haven't you two discussed it?" her father asked.

"I can't talk to him about it right now."

"Since you were little, when you got overwhelmed, you'd shut down," her mom said. "When horrible things happen, you need each other, don't shut him out, honey."

Rachel took another sip of the water; she was glad her mother didn't listen to her when she'd claimed she wasn't thirsty. Maybe she was dehydrated from all the crying she'd done lately.

"I thought talking to the two of you would help, but this is all just too much right now." Rachel put her purse over her arm and stood.

"Don't go," her mom said, crossing to Rachel. "We won't talk about it anymore, there are lots of other things we can talk about, and I have cake." Rachel sighed as her mom ran off to the kitchen again. "Do you want fresh strawberries and whipped cream with it?" her mom called out.

Her father raised his eyebrows and tilted his head at Rachel. Rachel knew he was telling her to let her mom feed her. She didn't want cake, but even more, she didn't want to disappoint her mom more than she already had.

Her mother brought Rachel a large piece, piling it with strawberries and whipped cream. Rachel picked at her cake while her parents gossiped about various people Rachel had grown up with.

I wonder if other people's families are talking about me, Rachel thought. She listened to their banter for as long as she could tolerate, then told them that she needed to get going.

"I have an idea," her mom said. "How about if I take you for afternoon tea this week?"

Afternoon tea was something Rachel's mom had been doing with her since she was young. Whether they were celebrating something, or Rachel was having a tough time, it was her mother's idea of doing something nice for Rachel.

"I don't know, Mom, I'm not in the best place."

"I think it will be a good distraction."

Rachel thought for a minute. She knew how important it was for her mom to feel like she was doing something to comfort her. "Okay.

Can I ask my friend Katie to come with us?"

"Of course," Leah said. "I'd love to meet her."

Rachel filled her mom in about Katie's pregnancy and how she didn't have the support system Rachel had. Her mom promised she'd make sure Katie had a good time.

Rachel's parents walked her to the door but before they let her leave, they pulled her into a family hug. Rachel recalled what it was like to have no responsibilities and to just be a little girl with parents who loved and watched over her. She was so caught up feeling safe in their embrace that she almost reconsidered leaving.

When Rachel got to her car, she reached into her purse for her sunglasses, but couldn't find them. She had a flash of putting them down on the entry table in the house. When she found the door unlocked, she let herself in and grabbed her glasses. As she was closing the door behind her, she heard her mother crying and her father trying to comfort her. Rachel knew she should leave, but her feet stayed planted where she stood, the door half open.

"I can't imagine how much stress Rachel's under, I'm so

worried about her," her mom sobbed. "It's killing me that she's in that much pain and I can't do anything to help her."

"You got through your pregnancy, honey, Rachel will get through this, too," Rachel heard her father say.

"It's going to destroy her if she can't ever have a baby of her own, and it's tragic because she'd make a great mother. I'd never want Rachel to know this, but selfishly, I can't imagine going through life without a grandchild."

Rachel covered her mouth to hold back a sob that was lodged in her throat. As quietly as she could, she closed the door behind her.

The moment she sat in her car, the avalanche of tears broke through, and she was submerged in a flash flood. Driving while sobbing was dangerous, but Rachel couldn't let her parents spot her sitting in front of their house. She drove a half-block down the street, pulled over, and punched in the number of the only person she could talk to.

Rachel told Katie what she'd overheard.

"Of course they're upset, they love you and they want you to be happy," Katie said.

"My mom was crying harder than she did at her father's funeral." Rachel turned up the air conditioning, the sweltering heat of the afternoon sun exploding through her windshield. "It's not like I didn't know that she would be sad without a grandchild, but hearing her say it out loud made me feel like a failure as a daughter."

"You're not a failure. Yes, maybe your mother is sad for herself, but she's also grieving with you. I think it's a gift that they care so much."

"I must sound insensitive and thoughtless after all you've been through with your parents."

"No, I'm glad you have them," Katie said.

Rachel nodded, even though Katie couldn't see her. Then she raised her armpits in front of the air that rushed out through the vents. "Oh, and my mom's solution to my misery is for her to take me for high tea," Rachel said sarcastically. "It's a known fact that hot tea fixes all." Even through her tears, she laughed at the absurdity.

"You sound thrilled."

"I'm not. I haven't felt like going anywhere, but if it makes her think she's fixing something for me, then I'll go." Rachel put her face up to the air vent; her hair flew in the breeze. "I hope it's okay that I asked her if I could invite you to come with us."

"Really?" Rachel heard a gleeful tone in Katie's voice.

"My mom wants to meet you." "That's so nice," Katie said.

"So, you'll come?"

"Sure. I'd love to meet your mom, and I've never had high tea before, maybe it'll fix me, too." Katie laughed.

"I need to warn you though, she's going to ask you every detail of your life. You may not want to be my friend after that," Rachel said.

"It will take more than that to get rid of me."

Rachel felt better after talking to Katie, but she didn't want to go home. She drove around, not sure where to go, and before she knew it, she'd pulled into the parking lot of Studio City Recreation Center. When she was growing up, everyone just called it Beeman Park, since it was on Beeman Avenue. She and her mom would go to the Studio City Library, then walk down the street to the small, neighborhood park and rec center where Rachel took gymnastics.

She opened her trunk, threw her sandals in, and took out a pair of Nikes. Brett had urged her to keep an old pair of shoes in her trunk in case of an earthquake or a disaster of some kind. Deciding if she should terminate the pregnancy counted as a disaster, but probably not the kind he had been referring to. As she made her way around the perimeter of the park, her feet sank into the freshly mowed grass, and the aroma of barbequing hot dogs made her nostalgic for her youth.

It was late afternoon and the sky had clouded over and turned to a dusty gray. The sun hid as if it was afraid to come out and add light to this bleak day. Rachel ambled around the park, her thoughts ruminating endlessly as if she were lost in a corn maze and every turn was a dead end.

She looked up at the sky. *God, I haven't asked for much, but I need help. Please give me the courage to come to terms with what the right thing to do for this baby is.*

She came upon a group of girls, maybe seven years old, playing soccer and stopped to watch. In first grade, her parents signed her up for a team, which she hated because she was the only kid who cared about winning and her team lost every game. She wanted to quit, but her parents insisted she finish out the season. They told her she'd made a commitment, and in their family, they didn't quit.

Would they think I was a quitter if I cut short this pregnancy? Have I made a commitment to this baby to see that she's born?

Rachel walked quickly away from the game, her pulse beating

out of her arm. Around a corner, she found three picnic tables filled with people laughing, talking, and enjoying themselves. The tablecloths weren't the cheap paper ones, they were the linen ones you would buy for important celebrations. A banner hung from a tree read, 'Happy Retirement Marvin!' Rachel wondered if she'd ever have something to celebrate again.

When her legs got tired, she found a bench next to a majestic elm tree. Kids and their parents rode bikes, walked their dogs, or played on the swings. Everyone going on with life; she wished she had that luxury, too. She placed her hands on her belly.

My sweet girl, if I set you free now, maybe your soul will come back to me in a healthy body.

A dragonfly flew next to her, flapping its wings wildly. Rachel had read that a dragonfly was a symbol of self-realization and understanding a deeper meaning. The dragonfly stayed near her, even stopping briefly on the arm of the bench. It didn't seem to be scared of Rachel at all, it seemed almost fascinated by her.

She was sure this was nature's way of giving her a sign. No more pretending this was a pregnancy with a baby she'd be nurturing at the end of it.

I don't know why I'm being put through all this, but hopefully someday, I'll discover a reason.

Brett had the newspaper spread out and was reading the sports section when Rachel got home. Honey and Molasses were sleeping at his feet.

She sat next to him, folding her arms across her chest. "I'm going to terminate the pregnancy."

"When did you decide that?" he asked, his mouth falling open.

"Today," Rachel said.

"Without talking to me first?"

"I want to get this over with. Our daughter's going to die, and I need to start grieving her."

"I know, but you didn't let me be part of the decision. In fact, you've never asked how I feel."

"I'm sorry, but I can't deal with anything else," she said, getting up. Brett stood also, dropping the newspaper on the floor, startling the dogs, who got a burst of energy and ran around, scattering the pages everywhere. "I do care how you feel, but I'm having a hard enough time with my own feelings. I can't handle talking about this with you." Rachel went into the kitchen.

Brett followed her. "It doesn't seem like you do care how I feel. What if I need to talk about it? Who am I supposed to go to?"

Rachel's eyes softened. "Okay, so, what do you want me to do? End the pregnancy, or go the nine months?"

Brett's eyes drooped and tears pooled in the corners. He opened his mouth but didn't answer right away.

Rachel continued, "Okay, then it's good I called the doctor on my way home and set up the termination."

"You already made the appointment?" Brett said, getting his voice back.

"Yes. I'm sorry," was all she could vocalize. Rachel went to the pantry and got a box of spaghetti, then pulled a pot out of the cabinet, filled it with water, and put it on the stovetop on high.

"I'm not hungry," Brett said and retreated into what would've been the baby's room, closing the door loudly.

"Fine, because I didn't want spaghetti anyway," she called after him. She turned the burner off on the stove, poured the water out, and dropped the pot in the sink.

* * *

A couple of days later, Rachel handed her keys to the valet at The Beverly Hills Hotel. She knew he'd park her Nissan Altima somewhere far away from the Bentleys and Ferraris in front. Rachel tried to get out of the way of the bustling bellmen who scurried to open car doors before the affluent patrons had a chance to reach for their handles. A wide red carpet extended from the driveway up to the front entrance. No matter how many times Rachel had walked into The Pink Palace, she was still impressed by its grandeur.

The lobby was crowded with people talking quietly on the beige couches, nestled between bright red accent pillows.

Rachel made her way to the Polo Lounge, gave her mother's name to the hostess, and was told she couldn't be seated until at least one other guest had arrived. Rachel leaned against a pillar, balancing her weight back and forth and watching women in Gucci and Yves St. Laurent glide past her Banana Republic ensemble.

Katie arrived, looking even prettier than usual. Her messy ponytail was juxtaposed with a smoky shadow that made her sapphire eyes stand out.

"I wasn't sure what to wear," Katie said.

"You look great." Rachel caught the hostess's eye. "My mom's not here yet, but the hostess will seat us now that you're here."

They were taken to a table overlooking the patio with

exquisite fuchsia bougainvillea and swaying palm trees. It didn't get more Los Angeles than that. Rachel was used to the emerald walls and elegant white tablecloths but seeing them through Katie's eyes made it seem new again. Katie picked up the embroidered linen napkin from the table as if it were a fragile treasure and placed it on her lap.

Rachel's stomach growled as she gazed upon the dark chocolate ganache-filled macarons being carried to the table next to them.

"I've never been to a restaurant this nice before," Katie said.

"It's pretty special." Rachel spied Leah at the hostess desk. "I hope it's okay that I told my mom about your pregnancy. I knew she'd bombard you with all kinds of questions, and I didn't want to put you on the spot."

"That's fine," Katie assured her.

"If she asks you anything that you don't want to answer, kick me under the table and I'll jump in."

"Don't worry, I'm good at distracting people with my wonderful personality."

Katie stood and reached out her hand to shake as Leah went in for a hug.

"Mom if you keep holding her that tight, she's going to pop the baby out right now," Rachel said.

"My daughter thinks I'm a little overbearing," Leah smirked at Rachel as she let go of Katie, who looked happy and flushed.

"When you two hugged, you were a tangle of blonde hair," Rachel said, and Katie and Leah laughed.

The waitress poured them water from a crystal pitcher into three long-stemmed glasses.

"I'm glad you could join us today," Leah said to Katie.

"Thank you, Mrs. Kagen, I'm happy to have been invited."

"You're welcome, and please, call me Leah." Leah put her hand on Katie's hand. "I'm grateful that Rachel has had you to talk to."

"I'm the lucky one," Katie declared.

"And it's crazy how much we have in common."

Katie agreed and then reached for her water. "These glasses are so delicate, I'm afraid to drink out of them." She shook her head and laughed. "They probably cost more than I make in a month."

"They probably cost more than my mortgage," Rachel said sarcastically.

Leah clapped her hands together. "You two are so cute."

An entire cheesecake was carried past them, and the women all watched it go by as if they were going to snatch it off the tray.

"That looks so good," Katie said. "Cheesecake's my favorite dessert."

"It's Rachel's also," Leah said and put her hand on top of Rachel's hand. "And the Polo Lounge is known for theirs, just wait until you taste it."

"My tastebuds are already doing a happy dance," Katie said. "I was telling Rachel that I've never been to a place this elegant."

"I remember the first time I brought Rachel here; she was so enthusiastic."

"I was a little kid. I would've been more enthusiastic if you'd bought me a Malibu Barbie," Rachel said.

"Oh Rachel, you loved it." Leah turned to Katie. "I remember the first time I came here with my mom. I was thirteen, and she brought me here to celebrate my first period."

"TMI, Mom." Rachel scrunched up her face.

Leah batted her hand in Rachel's direction. "We're all women here." Leah signaled their waitress and ordered three herbal teas with an assortment of mushroom bruschetta, tea sandwiches, little quiches, and cheesecake for dessert.

"Mom, we're pregnant, not just rescued off a deserted island," Rachel said.

"My daughter thinks she's so funny," Leah said to Katie but was looking at Rachel with love in her eyes. "I want Katie to be able to taste as many things as possible."

Rachel raised an eyebrow at Katie, who didn't seem to notice.

"That's so nice of you," Katie said. "Everything sounds great." Leah cleared her throat and lowered her voice. Rachel knew what was coming and tried to tap her mother's foot but instead smacked her toe on the leg of the table. She held in the curse words that came to mind.

"I'm so sorry you're going through so much with your pregnancy." Leah's voice was solemn.

"I'm sure she doesn't want to talk about that right now, Mom," Rachel said, trying to catch her mother's eye.

"It's okay," Katie said to Rachel, then turned back to Leah. "I'm trying to be optimistic and pray my daughter will be okay."

Rachel focused on the napkin in her lap. She knew her mother was wishing Rachel's daughter would be okay, too.

Three pots of steeping tea were put in front of them. Leah poured some into her cup, blew on it, and took a sip. "Rachel told us your parents aren't in the picture. Do you mind if I ask where they are?"

"Mom," Rachel said sternly.

Katie cocked her head at Rachel and nodded as if to say it was fine. "My dad left my mom and me when I was nine and I thought he was going to come back, but he never did. After I turned eighteen, I tried to find him, but eventually, I realized he didn't want me to find him."

"That must've been hard. What about your mom?"

"I haven't talked to her in a long time, she's been an alcoholic since he left." Katie's eyes misted over.

"Mom, you're making her cry," Rachel said.

"Oh no, that wasn't my intention at all." Leah sounded sorry.

"Don't worry, it's fine, I cry all the time now." Katie waved it off. Rachel reached in her purse for a tissue. Katie had been the one always handing Rachel tissues, so now it was Rachel's turn.

Katie wiped her eyes and the tears stopped. "See, it was only a second."

"I remember when I was pregnant," Leah said. "I cried at the stupidest things."

"I know, I even cry at dog commercials, and commercials with old people," Katie said.

"Or commercials with dogs chasing old people," Rachel added. Rachel started laughing, then Katie, then Leah. They laughed hard, then they all snorted, then laughed even harder.

"I can't believe you snort also," Leah said to Katie. "I'm not sure that's a good thing, Rachel and I are always getting dirty looks."

"I learned not to care a long time ago," Katie said.

A three-tiered silver serving dish with all the finger foods Leah ordered was put on their table. Then the waitress placed before each of them a cream-colored plate with a delicate floral pattern around the rim.

"These plates are too pretty to get dirty," Katie said, then reached for a cucumber tea sandwich and a quiche. "But I'm starving so I don't care."

Leah picked up one of the bruschetta and put it on Katie's plate.

"Are you going to keep working after your daughter's born?" Leah asked Katie.

"I have to, I don't have any other source of income. At least I work in an office that's all about mothers and babies. My boss will be very understanding if things come up."

"Who's going to watch the baby while you're at work?" Leah asked.

"I haven't figured that out yet." Katie squirmed in her seat.

"Is your home big enough for the two of you?" Leah asked.

"My apartment's small, but I can't afford to move right now, so I'll make it work."

"Mom, can you stop with all the questions," Rachel pleaded.

"It's kind of helpful," Katie said. "With everything else I've been dealing with; I haven't thought about the everyday things that go with having a baby. And to be honest, I appreciate you asking."

"I know you both have a lot on your plate," Leah said, looking directly at Rachel.

Rachel picked up her fork, then put it back down and sighed. "I'm going to terminate the pregnancy," she said, much stronger than she felt.

Leah swallowed hard, then took a sip of water. "You and Brett made the decision?"

"Yes." *Well, I did*, Rachel thought.

"I'm glad you guys settled on what to do," Leah said. Rachel couldn't look her mother in the eyes; Leah was always able to tell when Rachel was holding something back.

"Your father and I would support you and Brett no matter what you decided."

"I know," Rachel said.

"When are you planning on doing—" Leah started to ask when Rachel cut her off.

"I just wanted you to know so you could tell Dad. Can we talk about something else?" Rachel asked softly. Rachel knew Leah would respect her request, even if she wanted more details about her decision.

Rachel changed the subject to a movie she had watched on Netflix. It turned out both Katie and her mom had seen it, too, and they had all loved it. As they finished eating, they had a lively discussion about who figured out the unbelievable twist first. The server cleared their dishes and put a slice of cheesecake in front of each of them.

Katie dug into her dessert first. "This is delicious," Katie said, licking her lips.

"It is, isn't it?" Rachel agreed.

It got quiet as they indulged in the creamy, fluffy, rich dessert.

"I'm having such a nice time," Katie said. "Thank you both for including me."

Leah took Rachel's hand. "It was our pleasure." Leah reached in her purse and took out a small piece of paper and a pen and wrote something down. "Since you don't have family here, if you ever need something, or someone in an emergency to watch your baby, please don't hesitate to call me. Anyone who's a friend of Rachel's is special in my book."

Rachel smiled warmly at her mother.

"Thank you," Katie said, taking the paper, "I can't tell you how much I appreciate that."

Chapter Fourteen
Katie

21 weeks pregnant

Sandra pulled her food out of the microwave and joined Katie at a table. The breakroom had three round tables, each with four chairs and a vase with a bouquet of silk tulips. At one table were two doctors, both with their heads in a book, as if they forgot they were sitting together. There was a refrigerator, a coffeemaker, and a vending machine, which Katie had to pretend not to see, or her lunch would've been potato chips and jellybeans.

Katie reached into her flowered lunch bag and pulled out a huge Caesar salad with grilled chicken, a baguette, and an apple.

When Sandra sat down with her lunch, Katie couldn't help but scrutinize it. "What are you eating?" she asked.

"Cauliflower pasta with almond cheese and zucchini

179

blossoms. I'm trying this new vegan diet to lose the weight I gained last week." "Yeah, I can see that eighth of a pound settling on your hips. I can only imagine how tight your clothes must be." Katie put her face directly over Sandra's food and inhaled, then covered her nose and turned away. "Gross! That smells like something I'd give Mr. Morrison, although he wouldn't eat it, and he eats mice."

"That's mean. I got up early this morning to cook this," Sandra said. "Are you sure you read the recipe right?"

"Nice, coming from someone who doesn't have to worry about gaining weight." Sandra took a bite and made the same face Katie had made. "This is awful." She dumped the rest of her lunch in the trash, then took Katie's fork and ate a bite of her salad.

"You aren't concerned about taking food from my baby's mouth," Katie said.

"I'm being a good friend. I'm helping you learn how to eat faster before your toddler knocks your food off the table."

Katie rolled her eyes, then took back her fork and dug in.

Julianna and Margarette sauntered in holding bags from McDonalds. The smell of warm, salted fries hovered over Katie's head like a delicious drone.

Katie reached over and nabbed four fries from each of them. She offered two to Sandra, but Sandra shook her head no. Katie ate each fry slowly, savoring the flavor; wanting them to last as long as possible.

Sandra went to the vending machine for a protein bar.

While Katie finished her lunch, Julianna and Margarette got into a spirited discussion about which one of them was better at pickleball.

When there was a break in their conversation, Katie shoved her hands in the pockets of her scrubs. "There's something I haven't told you guys about my pregnancy," she said, bouncing her leg.

Julianna and Margarette looked at her with expressions of concern.

"What do you mean?" Julianna asked.

"Are you and the baby okay?" Margarette asked.

"I am, but my daughter may have Down's syndrome." Katie's voice shook.

"Oh no." Julianna put her hand over her mouth.

"I'm so sorry," Margarette said, pushing the rest of her food away from her. "We had no idea there was anything wrong."

"I didn't want to say anything until I figured out what I was going to do."

"What did you decide?" Margarette asked tentatively.

"I want her, and whatever happens, I'll deal with it," Katie said, her voice stronger.

"We'll help you any way we can," Julianna said.

"Yep, and I'm going to be the baby's fun mom," Sandra said. "I'll teach her how to crawl out of her crib, how to flirt with boys, and how to sneak out of the house when her mom grounds her."

"And I'm going to teach her not to listen to you," Katie smirked.

"Just let us know what you need," Julianna said.

"Thank you, you guys are the best." Katie felt so much support at that moment. Maybe she could handle whatever life threw at her.

The lunch hour was over, so Julianna and Margarette threw the rest of their food in the trash and left.

"How can Julianna throw away good fries like that?" Katie asked.

"If you weren't here, I can't promise that I wouldn't fish those out."

"I'll pretend you didn't say that," Sandra said.

"So will I."

"I've missed you. It's been a while since we've had a girls' night." "I haven't been going out a lot lately," Katie said.

"I get it. Whenever you feel like it, just call. And if you don't want to go out, we can just hang out at your place and watch a movie."

Katie thanked her and hoped Sandra wouldn't be able to tell she was lying. Katie had been going out, but Rachel was the only person she'd felt like spending time with.

Now that Katie had told her friends, she felt stronger, and it was time to tell Father George about her decision. Each day, she promised herself that she'd go by the church after work, but by the time the day was over, all she wanted to do was lie on her couch and fall asleep. Today, she was determined to go see Father George, no matter how exhausted she felt.

When she walked into the sanctuary, she worried that the sound of her flip-flops smacking against her feet might bother the other people, but no one was there. No parishioners, no one playing the organ, no one in the pews. Ordinarily, she would've loved having the church to herself, but today the silence felt almost foreboding. She made her way to the altar to light a votive candle and pray for her daughter, but when she was halfway down the aisle, she realized someone was kneeling in front of a statue of Jesus.

She wasn't alone after all.

Not wanting to intrude, Katie sat in a pew to wait. She closed her eyes and tipped her head back but opened them when she felt a slight quiver in her belly. It was as if a hummingbird was flitting around inside her, lightly touching the insides of her body. Katie put her hands on her belly, her favorite thing about being pregnant was her daughter moving inside her. It reminded her that she was growing a real human being and in only a few more months she'd have this other person to take care of. *I'm going to be somebody's mother*, Katie thought. *How preposterous is that?*

The man who'd been in front of the statue turned and Katie recognized him as the youth director who interrupted her and Father George the last time she was there.

Hunky, gorgeous, chiseled, striking, well proportioned . . . was the list of adjectives that came to Katie's mind. Did he fit all those words, or could she just be sexually frustrated? He was handsome. He reminded her of an older version of her high school boyfriend, although she'd heard he went to prison for embezzling money from little old ladies.

Katie felt as if parts of her body were getting an electric shock, and she stopped herself from jumping up and screaming for him to come over and talk to her.

Okay, maybe she was sexually frustrated.

Get it together, she thought. *Do not make a fool of yourself.*

She could tell the exact moment he spotted her by the way his face turned from somber to a smile.

Daniel's coming over. Will he think I'm a stalker if I admit that I remember his name?

"Hi," he said, "I don't know if you remember me, but I'm the guy who interrupted your meeting with Father George."

Katie massaged her face, hoping to disperse the blush she couldn't stop. "Oh . . . yeah, that's right."

"I'm Daniel."

"Katie." She put her hand out to shake his.

He tilted his head and pointed toward the empty seat next to her. "Mind if I join you?"

Daniel had more than enough room to sit down on the aisle next to Katie, but she was so flustered that she moved toward the aisle, so Daniel had to crawl over her.

"I hope I'm not intruding," he said when he sat.

"No, I was about to go light a candle."

"I don't want to keep you from that."

Katie stood up but didn't move right away. She looked back, worried that he'd leave while she was gone.

As if he were reading her mind, he gestured for her to go. "Take as long as you need. I'll wait here."

Katie lit a candle at the altar, then knelt and prayed. "Dear Lord, please help my beautiful daughter come into this world healthy and happy. And if she does have Down's syndrome, give me the strength to know how to nurture her and help her become the best possible version of herself." Katie was weighed down by all the emotions running through her as she made her way back to Daniel. She kept her head down, but even a blind man would sense that she was distressed.

"Are you okay?" Daniel asked when she sat back down.

Before Katie could answer, she was weeping. Daniel gave her a few minutes while she pulled herself together.

"I'm so embarrassed," Katie said, wiping her eyes with her fingers. "I don't usually cry in front of strangers."

"It's not a big deal, churches tend to make people more emotional. Besides, I work with kids, I've seen lots of tears. At least you aren't crying because I stopped you from eating dirt."

"I gave that up when I found out chalk tastes better." Katie couldn't help but smile.

Daniel pointed to her face. "You have an eyelash on your cheek."

Katie put her palm to her face and brushed it back and forth. "Did I get it?"

"No. May I?" he asked.

Katie nodded and Daniel gently rubbed his fingertips across her cheek.

When he finished, her eyelash was on his finger, and he held it out towards her. "Make a wish."

As hokey as that sounded, Katie closed her eyes. *I wish that this man doesn't disappear.* She blew on the eyelash, and it flew into the universe to make her wish come true . . . or it could've dropped on the floor and would be swept up by the janitor.

"I'm such a mess," she said. "Even my eyelashes are stressed out."

"I would imagine being pregnant isn't easy . . . but that's just a guess, so far I haven't been pregnant yet." Katie laughed.

"You have a great smile," Daniel said.

She ran her fingers through her hair, hoping her cheeks had stopped blushing. She glanced as inconspicuously as possible at his ring finger. Her chest expanded with relief when she didn't see one, but then she remembered Dylan hadn't worn one. She scooched over, leaving a little more space between them.

"Are you married?" she asked.

"Not the last time I checked. Are you?"

"Nope."

"I'm glad," he said lightheartedly.

"You might not say that if you knew my story." Katie gave him a modified version of why she was pregnant and not married. Daniel leaned in and Katie observed how intently he listened to her and was pleased that his expression was empathetic. "At first I thought I was an idiot, but then I realized that sometimes you just make a mistake and it's not your fault."

Daniel shook his head. "I have idiot radar and I can tell you're not one. My mom was a single mother, also."

"Really?" Katie said.

"Yeah, similar thing to you. I never knew my dad, and my mother wouldn't talk about him. Whatever happened between them, must've been bad," Daniel said.

"Are you close with her?"

"I was, she died from cancer eight months ago."

"That's terrible, I'm so sorry."

"She was the youth director here until she got so sick and had to step down. The church supported me through so much, so I asked if I could take over for her." Daniel's voice was rich with emotion. "I wanted to give back to them, and being a social worker, I knew a lot about working with kids."

Katie looked into Daniel's eyes, the same eyes that took her breath away the first time she saw him. There was something about this man that made her feel as if she were wrapped in her favorite flannel quilt.

"Are you close with your parents?" he asked.

"No. Let's just say, I didn't have the best role models."

When the door to the church opened, Katie squinted. The sunlight that bounded in from outside blinded her for a minute, and she couldn't see who'd come in. When her eyes adjusted, she realized it was Father George carrying a Starbucks Frappuccino, which made Katie salivate. The priest smiled at them, then walked around the opposite side of the church toward his office.

"I need to work on my sermon for Sunday," Father George called out as if they'd asked him where he was going, then he continued to his office. Katie felt like she'd been caught in the most sacred of places making out.

"He's a good man," Daniel said.

"Definitely. The priest at my church in Arizona was standoffish, and he never asked me if I was okay when it should've been obvious that I wasn't. I felt invisible a lot of the time."

"That's not okay. I would've checked in with you."

"And that's why I bet you're a good social worker."

"I think so," he said and chuckled. They talked for a while longer. "I know we just met, but would it be weird if I asked you out sometime?" Daniel cracked his knuckles.

He seemed so confident until he asked me out, she thought. *How sweet that he's nervous.* "Are you sure?" she asked. "My situation's pretty complicated, in case you hadn't noticed, I'm pregnant."

"And here I thought you'd just eaten a big sandwich for lunch."

"Why thank you." She giggled.

"It doesn't bother me that you're pregnant, as long as there isn't some huge guy that's going to kick my butt."

"Fresh out of those."

"Then I'd like to get to know you better," Daniel said.

Katie was sure the wish from the eyelash was coming true. "Then I accept."

As they exchanged contact information, a loud clomping noise sounded behind them. A boy around six years old came rushing in, his light-up Skechers echoing off the wood floor.

"Daniel!" the boy yelled. He climbed over Katie's legs and threw himself into Daniel's arms, almost knocking Daniel off the pew. "My mom's waiting in the car, I forgot my painting in the art room."

"No problem, Andy." Daniel turned to Katie. "I need to get this young man his artwork. I'll call you soon."

After Andy dragged Daniel away, Katie went to Father George's office. The door was open, and Father George was busy writing on notecards. She knocked on the open door and he put his pen down and motioned for her to come in.

"It's nice to see you looking more relaxed," he said.

Katie was in a better place, but Father George could've also been seeing the afterglow she possessed from her conversation with Daniel.

"I wanted to let you know that I've decided to keep my daughter, even if . . ." Katie had a hard time accepting that there could be anything wrong with her baby, even though she knew the odds could go against her.

"The most important thing that a child needs to know is that they're loved, and you're already doing that by deciding to raise her."

"I appreciate all the support you've been giving me, Father." Katie stood to leave.

"I'm glad you're getting to know Daniel. I think you two will have a lot in common."

Katie nodded. She didn't tell him that Daniel asked her out; she was skeptical that it would happen.

On her way home, Katie got stuck at a railroad crossing waiting for a commuter train to go by when she heard her phone vibrating inside her purse. She stared at the text from Daniel that he was looking forward to getting together. *Is this man too good to be true? Will he back out when he finally grasps that I'm going to have a baby in a few months? I may be overly optimistic, and I've been wrong before, but I think this guy meant what he said.*

Chapter Fifteen
Rachel

20 weeks pregnant

Brett and Rachel pulled up to the surgical clinic which was located in a nondescript single-story building. No sign was visible from the street, although it might have been hidden by the leafy vines that had trailed up both sides of the structure. Rachel hadn't spoken a word during the ride over, and she had watched Brett staring through the windshield as if he had no idea he was driving.

Brett turned off the engine and got out of the car, but Rachel didn't open her door.

Brett trudged around the car and gently tapped on her window.

"Are you coming?" he asked, his voice distorted through the glass.

Rachel turned and looked at him as if she didn't know who he was. Brett opened her door and offered her his hand.

She didn't take it. Getting out, she steadied herself on the curb before following a few steps behind him.

They made their way to the front of the clinic which was painted the same pale pink as the peonies in Rachel's garden. Her insides jumped around as if all her organs were preparing to flee from her body.

Rachel stared into the opaque glass on the front door.

What would she find on the other side? She couldn't even detect a shadow.

Brett opened the door, put his arm on her lower back, and eased her through it as if she were a scared toddler going to preschool for the first time.

They entered into a small waiting room, painted in an even lighter shade of pink than the exterior. Other than soothing instrumental music, it was as quiet as a library, and they were the only ones there. Eight plush chairs were scattered around the room, but nothing about the place made Rachel feel relaxed.

The receptionist was behind another opaque window as if the whole clinic and its employees were hiding behind glass.

Rachel picked at the dry skin on her thumb as the receptionist slid the window open. She was an elderly woman with her hair up in a knot and two knitting needles sticking out of it. She had two balls of yarn on the desk next to her. She greeted Rachel by name.

"How does she know who I am?" Rachel whispered to Brett. Brett, indicating the empty room, gesturing with his hands as if to say, *who else could you be?*

Rachel inched over to the window; Brett sat. Knowing this

woman was witnessing what Rachel was about to do made it all the more real. The guilt she'd been living with for weeks was screaming so loud, she thought she was going to scream back.

The receptionist was as friendly as if she and Rachel had met before in a much happier place. She handed Rachel paperwork to complete.

Rachel took the clipboard with the forms and sat next to Brett. Her hand was shaking so hard she could barely print her name.

Brett took the clipboard from her and filled everything out. "Are you sure you want to do this?" he asked when he was done.

Rachel wondered if he was asking because he wanted to run as much as she did. "No, I don't want to do this. I want to give birth to my daughter and braid her hair and take her to Disneyland and help her dress for the prom, but none of that's going to happen." Rachel's voice shook.

Brett handed the paperwork back to her, and Rachel knocked on the glass window. The receptionist looked through the pages and asked for her signature on one last form.

"Is all this necessary?" Rachel asked; her hand holding the pen trembled.

"I'm sorry, but it is," the woman said. Rachel assumed the woman was someone's mother and was hired because she appeared so compassionate.

Rachel scribbled something illegible that barely resembled her name. The receptionist thanked her and closed the window. Rachel paced almost in circles around the waiting room.

Brett came up behind her and tried to hug her, but her body stiffened, and she pulled away. She didn't want to be touched.

Rachel stared at the door, praying that she would be sucked into another dimension. *I'd rather stumble into quicksand with an alligator chasing me,* she thought.

When she was called in, she handed Brett her wedding ring to hold onto and noticed the corners of his mouth were drawn downward, the results of what she was about to do written on his face.

In the changing room, Rachel took off her clothes and put on a faded green medical gown that matched her dull complexion. She took time to fold her clothes neatly and put them in the locker while the nurse waited to escort her to the surgical room.

"You can have a seat here." The nurse pointed to the metal table. "Dr. Thatcher will be in to talk to you in a minute."

Rachel replied, but the words came out so softly, she wasn't sure she said them out loud until the nurse nodded and left.

Rachel was alone, more alone than she'd ever been. All kinds of ominous-looking machines surrounded her, and the shrill ticking of the wall clock was foreboding.

Every second that went by, meant she was getting closer and closer to no longer being pregnant.

Rachel felt all around her the aura of other despondent mothers who desperately wanted their babies. She wished she could talk to them and ask how they got through it and how they were doing now.

"Hi, Rachel, I'm Dr. Thatcher." The doctor startled Rachel as she walked into the room.

"Hi," Rachel said somberly; she hoped she wouldn't faint.

"I know the nurse went over the procedure with you on the phone, but do you have any questions before we get started?"

"I . . . I . . . Will I still be able to have a baby after I . . . I mean after this?" Rachel played with the tie on her gown, pulling and tugging at it until it almost ripped.

"Yes, many of the mothers who've been where you are have healthy babies now." Rachel nodded and tried to be assured that everything would be okay, but her heart wasn't optimistic, and she wasn't sure if it ever would be again.

"I'm going to do a quick ultrasound, to get an idea of the position of the fetus," Dr. Thatcher wheeled the ultrasound machine over to Rachel. Rachel laid down automatically; she knew the drill by now. Dr. Thatcher squeezed gel onto Rachel's belly, then placed the probe on her.

The doctor put headphones on, which Rachel figured was so she wouldn't have to hear the baby's heartbeat.

As Dr. Thatcher looked at the ultrasound, Rachel started shivering. She wasn't sure if she was cold, or if her anxiety was so heightened that it was causing her to shake.

All she was sure of was that she couldn't control her body or anything else that was about to happen to it.

"Would you like a blanket?" Dr. Thatcher asked.

"Yes, thank you," Rachel said.

The doctor grabbed a blanket out of a cabinet under the sink and laid it across Rachel's legs. Rachel stared at the ceiling. First, she counted the tiles, then she counted the recessed lights. When she realized how hard she was grinding her teeth together, she stuck her tongue in between them to stop. Finally, Dr. Thatcher wiped the gel off her midsection and turned the machine off.

"It won't affect the procedure, but it seems as though the fetus has died in utero." She sounded as if she were telling Rachel what time it was. She moved the ultrasound machine back to the corner of the room.

"She died?" Rachel gasped, sitting up.

"Yes."

"When? I mean, I thought I felt her moving this morning, or was that yesterday, or the day before? I'm not sure anymore," Rachel babbled. Her hands automatically went to her midsection, but she dropped them as if her abdomen was combustible.

"I can't tell you when it happened, I can only say the fetus no longer has a heartbeat. It's common in cases like this."

Rachel swallowed hard. Even though she was about to end the pregnancy, she couldn't believe her daughter was already gone.

"So what does that mean, as far as . . . this?"

"Not a lot, we'll still be putting the dilators into your cervix, and then . . ." As the doctor went on to describe the procedure, Rachel was so busy crying that she barely heard a word.

"I'll give you a few minutes," Dr. Thatcher said. "Do you want me to get your husband?"

"No." Rachel wiped her nose on the gown that she despised. "I want to get this over with."

"Okay, I'll send in the anesthesiologist," the doctor said and left.

Rachel slammed her hands down on the exam table. "How could I not have known that she died? I'm her mother, shouldn't I have felt something?"

She went over to where the ultrasound machine was positioned.

"I hate you!" she yelled, holding herself back from pounding on it. "None of this makes sense, but nothing has made sense for a long time." She was sobbing and shaking, her body crumpling beneath her. When she felt like the muscles in her chest had locked up, she sat back down on the surgical table, worried that she might have a panic attack. She took a big breath, trying to gain her composure, all she wanted to do was get through this day.

She spent the next few minutes concentrating on taking slow, big breaths. When she was breathing normally again, a strange, surprising sense of relief began to wash over her.

I don't have to terminate, she stated emphatically to herself. She looked up, *Oh, thank you, God, for taking the decision out of my hands.* Tears were streaming down her face, but inside she felt a small bit of peace.

When the anesthesiologist came in, Rachel felt slightly more relaxed that both the doctor and the anesthesiologist were women. Rachel watched while the anesthesiologist prepared her IV. Rachel hoped this angel in a white coat would give her enough anesthesia to make her forget everything. She spotted the needle that was to go in her arm. Ordinarily, needles made her even more jittery, but the anesthesiologist had an ethereal presence and warm disposition, which quieted Rachel's anxiety, at least for a few minutes.

"I know this is going to be hard but do your best to stay still," the anesthesiologist said as she inserted the medication into Rachel's arm. The last thing she remembered was the anesthesiologist asking her to count backward from one hundred and reaching only ninety-six. When Rachel woke in the recovery room, Brett was at her side, holding her hand. At first, she didn't remember where she was. She looked around, saw the ultrasound machine, and it all came back to her.

She wished she was still comatose.

She tried to sit up, but her head was spinning, which forced her to lay back down.

"Is it over?" she asked Brett.

"Yes." She didn't look down at her body for fear if she saw that her midsection was even a little flatter, she'd lose it.

"They said the baby had already died." Brett had tears streaming down his face. "I can't believe she's gone."

"Me either."

Brett wiped his eyes with his sleeve. They heard a soft knock on the door, and the nurse who'd first brought Rachel into the surgical room came in to go over post-surgical instructions with them. Rachel had a hard time focusing, but she knew Brett would be listening. All she heard was 'drink a lot of water and take it easy for a couple of days.' "Rachel, do you have any questions for me?" the nurse asked.

Rachel just wanted to go home. Without her baby, she didn't see the point in taking care of herself. Brett assured the nurse that he'd watch over her.

"Take your time, it's fine if you'd like to stay for a while to say goodbye in your own way."

"I just want to get out of here, now," Rachel said strongly without looking at Brett.

"No problem, some parents need time to feel like they have some sort of closure."

"Parents? We aren't parents. We were almost parents . . ."
Rachel couldn't catch her breath; her words were stuck in her throat. The nurse asked if she was going to be okay. Brett nodded. The nurse held out the post-op instructions to Rachel. Rachel just

sat there, so Brett took the papers, folded them up, and put them in his pocket. The nurse quietly closed the door behind her.

"Maybe we need to say a prayer or something," Brett said gently. "It might give us closure."

"Closure is going home without my baby."

Rachel got up quickly, holding onto the table. She still felt dizzy but didn't care.

"She wasn't just your baby." Brett's voice rose a little at the end of the sentence. Then he took a big breath and the look on his face broke Rachel's heart.

"I know, but she's gone, and dealing with that is hard enough. I need to get this nightmare out of my head, not add to it by spending any more time in this place," she said. Rachel was completely drained of tears; she was an empty shell of a person.

"Okay." He put his hand in his pocket and nervously jingled his keys.

The drive home was as quiet as the sound of a jellyfish swimming in the ocean. Brett didn't even bother to turn on the radio, and Rachel was looking at her phone. When they pulled into their driveway and Brett helped her out of the car, she couldn't look at him. If she did, his anguish would be too much for her to bear.

The dogs ran over to her, craving attention after being alone for so long. Rachel gave them each a quick pat, then hobbled over to the couch. Her body hurt, but that was nothing compared to her soul. She wrapped herself in the afghan her grandmother had given her as a wedding gift, then picked up the remote and turned on . . . something. It didn't matter.

Brett asked if she was hungry. She had no appetite.

When he sat next to her, she turned away.

He asked if she was mad at him. Rachel wasn't; she just didn't want to talk. All she wanted was to be alone.

Brett was in the kitchen when the doorbell rang. "Who could that be?" he called out to Rachel, who didn't answer.

Brett answered it. Rachel turned toward the front door and saw Katie holding a bouquet.

"Hi, I'm Katie," she said to Brett.

"I'm Brett." Brett couldn't see that Rachel was slowly making her way to the front door. "Rachel isn't up for visitors right now."

"Oh, my god, I'm so sorry, I must've misunderstood when you texted me and asked me to come by," she said to Rachel.

"She did?" Brett asked incredulously. He turned to Rachel. "You did?"

"I don't want to interrupt," Katie said and handed the flowers to Rachel. "I'll call later." She turned to go.

Rachel stopped her. "Wait, no I want you to stay. I'm glad you got here so quickly."

Katie turned back around and came in, giving Rachel a gentle hug. Rachel thanked her for the flowers.

"Are you sure you're up to this, Rachel?" Brett asked. "The nurse said you're supposed to be resting."

"Talking to Katie will help me," Rachel said, then turned to Katie. "Do you want something to drink?"

"Thanks, but I always bring my own." Katie pulled a sports bottle out of her oversized purse and sat next to Rachel on the couch.

Rachel offered Katie some of her afghan to drape across her legs.

"How're you doing?" Katie asked.

"Awful." Rachel teared up.

"We can talk if you want, or we can just sit and watch TV. I'm here for whatever you need," Katie said.

Without saying a word, Brett picked up his keys and left the house.

Chapter Sixteen
Katie

23 weeks pregnant

"All I want to do is go home and sleep," Katie said to Sandra as they walked into the Tower Bar at the Sunset Tower Hotel. Katie closed her eyes, held her arms straight in front of her, and did the Frankenstein walk. When she opened her eyes, she saw the bartender giving her a curious look.

"I tried to tell that to Julianna and Margarette," Sandra said, "but they insisted on taking you out before the baby comes. I'll get you out of here early, even if I have to throw a drink on you and say your water broke."

"Very funny."

The Tower Bar was a chic Hollywood staple, located in what used to be Bugsy Siegel's apartment. The dark wood-paneled walls gave it almost a masculine vibe, but the red chairs added a touch of femininity.

Katie laughed at how out of place her teal polka-dot wrap dress and wedges were. She no longer cared what people thought. When you have tiny hands and feet poking you from inside of your belly, you stop worrying if anyone is judging you for your taste in clothes.

Sandra and Katie didn't see Juliette and Margarette or any empty tables, so they went to the bar. Katie's sense of gravity had changed since her belly had popped out more, so lately her balance was off, and getting onto a barstool was going to be a feat. Hopefully, some nice people would notice her and offer their lower table, the way people on a bus are supposed to offer a pregnant woman their seat. She looked around but no one was even looking in her direction.

Katie tried to calculate how high the chair was and how far off the ground she'd have to jump to land in the seat. She wasn't about to ask Sandra to pick her up, so she placed her hands on the bar and hoisted herself up and into the seat as if she were doing dips in the gym. When she landed, her belly jiggled against her dress.

Sorry, sweetie, it's not an earthquake. Just your mother sitting down.

"Here you guys are," Julianna said as she approached them. "Margarette and I've been holding a table." Julianna pointed to a booth where Margarette was waving. Katie and Sandra followed her over. Margarette had a large shopping bag sitting next to her.

"What took you so long?" Margarette asked. "We all left the office a while ago."

"I had to fix my makeup after we changed our clothes." Sandra signaled the waiter.

"And I don't walk fast," Katie said. "I'm worn out just getting from the valet to the entrance."

"So, one of you is vain and the other's big and slow," Margarette snickered.

"Exactly . . . So, which one of us is vain," Sandra said.

"Katie, you're not even six months," Julianna said. "Are you really that exhausted?"

"You try carrying another person inside you," Katie grumbled. Julianna ordered herself a Southside Fizz, Sandra got a Cucumber Mojito, and Margarette wanted a Cosmo. Katie ordered a club soda and bread for the table.

Margarette opened the shopping bag, taking out three boxes of various sizes all wrapped in baby pink paper with little white ducks.

"These are from Julianna and me. We went a little crazy last week at Nordstrom's." Margarette pushed the boxes over to Katie.

"You guys are so sweet," Katie said. She unwrapped the gifts and *oohed* and *ahhed* at the stuffed elephant, the onesies, bibs, and a tiny pink dress, tights, and white Mary Jane shoes. Katie put her hands together and pressed them to her lips. She couldn't begin to thank them enough. She put all the presents back in the bag and under the table.

The waiter put the women's drinks and the bread before them. Sandra leaned toward Katie, trying to be heard over the din of the other voices. "Are you going to tell them about Daniel?"

"Who's Daniel?" Margarette asked.

Katie crossed her arms and squinted at Sandra. "No one?"

Katie hoped the server was going to come over at that moment and take their order.

"We want to hear about Daniel," Julianna said.

"He's a guy I met at church, who asked me out. It's no big deal."

"Does he know you're . . . pregnant?" Julianna asked as if it was a state secret.

Katie pretended to whack herself in the head. "I knew there was something I should've told him."

"Ha ha," Sandra said. "Of course he knows she's pregnant. How could she hide that?" Turning to Katie, she said, "No offense."

"I envy you," Margarette said. "I'm having trouble getting a date and I'm not even carrying someone else's baby."

"Don't get too excited," Katie said, taking a bite of sourdough bread and chomping on the crust so loudly the women leaned in so they could understand her. "I'm not sure it's going to work out."

"Why so negative?" Margarette asked. "What's the worst that can happen?"

"You have no idea," Katie said.

"Katie's had some crazy dating experiences," Sandra said, laughing. "Has she ever told you about the guy who took her to see the last *Jason Bourne* movie?"

Margarette and Julianna shook their heads, put their elbows on the table, and leaned in closer.

Katie went on to tell the story about how this guy asked her out to the movies, but when they got to the box office, there were only two seats left and they were on opposite sides of the theater.

The guy was a huge Matt Damon fan, so he still wanted to see the movie. After it was over, she waited in front of the theater until she realized her date had left without saying anything to her.

Margarette chuckled. "Sorry, but you can't tell me that's not kind of funny."

"And that wasn't even the worst date I've had," Katie said. She told them about this one blind date she went on with a guy who kept saying how everyone told him he looked just like Ted Bundy. Her date was intrigued by serial killers, and he knew every fact about every woman Ted Bundy had killed. Katie got so freaked out, she went to the bathroom and called a friend of hers who was a police officer. She got him to come to the restaurant and tell her that her apartment was robbed, and she had to go with him to identify the thief.

"My date didn't even question how this cop knew that I'd be at that restaurant, or how I could know what the thief looked like."

"Okay, clearly you date psychopaths." Julianna shook her head and giggled.

"Yep, and now it's somebody else's turn to be humiliated," Kate said.

The three other women entertained each other by relaying their horrible dating stories.

Katie clasped her hands and pretended to be paying attention, but she'd gone deep inside.

She reflected on how men had been letting her down her whole life. She couldn't bear to be disappointed by another man. She wondered if it would be best if she gave up before Daniel could break her heart.

"Katie?" Sandra waved her hand in front of Katie's face. "Where'd you go?"

It took a second before Katie realized she had zoned out. "Oh, sorry. I was just thinking about . . . what if Daniel's like all those guys who reeled me in, and then disappeared?"

"That could happen. Or he could be on the FBI's Most Wanted List and hiding out at your church," Julianna said.

"Or he could be a gigolo and have a long list of clients," Margarette offered.

"You guys are freaking me out even more," Katie said.

Sandra stepped in. "I doubt that a man who takes over for his mom as the church youth director is any of those things. It might work out, and it might not, but until you go on the date, you'll never know."

"You're right," Katie said. "I need to take one day at a time. Or maybe one second at a time."

"Good idea," Julianna said. "But just in case I'll be watching America's Most Wanted."

"Can we now finish getting buzzed?" Margarette asked. Then to Katie, "And you can watch us."

"I think some of 'us' are already there," Katie said. "You're lucky I'm the designated driver. But be forewarned, when this kid stops breastfeeding, you all better watch out."

* * *

As Katie brushed her teeth, her body swayed to music that was only in her head. She'd been looking forward to this day for a week. Daniel wasn't picking her up for three more hours, which gave her time to scour her closet for a cute maternity outfit. One by one, she tossed various items on her bed, realizing nothing looked good enough for a man who'd planned an entire day all for her. She should've gone shopping. What would Sandra's Dolce and Gabbana dress look like on her now; she giggled just thinking about it.

She decided on white maternity jeans with slight fraying on the knees and a navy and white flowered tank top.

Katie couldn't believe she had to pee again. *I hope he's okay with having to stop at a lot of bathrooms.*

Two minutes before Daniel was due at her house, Katie was pacing, convinced he wasn't going to show up. The cat sat on a chair watching her. "How much do you want to bet, Mr. Morrison, that Daniel's still at home, figuring out how to get out of this date. He's probably trying to come up with a believable excuse, so it won't be awkward if we run into each other at church. What was I thinking agreeing to go out with him, I'm only going to get hurt . . . I always get hurt."

There was a knock on the door. "He's here, Mr. Morrison. I knew he'd show up." Mr. Morrison purred. "Okay, I was hoping he would. Better?" She patted the cat on the head.

Katie got to the door quickly, then started counting to twenty, not wanting to look too eager, but she only got to twelve before she opened it.

Seeing Daniel again aroused all the parts of her body that hadn't been touched since Dylan.

"Hi." Katie tried to lean against the door jamb in the sexiest way she knew how.

"Hi," Daniel said, his smile reaching out and caressing her

face. Daniel looked adorable and stylish in a blue and yellow tropical print short-sleeved button-up shirt with khaki shorts and pure white sneakers.

"Are you ready to go?" Daniel asked.

"Let me grab my purse." Katie left him standing at the door as she went to get her things. She was already buoyed by what a gentleman he was. *At least he's not trying to maneuver his way into my bedroom like Dylan did.*

As she locked the door, she noticed Daniel looking down at her feet.

"I'm glad you wore sneakers," he said.

And I'm glad you wore those shorts that hug that perfect butt of yours, she thought, but said, "They're the only shoes that fit right now. My feet are so swollen, LeBron James and I wear the same size." Katie clenched her teeth. She couldn't believe she said something so unsexy. When Daniel laughed, though, she wanted to kiss him right then.

Daniel opened her car door, waited until she got in, and put her seatbelt on.

"I thought maybe we'd start with a round of miniature golf, then I planned a picnic at Lake Hollywood Park for lunch," he said.

"That sounds great. I must warn you though, I'm a professional mini golfer," Katie said. "I've spent many days perfecting my skills." *Oh my god, did I just say I miniature golf all the time, what a nerd.*

"Then we can go on the circuit together."

The miniature golf course was busy with three kids' parties going strong. By the time Daniel and Katie got to the eighth hole, two teams of kids had already gone around them, complaining that they moved too slowly.

"This hole is my favorite," Katie said.

"Then I can't wait to watch you in action."

Katie was supposed to hit the ball into a chute and avoid the arms of a windmill. She'd done it a hundred times and never missed. She took her time, aimed, and swung hard. The ball hit exactly at the wrong moment and whacked into one arm of the windmill. Katie didn't duck quick enough, and the ball ricocheted back at her like a rifle shot into her arm.

She stood still, holding her triceps, and praying the sting would go away and a big ugly bump wasn't forming.

Daniel moved to her. "Are you okay?"

Katie laughed, too embarrassed to cry. "Yes, I'm fine."

Daniel examined her arm. "I'll go get ice from the concession stand."

"No, seriously, it doesn't even hurt," she lied, but at least there was only a small red mark. "My arm can take a lot." She made a muscle to prove it still worked.

"Nice, but I hate that you got hurt."

Katie picked up her club to show him she was a good sport. She hit the ball again, this time it went perfectly into the windmill chute and came out the side and right into the hole.

"See?" she said, "I can still get a hole in one . . . or is that two?"

"Either way, it's impressive. You might be better than me, and I'm pretty darn good," Daniel said. As they continued to the next hole, the pain Katie felt faded into the background.

By the time they got to Lake Hollywood Park, Katie was having so much fun with Daniel. Daniel opened the trunk of his car and pulled out a blanket and a picnic basket. When he took her hand to lead her across the street, Katie grasped it tightly, not wanting him to let go; she enjoyed the feel of his palm in hers.

It was eighty-two degrees; the sky the color of faded blue jeans. Daniel led her to a perfect spot in a corner under a white birch tree that was so tall it looked to be embedded in the clouds.

He laid the blanket out, smoothing out the wrinkles. Katie sat, trying to get her expansive body in a comfortable position. First, she leaned to the side, with her arm supporting her. She wanted to look as if she were a pregnant centerfold, however, within a minute, her wrist cramped up. She turned over on her back. Having her pregnant belly sticking straight up made her feel like she was harpooned, which wasn't the message she wanted to send. She sat up with her legs slightly crossed, and that seemed to be the most comfortable position, or as comfortable as she was going to be sitting on the ground.

The process of sitting took so long that her face was glistening with sweat, and pieces of her hair were sticking to her cheeks. She envied how easily Daniel plopped himself down, sitting cross-legged, his hair still perfectly coiffed to the side. He looked as if he'd walked off the runway at a fashion show. Katie thought she must've looked like she'd walked off a runway, an airplane runway where she'd been sucked into the engine.

Daniel set up a little Bluetooth speaker, then turned on a playlist. He opened the picnic basket and took out two paper plates, napkins, four sandwiches, two salads, crackers, and two kinds of cheese. Katie noted they were only hard cheeses, so he must've done research as to what a pregnant woman could eat.

Lastly, he took out two pieces of apple pie, bottled water, and sparkling apple cider.

"That's a lot of food," Katie said.

"I didn't know what you liked, so I brought a little of everything."

He's so thoughtful, she thought.

The two of them talked and ate as they listened to Ed Sheeran's "Perfect," followed by Jason Mraz's "I'm Yours," followed by Bruno Mars' "Just the Way You Are."

"How did you know all my favorite songs?"

"Okay, I have to confess. I did a little recon on social media and saw some posts of various artists you've seen in concert." Katie thought she could see his face redden. "I hope that doesn't scare you away."

"Not at all. That is beyond sweet," she said.

Daniel seemed to let out his breath, and there was a slightly awkward silence.

Katie took a bite of the chicken curry salad, which was delicious. "What made you decide you wanted to be a social worker?" she asked, breaking the silence.

Daniel relayed how when he was growing up his mother was always doing charitable work, and she'd take him with her. He would watch how his mother helped change people's lives, and how happy that made her.

"That's the same reason I work at an infertility clinic. I like helping women achieve their dreams of having a family. The only bad part is, for every woman who walks out happy, there's two more that are crying."

"I know. I like my job except when I have to deal with a really bad domestic situation," he said.

Katie reached her hand toward the picnic basket. As if Daniel knew exactly what she wanted, he handed her a bottle of water, and she thanked him.

Daniel told her how he's had to be responsible for taking kids from their homes and putting them in foster care. "Even though the parents were unfit, and the situation was dangerous, the kids didn't understand why I was breaking up their family. It tore my heart out and no explanation could make them feel better."

Katie looked down at the ground so Daniel wouldn't see her getting emotional. He put his hand on her chin and raised her face to him.

"What did I say?" he asked.

"It's just that I was one of those kids." Katie told him how her dad left when she was young, and her mom coped by drinking her body weight in alcohol every day. "I didn't have a childhood, I couldn't have friends over, and being an only child, I had no one." Daniel put his hand on hers. "And as awful as all that was, I still would've been terrified if some stranger came in and took me away from my mom." Katie could tell from his expression that he cared deeply about what she'd gone through.

Out of the corner of her eye, she spied a soccer ball flying toward them. Daniel jumped up to block it but wasn't quick enough, and it whacked into her forehead.

"Oh no!" Daniel exclaimed. He grabbed the ball and tossed it back to the kids.

"I must be a magnet for balls today." Katie put her hand to her forehead.

"I'm a gentleman so, I won't touch that statement," Daniel grinned.

Katie felt her cheeks get hot. "You know what I mean," she said, laughing.

"Let me look," Daniel eased her hand away. "It's red."

"Is there a bump?"

"Not yet. I'm going to get you some ice." He rummaged through the picnic basket, trying to find ice.

"Do you think it means anything that this keeps happening?" Katie said.

"I think it means you're so pretty that even sports equipment is attracted to you."

Daniel presented a handful of ice and held it to her forehead. Unfortunately, the ice had mostly melted, so little droplets of water dripped down onto Katie's nose and chest.

"I'm sorry, you're getting all wet," Daniel said.

Katie wiped her shirt, then gently moved Daniel's hand away from her face. "You're so kind. But like my arm, my head is pretty hard." Katie switched her position to face the soccer game; she didn't want to be surprised by another ball coming toward her.

"You blow me away," Daniel said. "You handle life and your situation so well."

"You didn't see me falling apart for the first half of my pregnancy. Oh, wait, you did – I was completely losing it that day in church when we first talked."

"I have no memory of that at all."

"Yeah, me neither." Katie felt herself flush. "Hey, what about that apple pie? Or were you going to keep both pieces for yourself?"

"How could I do that after all you've been through today?" He handed her one of the pieces. "You have something in your top front tooth," he said matter-of-factly.

Katie closed her mouth tight. "Oh god, how embarrassing."

"Oh please, it's no big deal."

Katie turned her head away from him and stuck her nail between her front teeth. When she realized she got out a piece of lettuce, she turned back.

"When we're done here, I have one more place I'd like to take you."

"We aren't playing dodgeball, are we?" Katie teased.

"Nope. I canceled that part of the date," Daniel teased her back.

Katie was pleasantly surprised when Daniel pulled into a parking lot at the beach in Santa Monica. As it was later in the afternoon, more people were going than coming, so it was easy to find a parking space even on such a perfect beach day. Katie slipped off her shoes and socks. She hadn't been to the beach in a year; she missed the ocean breeze blowing her hair.

Daniel took her hand, and they walked across the warm sand toward the surf that slowly rolled to the shore. A large wave came at them, surprising Katie, who squealed and jumped back, cold water washing over her feet. The hem of her white jeans was soaking wet and turning brown.

"Your pants are getting dirty," Daniel said.

"Yes, they are." She flashed him a huge smile. At that moment she didn't care if she could never wear them again, it would've all been worth it to be taking a romantic walk on the beach with a gorgeous man.

They stepped out of the water, back onto the sand. Daniel was relaying a story about a prank phone call he and his best friend made when they were in elementary school when Katie stumbled and grabbed onto him. "Ouch," she said, hopping off her right foot onto her left. She lifted her foot and found that she'd stepped on a bee, the stinger sticking out of her foot.

"Are you allergic?" he asked, furrowing his brow.

"I don't think so, but I've never been stung before." Katie leaned against Daniel as he pulled the stinger out of her foot. She put her foot down and tried to walk but she could only limp. She grimaced with each step.

"You're in pain, let me look at it again."

Katie held her foot up again and Daniel scrutinized it.

"We need to take you to urgent care; the bottom of your foot is swelling up."

"Give it a minute, I'm sure it'll go down." Katie didn't want this beautiful date to end, let alone go to urgent care. "I can take Benadryl."

"You're pregnant, we can't take any chances." Daniel scooped her up in his arms and carried her across the sand. Katie wanted to enjoy how gently he was treating her, but all she could think about was her extra weight and how he was going to need urgent care, too. Daniel placed her gently on the passenger seat, helped her with her seatbelt, then jumped in and drove off.

Two and a half hours later, Katie limped up to her apartment door, holding on to Daniel's arm. "Do you want to come in?" she asked.

"If you're sure it's okay?"

Katie nodded and Daniel helped her to the couch and put a pillow under her foot.

"I want to get you ice for that foot, where do you keep your plastic bags?" he asked.

"I'll show you," Katie said, trying to get up.

"No, you should stay off that foot, just direct me."

Katie closed her eyes and imagined her kitchen setup, then directed Daniel to the correct drawer. Daniel must've gotten confused because he told her he'd found screwdrivers, scissors, hooks to hang pictures, and an X-acto knife.

"I don't think you want me to cut off your foot," he laughed holding up the knife.

"The bags are in the drawer two over from that and down one," Katie called out.

"Ah hah, pay dirt," Daniel said.

Katie could hear him getting the ice out of the ice maker. He came back, lifted her foot onto his lap, and held the bag of ice to it.

"I need to apologize for everything that happened today," Daniel said.

"Are you kidding? This is the best date I've ever been on."

"You got hit by two different balls and then stepped on a bee."

"You took care of me the way no one else ever has. You drove me to urgent care and waited with me for over an hour, only to hear, 'Put ice on it.' Most of the guys I've gone out with would've barely stopped the car and had me roll out."

"You're just saying that to make me feel better."

Katie leaned over and gave him a quick kiss on the cheek. "Does that feel like I'm just trying to make you feel better?"

"I'm not sure, I may need a few more of those to convince

me." Daniel dropped the ice on the ground and took Katie's face in his hands. He looked deep into her eyes. She couldn't look away and wouldn't have wanted to. He moved toward her, her eyes losing focus, then closing as he gave her a long, slow, kiss. Her heart beat so fast and she didn't want him to stop. When he pulled away, Katie put her hands on each side of his face and brought him back and things got heated.

When they took a break, Daniel noticed the ice had leaked out of the plastic bag and melted all over her floor.

"Great, now you're going to slip on the water, break your neck, and I'll have finished the job. Every pregnant woman will want to date me after that."

"No, only one pregnant woman." Katie kissed him again as Mr. Morrison licked the water off the floor.

Chapter Seventeen
Rachel

A long line of strollers was parked along one wall outside the children's museum. Rachel and Katie proceeded inside. The building was two floors, but the lower level was where the kids spent most of their time.

They almost got knocked over by joyful rugrats running toward each other like magnets to a refrigerator. "Kids seem to love it here," Katie said.

Katie was now almost eight months along, and Rachel envied how much she'd settled into her pregnancy. Katie's skin was dewy, her eyes sparkled and if you saw her from behind, you wouldn't have known she was pregnant. From the front was a different story. Katie looked as if she were hiding a wine barrel under her lavender maternity dress. Rachel's boyfriend jeans were too relaxed in the legs and being held up by a white belt hooked into its last hole. She'd lost all of her baby weight and five extra pounds in the last few months, which on her tiny frame, made her look slightly emaciated.

"I appreciate you coming with me today," Rachel said. "I was supposed to come here weeks ago for a guided tour to see if it would work for a field trip for the new school year, but I wasn't up to it."

The museum housed different themed rooms and areas for playing and exploring. One room had a life-sized ambulance, one had a rescue boat, and there was even a doctor's office. In each area, there were various costumes that the kids could try on. Katie and Rachel came around a corner and found a girl wearing a firefighter costume and a boy wearing a banana costume pretending to fight a fire. Their mothers sat off to the side watching them.

"Don't you think it's weird that we're thirty-something-year-old women at a children's museum without a child in tow?" Katie asked.

"Maybe we're bad parents who let our kids create havoc while we hide from them and chat," Rachel said.

"That does make me feel less creepy." Katie chuckled.

They sauntered into the next room where they discovered an inflatable motorboat sitting in a pool of blue balls meant to look like water. Inside the "water" were four toddlers with runny noses pelting each other with the balls.

"Is this what I have to look forward to?" Katie asked. "A battle to see who can pick up the most germs?"

"I'd be okay with that." Rachel's shoulders dropped.

"I really should think before I speak." Katie put her head in her hands. "You have been so amazing about my pregnancy, but it must be hard on you."

"It is, but I can still be happy for you," Rachel said. "At least most of the time."

The next area they came upon was set up like a grocery store, where two boys were pretending to sell fake fruits and vegetables. The boys were in the middle of an argument over the price of a corn cob. A young girl asked to play with them, and the boys told her to go away. She began crying and calling out for her mother.

"Are you sure you want to bring sixteen kindergarteners here?" Katie asked Rachel. "Seems like a lot of work."

Rachel shrugged. "It's always a lot of work, but I love teaching this age. They're so innocent and have no concept of the terrible things that can happen in life which will destroy them emotionally. Oh, sorry, I promised myself I would stop being such a downer."

Rachel put a hand on each side of her mouth and pushed the corners up, so it looked like she was smiling. "Look, I'm happy."

"You look like the count in Sesame Street," Katie said, and Rachel dropped her hands.

Katie stopped at a water fountain and tried to drink without having the water splash down the front of her dress.

Rachel waited until she finished, then asked in a sing-song voice. "So, how are things with you and Daniel?"

"Surprisingly good," Katie said and moved over so Rachel could take her turn at the fountain. "We've gone on . . . ."

As Katie counted on her fingers, Rachel jumped in. "Eight dates in the last three weeks."

"I can't believe you know that."

"I'm invested in people I like."

Katie beamed at her. "And I still haven't found anything wrong with him. Although, there's still time for the shoe to drop."

"What if there's no shoe?"

"There's always been a shoe, and it's usually something with spike heels that hurts a lot," Katie said. "But I'm hoping that's in the past. Daniel's different from other guys I dated."

Rachel motioned to Katie to follow her over to the boys who were working in the grocery store. Rachel offered to buy two tomatoes and three potatoes from them. The boys looked at each other and nodded, then asked Rachel for a million dollars. Katie told Rachel she thought that was a good price, and Rachel agreed and gave the boys imaginary money. The boys looked at each other as if they found two of the dumbest adults. When Katie asked how much it was to buy the grapes, the boys asked for two million. Rachel and Katie told them they were now broke and would have to go to the bank for more money. The boys went back to finding other suckers to buy their food.

Rachel pointed to a kid-sized table in the corner of the room and suggested they take a break. Katie eyed the miniature chair, then tried to sit in it.

"I bet whoever's monitoring the security cameras is getting a big kick out of watching me try to squeeze my body into a seat that wouldn't be big enough for Tiny Tim," she said. Then she wiggled back and forth until her hips were wedged between the arms of the chair. "I hope I can have the baby here because I'm not sure I'll ever be able to get out of this thing."

"I promise to peel you out of there when it's time to leave." Rachel giggled.

"Thank you," Katie said. "So, how are things between you and Brett?"

"Not good." Rachel described how at dinner their conversations were about their dogs, the same way people who don't know what to say to each other talk about their kids. Then after dinner, she'd go into their bedroom to read, and he'd stay in the living room to watch TV.

"And the best part is we haven't had," Rachel dropped her voice to a whisper, "sex in months."

"You have to try to get him to talk," Katie said. "When men grieve, they often shut down. I've seen it a lot at work."

"It's me who doesn't want to talk. I don't want to discuss what happened."

"I get it. Is Brett on the same page?"

"No. I want to move on, but he seems stuck. I'm finally getting to the point where I can sleep without having nightmares." Rachel squeezed one of her fingers, hoping the pain would distract her from her intrusive thoughts.

Katie rested her elbows on the table. After a minute, she said, "Hear me out. I wonder if you got pregnant, would Brett still feel stuck?"

"I don't know."

"I don't want to overstep but think about it. If you got pregnant again, you and Brett could move forward, and you both would have something good to focus on."

"I'd like to be pregnant again, even if it would be scary."

Rachel's breath quickened just thinking about it. "Brett and I were so happy before we got the baby's diagnosis."

"That's what I'm talking about," Katie said.

"Maybe you're right." Rachel nodded vigorously as if she were a bobblehead being attacked by a teenager. "Being pregnant again would take us back to that place." She began to feel more optimistic than she had in months. She clasped her hands together. "You're pretty wise."

"Remind me of that when my daughter becomes a teenager."

A child at the next table was crying, but Rachel tried to tune it out. Crying had been the background music at the museum. "So, when do I get to meet Daniel? You've told me so much about him, I want to see for myself if he lives up to the hype."

Katie assured Rachel that if he was still in her life after she had the baby, she'd introduce them. The child that had been crying began weeping and then screaming. Rachel and Katie turned around to see what the commotion was.

A young mom was trying to calm her daughter. "Mommy, I can't afford to buy the potato. I only have twenty dollars, and they want a hundred million," the little girl blubbered.

"Sometimes that happens, honey," the mother said. "We can't always get everything we want."

"Ain't it the truth, ain't it the truth," Rachel exclaimed as if she were the cowardly lion in *The Wizard of Oz.*

Katie grinned. "But we should never stop trying."

When Rachel got home, Honey and Molasses greeted her as if she'd just come home from war. To Rachel that wasn't so far off, as she felt like she was under siege every day. She got cheese and crackers and headed to the couch. Molasses ran over to one side of her, and Honey to the other side, both looking at her expectantly.

"You guys would never leave me if I couldn't give you a child, would you? You'll always be loyal and loving . . . As long as I share my snacks with you." Rachel gave each of them a cracker and the dogs swallowed them without even chewing.

Rachel picked up *Cosmopolitan* magazine off the coffee table. Saweetie was on the cover in an army green tank dress and in huge letters it read, 'Your New Sex Life Will Be Interesting.'

"New sex life, I'd take my old one right now, right girls?" she said to the dogs. Suddenly, they jumped up and ran toward the front door. "Too much information?" she called after them.

When she heard keys in the door, she steeled herself to have a conversation with Brett, who walked in carrying a six-pack of beer and a bag of groceries.

"Hi," Rachel called out over her shoulder, a lilt in her voice.

"Hi."

Rachel went into the kitchen. "I wish I'd known you were going to the store," she said. "I would've asked you to pick up a few things."

Brett shrugged and Rachel looked through the bags to see what he'd bought. She pulled out a carton of eggs and put them on the counter.

"I've been doing a lot of thinking about how we can go on after everything that happened," Rachel said.

"Me, too."

"I figured out a way that we can get back to our old selves," she said flirtatiously and moved closer to him.

Brett raised an eyebrow at her. "Tell me."

"We get pregnant again," a grin spread across Rachel's face.

"You must be kidding," Brett said, then quickly stepped back from her as if he'd received an electric shock.

"The doctor told us we could start trying, so why should we wait?"

"I'm still dealing with the loss of our daughter." Brett stared into his empty hands.

"I am, too, which makes getting pregnant a good idea," Rachel said, her mouth suddenly dry. *Please, please, please*, she thought.

Brett opened one of the beers and took a big gulp. "What if 'it' happens again?" he asked.

"The doctor said it was probably a random gene mutation, which means the odds are small that it would happen again."

"Small odds are not the same as never."

"You're overthinking this." Rachel slumped down in a chair.

Brett picked the carton of eggs up off the counter. As he carried them to the refrigerator, one egg fell out, breaking and splattering all over the floor. Brett stared at the broken egg but didn't move. Rachel jumped up to grab a paper towel, trying to erase the mess.

"Are you saying you don't want to try again?" Rachel asked, throwing the towels away.

"I'm not ready, I need time."

Rachel threw her hands up in frustration. "How much time?"

Brett clenched his jaw. "You don't want to consider how I feel. You just want me to go along with what you want, the same way you made the final decision to terminate."

"Did you think it was the wrong decision?"

"No, but we still should've talked it out."

"So, are you punishing me?"

"No," he said emphatically. "I'm grieving, and another pregnancy won't fix that."

"Well, I think it would!"

"This is one thing that you can't decide on your own," he said. "And this conversation isn't going anywhere."

Rachel panicked; she was sure she could hear her heartbeat thumping outside her chest. "You're not being fair."

"You're the one who's not being fair." Brett strode to their bedroom, Rachel stayed on his heels. He pulled a large suitcase down from the top shelf of their closet.

"What're you doing?" Rachel asked.

"I'm going to San Diego to stay with my parents."

"You're leaving me?" Rachel's head felt like it was submerged in water. She was so stunned; she couldn't move, and she couldn't get any words out.

"I'm not leaving you; I'm just taking some time for myself."

Did she push him too far? Was he going to come back? She thought she was going to faint. "How much time?"

"I don't know!" Brett pulled socks out of a drawer and threw them into the suitcase.

"You're really going to leave?" Brett didn't answer and Rachel found herself going from shock to anger. "That's a lot of socks you're packing," she spit out.

He went into the closet and took shirts off hangers. Rachel marched into the bathroom, picked up Brett's toothbrush then dropped it in his suitcase. "Wouldn't want you to have bad breath while you're gone," she said, holding back hysteria.

"I'm not going away forever; I just need to clear my head."

Brett kissed her on the forehead. "I love you, but I just can't be with you right now."

Rachel went back into the bathroom and locked the door while he finished packing. She came out when she heard the front door closing. She slumped onto the carpet in her bedroom and cried as Honey and Molasses licked the tears from her face.

Chapter Eighteen
Katie

30 weeks pregnant

Katie sorted tiny onesies, PJs, bibs, and blankets on the gunmetal gray glider that was a gift from the doctors at work. Up against the right side of her bed was a white crib with a few nicks in the wood. Katie had bought it at her neighbors' garage sale. A mobile hung from the side, the air conditioning making Winnie the Pooh, Eeyore, Piglet, and Tigger dance in a circle. Katie had bought pink ballerina bedding, which she'd washed three times to make it as soft as possible and then ironed out all wrinkles. It was ready for a baby to dive into, even though she still had ten weeks left.

In a corner of Katie's bedroom sat a stroller, a car seat, and a changing table. The changing table shelves were filled with baby wipes, diapers, ointment, and burp cloths. Above the changing table were shelves lined with *Goodnight Moon, Hungry Caterpillar*, and the series *Pat the Bunny*. Except for Katie's bed, the room resembled a crowded baby store.

Katie held up a diminutive Dolce & Gabbana dress with large white roses and green stems and leaves on a black background, a gift from Sandra that came with a matching headband.

How can a small person who's still in a bubble have a better wardrobe than me?

When the doorbell rang, Mr. Morrison rocketed into the air and scampered to his hiding place under the couch. Katie peered through the peephole and saw Rachel standing outside with her eyes cast down at the ground. When Katie opened the door, Rachel picked up her head and her eyes were swollen and her face splotchy. "What happened?" Katie asked.

"Brett's gone." Rachel covered her mouth with her hand as if she might throw up.

Katie pulled Rachel inside. "What do you mean gone? Did he get in an accident?" Katie's heart pounded.

"No, he left town yesterday, we had a fight, and he went to his parents' house in San Diego."

Katie nodded, she wasn't surprised, as men leaving was something she had come to expect. "What did you fight about?"

"He doesn't want to have a baby with me anymore."

"He said that?"

"He might as well have." Rachel stuffed her hands in the pocket of her jeans. Katie followed Rachel into the kitchen and opened a bottle of chardonnay and poured Rachel a glass, but before she handed it to her, she put her nose to it and took a big, long, delicious sniff. Rachel drank as if she was a nomad dying of thirst, then relayed the details of the fight she and Brett had.

"What I hear is Brett's not ready to try again yet . . . 'yet' being the operative word," Katie said.

"That's not the feeling I got."

"You're both still emotional, and you're jumping to the worst-case scenario. I'm sure he'll come around. He'll want an heir, most men do."

"But what if I can't give him one? Didn't they chop off the heads of women in England if they couldn't produce a kid?"

"That was Henry VIII, and you're not a queen in the fifteen hundreds."

Rachel walked into Katie's kitchen as if it were her own and took a nectarine out of the fruit bowl.

"The way you've described Brett, he doesn't sound like the kind of guy that's going to walk out on you forever if you can't have his baby."

"I'm not so sure. He's only called once, and that was to tell me he made it to San Diego," Rachel said, grabbing a paper towel for the nectarine juice.

"He hasn't even been gone a day," Katie said. Rachel shrugged her shoulders. "Give him some time, he's been through a lot."

"So have I. What if he went to San Diego to find a fertile wife?" Rachel choked out.

"You have to change the way you're looking at this."

"What other way is there to look at it?"

"That so far things have sucked in this one area, but that doesn't mean they always will." Katie's face contorted and she hunched over and put her hands on the refrigerator to steady herself.

"Oh no, I'm stressing you out," Rachel said.

"It's not you. These Braxton Hicks contractions are not fun." Katie

bit her lower lip. "And if these are painful, what is the actual labor going to be like?"

Rachel took Katie's arm and led her to the living room just as another contraction hit. Katie bent forward and grabbed onto the arm of the couch with one hand, her other hand holding her side.

"If they're worse than this, I'm not going to have the baby," she said.

"Are you sure this isn't labor?"

"Yes, I was at the doctor's yesterday. I only have them once in a while, then they're gone for days." Katie's face softened and she dropped her hand from her side when the contraction ended. She sat on the couch.

"That's good. I know they hurt, but I'd take contractions any day." Rachel pursed her lips.

"I hope being around me isn't triggering you," Katie said.

"I'm dealing with it. You're the one who's kid is trying to kung fu its way out of you." Rachel drank more of her wine. "Maybe I'm just noticing it more, but it seems like the whole world is pregnant right now. Fifty percent of the moms of the kids in my class are having babies. I think it's a requirement that when your child starts elementary school, you have to start baking your next one."

"Don't make me laugh, I might pee," Katie said.

"Didn't you say Mr. Morrison peed on this couch once?"

Rachel joked. Hearing his name, Mr. Morrison poked his head out from under the coffee table and looked at them.

"I don't know how I'd go through all this without you. I'm scared out of my wits," Katie said.

Mr. Morrison always seemed to know when Katie needed him, and he jumped up on her lap. Rachel reached over to pet him, and he moved his face closer to her, purring loudly.

"Wow, he doesn't let anyone but me pet him," Katie said. "He must feel safe."

Mr. Morrison curled up against Rachel's body and fell asleep.

"He's been so tired; I think I've been keeping him awake at night. He sleeps with me, and I've been restless. I keep having this weird dream," Katie said.

"What's the dream?" Rachel asked.

"I've just given birth at my childhood home, and my mom cuts the cord, then she lays my daughter on my chest. In the dream, my mother tells me how much she's missed having me around and how she wants to be the best grandmother to my daughter. I always wake up crying."

"Maybe your subconscious is telling you to call her," Rachel said. "She is going to be a grandmother."

Katie noticed Rachel got quiet and wondered if Rachel was thinking how unfair it would be for Katie's mother to get that opportunity, while her own mother may never get that chance.

"I think I'm having the dream because a couple of months ago, my mom left me a voicemail that she finished rehab again. I didn't call her back because I've heard that so many times."

"Maybe this time's different."

"I don't know," Katie said, shaking her head. "She doesn't even know I'm pregnant."

"If she's sober, she might be able to be the mother you need. She can tell you what it was like giving birth to you, and hopefully allay some of your fears. I bet she'll say that having you was the best thing she ever did and how she couldn't imagine not having you as a daughter. Or some motherly things like that."

"You don't know my mother."

"People can change. Call her," Rachel urged. "She might surprise you."

Katie picked up her phone, then dropped it back on the table as if she'd burned her hand.

"I feel like it's going to be okay," Rachel assured her, picking up Katie's phone and giving it back to her.

Katie relented and dialed. When it started ringing, she hit the speaker button and Rachel got closer to her.

The phone rang several times. Katie shook her head back and forth and shrugged her shoulders. She let out a breath and was about to hang up when she heard her mother say hello. Then Rachel and Katie heard what sounded like the phone hitting the floor. In the distance, words were being said, but nothing Rachel or Katie could understand. It was as if her mother's voice was being muffled by a piece of paper.

A few more seconds went by until, "Hello? Who is this?" Katie's mother slurred and Katie knew she was drunk. "If you don't talk, I'm going to hang up."

Rachel nudged Katie to say something.

"Uh . . . it's me, Mom," Katie said tentatively.

"Katie? Well, isn't this a surprise." Her mother's voice oozed with sarcasm as if it was blood dripping from an open wound.

I must be crazy, Katie thought, then blurted, "I have some good news."

"If you didn't win the lottery, it's not good news." Her mother cackled hysterically.

"I'm pregnant."

"Is that a joke?"

"No, Mom, I'm having a baby."

"Well, thanks for inviting me to the wedding," her mother sneered.

"I'm not married."

"Figures. So, who's the father? I hope it's not a deadbeat like yours. That man didn't pay me a cent of child support."

Katie imagined her mother holding a bottle of vodka and taking gulps as she yelled at her.

"I'm having the baby on my own."

"Of course you are."

Katie could feel her mother's smug expression through the phone.

"This was a mistake," she mouthed to Rachel. Katie marched back and forth in a straight line, leaving footprints on the carpet as if she'd been asked to do a field sobriety test. "I didn't call to talk about how I got pregnant."

"Then why did you call?"

Katie fumbled with the phone, almost dropping it. She stopped walking and centered herself. She tried one last time, desperately wanting her mother to finally be there for her. "I'm scared to give birth and I was hoping you could tell me what it was like when you had me.

Was I an easy delivery or did it hurt a lot?"

"I don't know," her mother spat out as if she ate something bad.

"What do you mean? Don't you remember?" Katie looked at Rachel, whose eyebrows were scrunched together as if she was just as confused as Katie.

"I didn't give birth to you. You were adopted."

The ground fell out from under Katie's feet as her whole world collapsed. "I was adopted?" she said incredulously and shivered as if a bucket of ice had been dropped down her back.

"Yes, you were adopted," her mother said.

"Why didn't you ever tell me?"

"I thought it would make you feel bad."

Katie's knees buckled and Rachel rushed over to steady her. Katie took deep breaths in an attempt to calm her racing heart and avoid any more Braxton Hicks.

"So, who is my biological mother?"

"How the hell should I know?" her mother spewed. "I don't need you calling me just to complain about your life. I have my own problems." She hung up.

Katie fell back down on the couch, staring at the phone in her hand.

"Are you okay?" Rachel asked, but Katie didn't answer, she just flexed and unflexed her fingers as if she wanted to hit someone. "I'm sorry, I told you to call her."

"If you hadn't I never would've known," Katie said. She stopped flexing her fingers but started shaking her left leg up and down rhythmically.

"She's worse than you described. She's a monster," Rachel said, placing her hand on top of Katie's knee.

"My mom wasn't always that way." Katie had good memories of her childhood before her father left and her mother started drinking. "My parents used to love hiking Thumb Butte. On weekends in the spring, my mom would put baby carrots, string cheese, salami, and lots of water in a backpack and we'd sing songs as we walked. When I got tired, my dad would hoist me up on his shoulders. Then he'd reach back and tickle me, and I'd laugh so hard that I'd snort, and then worry that I might fall, but he always held on tight."

"That sounds nice," Rachel said.

"It was, until he left, and my mom blamed me, which at the time I believed." Katie's legs were starting to cramp, so she stretched them out in front of her. "Now, I don't belong anywhere. I don't have a family, not that I did before, but now it's final."

"I'll be your family."

Katie almost got teary. "You're sweet, but you already have a wonderful family."

"I also had a husband, but I think I screwed that one up."

"Take it from someone who doesn't have anyone in the world but her friends, you need to work that out." Katie got up and sat on the floor with her back against the couch. She sat quietly, trying to take everything in. The only sound was the cat lightly snoring.

"Is it weird that I'm not crying? Do you think I'm having a stroke or something?"

"You're not having a stroke," Rachel said.

Mr. Morrison jumped down from the couch and laid down

next to Katie's legs. As she ran her fingers through his silky coat, Rachel went to get Katie water, then she sat on the floor next to her. Katie drank a little, then put the glass between her thighs to prevent it from falling over and spilling.

"My friend Sandra's going to be floored when I tell her about this." Katie's eyes were moving back and forth rapidly, as they both sat in silence. After a little while, a half-smile crept slowly across Katie's lips. "I . . . think . . . I might be relieved. It's like there's been this thousand-piece jigsaw puzzle and I couldn't quite fit all the pieces together. Now I know why."

"What do you mean?" Rachel asked.

"I didn't resemble either of my parents. My mom is dark-complected and is tan year-round. She has curly hair the color of coffee grounds, and she's a lanky five-ten. When my dad left, he was already going gray, but when he was a kid, his hair was red. He was six-three and built like a football player that had let himself go. I have stick straight blonde hair, fair skin, a long torso and short legs, and am barely five-four. I assumed I looked like some relative I'd never met."

"I look a little like my dad," Rachel said. "But my mom and I share the same nose, and we both have really long fingers." Rachel wiggled her fingers toward Katie.

When Katie picked up her glass of water, a few drops sloshed onto her pants. She rubbed her hands across the wet spot on her inner thigh, then fanned her hand over it to try to dry it but gave up quickly; she had bigger problems.

"I guess I can stop worrying about getting the gene for addiction," Katie said.

"See, this is nothing but good news," Rachel said

enthusiastically. "You know, you can try to find your biological mother."

"Right, then I can have two mothers who didn't want me."

"You don't know why she put you up for adoption. What if your biological mother has always wanted to find you?" Katie looked at Rachel as if she was a little nutty. "I'm serious, you've heard of Ancestry.com, right?"

"Yeah, that's where you spit into a vial and send it in and they try to use your DNA, to find relatives," Katie said.

"Exactly, you could do it and see if you match with someone on their site."

"It sounds like a long shot, and I've had so much disappointment, I don't think I can take any more."

"Let me just show you, where's your computer?" Rachel asked.

Katie pointed toward the kitchen and Rachel brought it over and typed in the website. "You just need to fill out this form and put in your credit card and they'll send you the kit."

"You want me to do this, don't you?"

"Yep."

"Okay, fine," Katie said.

"This is so exciting," Rachel exclaimed, clapping her hands together. "It feels like we'll be solving a crime."

"The crime was living thirty-two years thinking that woman was my mother." Katie rubbed her hands over her belly. "My daughter will never feel as alone as my mother made me feel."

Rachel gave her a hug, and Katie let herself collapse into her arms. "You'll never be alone again, I'll always be here," Rachel said.

* * *

Daniel opened the car door for Katie, and they walked hand in hand toward Katie's favorite yoga studio.

"Thanks for coming with me. Forty-five minutes of meditation is probably not your idea of a fun afternoon," Katie said.

"Any afternoon with you is fun for me." Katie snuggled into Daniel's shoulder.

"Besides," he continued, "for the last few months you've supervised me hanging up pictures at my apartment, watching countless football games with me and my friends, and you've kept me company while I've done paperwork, without out ever saying you're bored."

"I figured if you were willing to date a pregnant woman, I'd do anything you wanted," Katie said.

"Anything?" Daniel said.

Katie looked down at her now thirty-seven-week pregnant waistline. "When this little one comes out, we'll talk," she said lasciviously.

"Sounds like a plan." Daniel kissed her on the cheek as they walked through the door of the studio just as a yoga class was letting out.

Katie's nose twitched at the pungent odor of sweat washing over her. "I wish I could still do yoga, but I can't get in any of the positions anymore and my balance is not what it used to be. I'm bummed because yoga helped with my anxiety."

"You're anxious?" he said in mock shock. "What do you have to be anxious about?"

She crossed her eyes at him and made a goofy face. He crossed his eyes back at her, and they cracked up.

"Meditation is going to be hard for me," Daniel said. "Getting my brain to shut off is not something I excel at."

"Me either. This brain of mine rattles around twenty-four hours a day."

"So, that's what all that noise is." Daniel snickered.

Natural light emanated through large windows and bounced off the floor as people were slowly coming in. Twenty meditation chairs with seat backs for support were spaced out around the room. Soft, soothing music played in the background.

"Let's hide back there," he said, pointing to the chairs in the back of the room. "What happens if, in the middle of the session, I freak out and need to open my eyes?" he asked above the soft chatter in the studio.

"Then they hit you with a gong mallet." Katie grinned.

"You're mean."

"Seriously, if you're really uncomfortable, you'll probably be hidden behind me anyway. It's not like I'm not big enough."

"I love your huge body . . . okay, that didn't come out the way I heard it in my head." Katie got on her tippy toes and kissed Daniel, who then guided her down onto her chair. He pulled another chair next to her.

The room was filling up with bodies of all shapes and sizes. The instructor, Madeline, went to the front of the class and sat on her mat facing everyone.

"Namaste," she said, and the class repeated it back to her. She asked everyone to set an intention for today before they began.

I intend to be grateful for however long Daniel's in my life, and to try not to stress that he's going to run away after I give birth, she thought.

Daniel's stomach growled loudly. "My intention is to devour a hamburger after we're done," he whispered.

Madeline described how important breathing was in meditation. She asked everyone to close their eyes and raise their arms above their head, inhale deeply, then breathe out slowly as they lowered their arms a few times.

"As you inhale and exhale, put out of your mind all the stresses in your life."

The air going in and out of bodies was the only sound until Madeline began to walk them through a meditation. Her melodic voice warmed Katie's whole body as if she were standing in front of a roaring fire on a rainy afternoon. Katie felt herself floating inside a fluffy cloud, transported across a deep blue sky, until she felt a strange wetness. *I must be really out of shape if meditating is making me sweat,* she thought. She opened her eyes and looked down and saw the crotch of her yoga pants was damp.

"I'm wet," Katie said almost to herself, but Daniel's eyes popped open.

"What do you mean?" Daniel asked.

Katie's heart pounded, but she tried to sound calm. "I think my water just broke."

"Oh my god," Daniel whispered.

"It's too early, I still have three weeks left," Katie said. "Maybe if I sit completely still, it'll stop." Katie froze every part of her body, then felt a gushing between her legs. "I don't think that's going to work."

"Your baby's leaking. Should I call 911?"

"No, but I think you should drive me to the hospital."

Daniel stood, took off his shirt, and wrapped it around Katie's waist. Even in Katie's state, she couldn't help but notice his abs.

Daniel helped her up and with Katie leaning on him, they headed to the door. Right before they crossed the threshold, Madeline asked, "Katie, are you okay?"

"Water broke, water broke, our baby is coming out!" Daniel said excitedly, his loud voice breaking through the tranquility. The rest of the class opened their eyes and started clapping, whistling, and wishing them good luck.

"That's not exactly what I meant by leave quietly," Katie said.

While Daniel drove Katie to the hospital, she called Sandra and asked her to meet them there. She also left a voicemail for Rachel.

When Sandra arrived, Katie was sitting at the admissions desk filling out forms. Daniel was standing next to her, holding her purse.

"I made it, I made it," Sandra said, huffing and puffing. "I think I cut off a cop, so if a tall guy with a wiry mustache comes in, say you haven't seen me."

The admissions clerk stared at her.

"I told you that you had time. Remember our childbirth class, things don't happen quickly," Katie said. "I'm not even having contractions yet."

"You can't predict anything. Remember that woman on the news who had her baby walking down the street? The kid fell right into her panties," Sandra said.

"That was her eighth kid."

"I still wasn't going to take a chance."

Katie introduced Sandra to Daniel, and while Katie finished the paperwork, Sandra and Daniel fed off each other about how eager they were to meet the baby. A nurse arrived with a wheelchair, just as the first strong contraction hit Katie.

"I can walk," she said breathlessly, hunching over and grabbing on to the sides of the wheelchair.

"Of course you can, but we prefer to bring you to your room in style," the nurse said as she helped her into the wheelchair.

"Are you coming?" the nurse asked Daniel as she turned to leave.

"Oh, he's not the father," Katie said smiling at Daniel.

Daniel kneeled down next to Katie. "I can come with you if you'd like me to."

"Thank you, but I'd prefer you not see me with my body parts spread out in ways they shouldn't be."

"Gotcha." Daniel handed Katie's purse to Sandra. The nurse wheeled Katie away with Sandra following behind.

"I'll be in the waiting room," Daniel called after them. "I'm not moving even to go to the bathroom until I hear you've had the baby."

"That's true love," the nurse said to Katie. "Although, he's going to end up with a kidney infection."

"At least he's in the right place for that," Sandra said.

In the labor room, Katie changed out of her clothes and got into bed. When another painful contraction hit, she yelled out in pain, trying to breathe through it.

"Someone needs to give this woman an epidural!" Sandra yelled to two nurses who were walking by the room, but neither one stopped. "Hello . . . Anyone? Please come and stop my friend's pain!"

"I'm okay, Sandra," Katie said. As the contraction stopped, a nurse came in to examine Katie.

"I know it hurts, but you're at the beginning, so it will be a while," the nurse said.

"It's going to get worse?" Katie said.

"Please give her an epidural," Sandra said. "I might need one, too."

"After Dr. Washington is finished delivering twins, she'll be in to check on you and let you know about the epidural," the nurse said and left.

"Dr. Washington is going to be tired after delivering twins," Katie said nervously. "What if she's so exhausted, she forgets what she's doing?"

"She doesn't have to be that alert to catch a slippery eel that's flying out of you."

Katie wanted to laugh, but another contraction hit, so all she could do was grimace.

"If you want, I can bow out and Daniel can be your birthing coach," Sandra said, giving Katie ice chips to suck on.

"Are you kidding? If he watches a head come out of my vagina, he'll never want to have sex with me."

"You mean have sex with you again," Sandra said.

"No. We haven't had sex yet. I didn't want him to see my body until it was back to normal," Katie said.

"Wow, this guy's so patient. I wouldn't wait that long to have sex with you."

Dr. Washington walked in, calm as could be, which relaxed

Katie. She examined her and announced she was six centimeters dilated. "That's good, right?" Katie asked. "The baby's coming out soon?"

"It's pretty quick for a first baby. How long have you been having contractions?"

"Not long, my water broke while I was at a meditation class."

"Well, that doesn't sound very relaxing," Dr. Washington said.

"Did you have any pain last night?"

"Just a few gas pains, but they weren't bad."

"That wasn't gas, that was the beginning of labor."

Katie's eyes opened wide. "I was in labor?"

"Most new moms don't realize it, but it's fine. I'll send in the anesthesiologist soon to put in an epidural." Dr. Washington smiled and left.

"Oh my god, Sandra, this is happening. I'm going to meet my daughter."

"Yes, and she'll be blotchy and squishy and covered in goo!"

"And all mine," Katie whimpered as another contraction hit. Sandra helped her breathe through it.

Ten minutes later, the anesthesiologist walked in and prepared to insert the epidural into Katie's back.

"That's a big needle," Katie said, her eyes wide.

"I think that's my cue to take a walk," Sandra said. "Is it okay if I go get some coffee?"

Katie nodded. "Right now I wish I could go with you."

When Sandra came back in, she brought Daniel, Rachel, and Leah with her. Katie was sitting up in bed, brushing her hair. She felt light and airy and soaring through the air like a paper airplane. "Hi, there," Katie said. "Welcome to my room!"

"Someone's epidural is working," Leah said.

"I don't feel anything!" Katie said in a sing-song voice. "This birthing thing is so easy."

"When that epidural wears off, everyone scatter," Sandra whispered.

"I hope it's okay that I brought my mom," Rachel said. "We were out shopping when you called."

"The more the merrier," Katie said. She held her arms out as if to give them all an air hug. "I'll assume you've all met each other at what has turned into my birth party."

Daniel kissed her on the top of the head.

"Thank you all for being here on the most important day of my life," Katie said.

"We're happy to be able to share it with you," Leah said.

"No matter what, this baby is going to know we are all here for her," Rachel said, looking at Katie, who nodded and mouthed 'thank you,' to her.

An hour later, Dr. Washington came back in and asked the group to move back so she could close the curtain and see how things were progressing.

"You're at eight and a half centimeters," she said.

"She's at eight and a half centimeters!" Sandra yelled out from the other side of the curtain.

"I'm great at this birth thing, right?" Katie said.

"Yes, you're a champ," Dr. Washington said. "It'll be time to push soon."

"I didn't dilate too fast, did I?"

"Not for me, I may actually get to see a movie tonight." She looked pleased as she pulled back the curtain. "Okay, everyone needs to say their goodbyes, this little girl is asking to come into the world."

Daniel, Rachel, and Leah hugged Katie, wished her luck, and went back to the waiting room. The nurse and the anesthesiologist were preparing for the birth.

"I'm going to decrease the epidural a tiny bit," the anesthesiologist said. "As long as you feel enough to push, were good to go."

"You shoot that sucker out; you hear?" Sandra said.

"I'll do my best." Katie looked up at Sandra. "I'm so grateful that you're here with me. I could never tell you how much it means."

"There's no place I'd rather be," Sandra said.

Katie's throat tightened as she realized she was going to be finding out very soon if her daughter had Down's. She knew it was a possibility, but until that moment, it wasn't entirely real. "What if . . . what if she does have . . ." Katie didn't finish; the rest of the sentence got stuck.

"You have a lot of people who're here to support you," Sandra said.

"I'm really scared, my whole life could change in a matter of minutes."

"No matter who that little girl is, your whole life is going to change, but you have a lot of love to give her. You're going to be a great mom." Katie grabbed Sandra's hand and held it tight.

A second nurse came into the room bringing more equipment and an incubator, followed by the pediatrician, Dr. Pine. Katie had met him once before when she was interviewing doctors.

Dr. Washington checked Katie one last time, told her she was ten centimeters, and it was time to push. Dr. Washington asked if Katie wanted a mirror to watch the baby come out, but that was one thing Katie didn't need to witness. Katie put her feet in the stirrups and one of the nurses got behind her and lifted her back for support so she could bear down. Katie squeezed Sandra's hand.

Please let my baby be okay, Katie thought.

A contraction hit and Katie took a big breath and pushed hard. When the contraction stopped, Katie panted, trying to catch her breath. Just as she felt like her heart rate was going down, another contraction hit, and she pushed again. Every time the doctor told her to push, she did, and it felt like it was going on for hours. Katie grew more and more tired and wondered if it would ever end.

"The heads out," Dr. Washington said, and Katie leaned just enough forward to be able to see the top of her daughter's pink head.

Finally, Katie thought. After the head came out, she was determined to push as hard as she could, hoping she wouldn't shoot the baby across the room.

When Katie pushed again, Dr. Washington said, "Hold on a minute, I want to get her other shoulder out."

Katie told herself over and over not to bear down, but her body was screaming at her to keep going. Finally, Dr. Washington told her to push, and with the final push, the rest of her daughter scrambled into the world, crying hard, followed by Katie crying even harder. Katie stretched out her arms for the nurse to hand her the baby, but the nurse didn't. The baby stopped crying.

"The baby's cyanotic," the nurse said as she wiped the baby

with a towel. The room exploded in activity and the pediatrician, Dr. Pine, stepped in to take over.

"What does that mean?" Katie asked, panicking.

No one answered right away. Dr. Pine grabbed his stethoscope and listened to the baby's heart. Katie looked at Sandra who was quiet, her face taking on a shade of gray.

"Does she have Down's syndrome?" Katie asked Dr. Pine.

"No, she doesn't." Dr. Pine put the baby in the incubator and asked the nurse to take her to the operating room, then he came over to Katie. "The baby has a slight heart defect, which can present like Down's."

"Is her heart going to be okay?" Katie asked, starting to freak out, feeling like she might pass out.

"It's a heart defect that limits oxygen in the blood. The pediatric surgeon will do the surgery now, and after she should be fine."

"You're going to operate on a newborn?" Katie held back a scream.

"I know it's scary," Dr. Pine said, "but they do procedures like this on newborns all the time. They're much stronger than you think. She'll be in your arms in no time," Dr. Pine walked toward the door. "I'll keep you posted," he said and left.

Dr. Washington still needed to deliver the placenta and get Katie cleaned up. Katie turned to Sandra. "Did he say my baby's going to be okay?"

"Yes, he said your daughter's going to be fine," Sandra said, and Katie burst into tears again.

Chapter Nineteen
Rachel

Rachel sat back and admired how she'd decorated her classroom. She'd put up new posters, arranged all the books in the bookcase, and had drawn a cartoonish happy face on the smart board. She couldn't believe the summer was over and it was the first day of school.

All the parents had left except for one mother who was sharply dressed in a navy pencil skirt, a cream silk blouse, a blazer, and navy pumps and was weeping.

"It's going to be okay," Rachel said, speaking softly and subtly moving her toward the door. "He'll be fine, and you'll see him in a few hours."

A diminutive boy ran up to the woman. "Mommy, I've already made lots of new friends!" he exclaimed joyfully and ran off. The woman cried harder.

"The first day of kindergarten is hard." Rachel handed her a tissue. "Do you need a hug?"

The woman sniffled loudly and wiped her tears. "I'll be okay," she said and allowed Rachel to escort her the rest of the way out of the classroom.

When Rachel had closed the door, she walked to the front of the room and clapped rhythmically to get her students' attention. A hush quickly fell over the room, and sixteen pairs of curious eyeballs looked up at her. Some of their faces appeared excited, others looked terrified that she might eat them.

Rachel asked them to take a seat on the oval rug which displayed all the letters of the alphabet inside red, blue, yellow, and green boxes. The room reverberated with boisterous and animated energy as the kids scattered to find a spot. Rachel sat in a big wicker chair at the top of the rug.

"Hello, I'm Mrs. Segal. This year we're going to have so much fun together, and I can't wait to get to know all of you. I'll be calling you up one at a time to get your name tag, and before you sit back down, I'll ask you to say one thing about yourself that you'd like the other kids to know."

Rachel began the process with the boy to her right and worked her way around the circle. As each kid came up, they revealed what they thought made them unique. They described their pets, their hobbies, and their favorite foods. The last child Rachel called on was a boy who reminded her of a miniature Peter Venkman, Bill Murray's character in Ghostbusters. The boy had the same cocky expression, he smiled at only the girls, and his backpack, which he refused to take off, resembled the proton pack.

Rachel asked him his name and held back a laugh when he

said it was Peter. She wrote 'Peter' on his name tag and stuck it onto his shirt.

"So, Peter," Rachel said, "what one thing would you like the kids to know about you?"

Peter looked as if he were deep in thought, then announced, "Every time I sneeze, I fart."

The kids began giggling. Peter hung his head and looked at the ground. One by one the kids yelled out "me, too," and "I do that." Peter's face lit up. Rachel had to pretend to get something out of her desk because she couldn't keep a straight face.

Her assistant, Mark, told the kids to line up for recess. Rachel mouthed "thank you" to him, and as Mark marched them all out, she heard him whisper to Peter that when he sneezes, he also farts. Peter high-fived Mark.

Rachel melted into the empty classroom. She was already exhausted, and the day had barely begun, but it was a welcome exhaustion. Being at work was easier than sitting home, wondering what Brett was doing in San Diego. Was he thinking about her? Did he miss her? When was he going to come home? Rachel sat at her desk, resting her head on her arms.

After what seemed like two minutes but was twenty, Mark came back in, followed by jubilant and energetic little beings. She didn't know what Mark did, or if it was just the fresh air, but the kids' body language had changed dramatically. The ones that had been hesitant and nervous were now joyful, bouncing around like they didn't have a care in the world.

I wish I only had to worry about whether I would learn how to read before first grade, Rachel thought.

She felt an enormous responsibility to take care of all these miniature humans. Her goal was to make them feel safe and help build their self-esteem, and she took that job seriously.

Rachel wondered what her daughter would've been like when she reached this age. Would she be scared of starting school, or eager? If she never could have kids of her own, would it be enough to take care of other people's? She pushed these thoughts away; the students didn't need a teacher who was curled up in a corner babbling to herself as she wept.

Rachel asked the kids to sit back in the circle so she could read them the book titled *Miss Bindergarten Gets Ready for Kindergarten*. The students were fascinated by everything she did with them that day, but that would wear off and it wouldn't always be that easy.

At the end of the day, Rachel was worn out. As she drove toward home, it hit her again that the only ones waiting for her were Molasses and Honey. She still hadn't gotten used to how empty the house felt without Brett. She'd missed the sound of his shoes on the hardwood, the way he hummed with enjoyment as he sipped his coffee in the morning, and even how he left his dirty socks on the floor next to the hamper.

Over the last six weeks, every time she and Brett talked, Rachel thought about asking him to come home, but she'd come to realize that he was waiting for her to apologize. She'd never been good at admitting she was wrong, even when she knew she was. It's her parent's fault; they never gave her a sibling to fight and make up with. The longer he stayed away, the worse their communication got.

"I'm sorry, Brett," she said out loud. "I'm sorry, I'm sorry, I'm sorry. I'm such an idiot. He'd like hearing that." She laughed at herself. She realized she'd made a wrong turn and missed the freeway onramp, ending up on a side street. "You need to pay better attention," she said to herself.

She was maneuvering a three-point turn to go back in the other direction when she saw a house across the street that had been taken down to the studs. Everything was gone, except the garage. Rachel slammed on her brakes, the car screeching to a stop in the middle of the street.

A white pickup truck sat in the driveway with a sticker on its bumper from the Great Dane rescue where she and Brett had gotten

Honey. Rachel cocked her head; *That looks like Brett's truck, but he's in San Diego.* Rachel's heart skipped a few beats as she pulled her car to the curb across the street then got out and went to look inside the truck. A blue and red flannel shirt was laying on the passenger seat, the shirt she'd given Brett for his last birthday. *Brett's in Los Angeles?*

Rachel ran back to her car, drove a few houses down, then pulled over. She dumped the contents of her purse on to the seat until she found her phone. She dialed and after it rang a few times, she assumed it would go to his voicemail.

As she was about to push the end call button, she heard the deep voice she'd always loved, say "Hi."

Rachel's greeting came out as a squeak. She made small talk for a minute, asking Brett how he was doing. She thought he sounded strained and harried when he said he was okay, and that work was fine.

It felt odd to Rachel, being uncomfortable talking to her own husband. "I wanted to check in. I hadn't talked to you in a few days," she said after another awkward pause.

"There's nothing new, I'm in Los Angeles checking on a job, but I'll be going back to San Diego in a few minutes," he said.

Rachel stared at the house through her side mirror and saw Brett come out of the garage, holding his phone to his ear.

"I'm sorry, Rachel, but I can't talk right now," he said. "Can I call you back tomorrow?"

She told him sure and hung up before he even had a chance to say goodbye. Rachel dropped her head onto her steering wheel. *He's so close to our house, and he didn't even call. Doesn't he still love me?*

When Rachel picked her head up, she noticed a young blonde in tight jeans and a lemon-yellow T-shirt come out of the garage and approach Brett. They seemed to be having an animated discussion.

Rachel clenched her teeth.

What have I done? I handed a great guy to another woman who's pretty and looks fertile.

A moment later, three kids, resembling triplets ran over to the woman, followed by another beautiful blonde woman who kissed the first woman on the lips.

Well, maybe not. But she's definitely fertile.

Brett waved goodbye to the two women, got in his truck, and drove away. Rachel ducked down, hoping he wouldn't recognize her car.

She never thought she'd feel this lonely and lost in her marriage. She and Brett used to be able to talk about everything, and when they had issues, they'd deal with them until they both felt heard. How had they gotten to this point? Actually, how had she not seen her part in everything?

Instead of turning toward home where her warm bed was waiting, she found herself driving into the hospital parking garage. She didn't want to unload on Katie, but maybe just hanging out with her would be a good distraction.

When Rachel walked into Katie's room, Katie was sitting in a chair, eating vanilla pudding, and reading *What to Expect the First Year*. The tray next to the bed had a plate filled with yellow sauce over what Rachel guessed was chicken. It smelled like the hallway of Rachel's first apartment when her neighbor's son played with his chemistry set.

Rachel gave Katie a hug.

"How are you doing?" Katie asked.

"I'd rather talk about how you're doing," Rachel said, and Katie nodded.

"I'm good. Except I was just reading about what it looks like when the baby's belly button plug falls off." Katie stuck out her tongue and put her finger in her mouth, mimicking throwing up, then she laughed until she snorted. She tossed the book on the bed. "If this book scares me, then I'm never buying *What to Expect When You Have a Teenager*."

Rachel walked over to the neonatal crib, peered inside, and saw that it was empty.

"They're doing the last test on her heart before they can release her to go home," Katie said. "Hopefully, she'll pass with flying colors."

"I'm sure she will. She's your daughter." When Rachel walked over to sit on the edge of Katie's bed, she got bonked by a bouquet of pink mylar balloons. There were eight smaller ones, with one large balloon in the center that was shaped like a heart, and read, "Welcome to the World, Olivia!"

"Olivia is such a beautiful name," Rachel said.

"Thanks. It means bringer of peace, like an olive branch."

"I love that." Rachel touched her heart. The room overflowed with various bouquets of flowers and a two-pound box of chocolates. "Looks like you've had a lot of visitors."

"Not really. Daniel's gone a little crazy." Katie looked sheepish, then rolled her eyes and blushed at the same time. She picked up the open box of candy and passed it over to Rachel. "Have ten. If I take this home with me, I'll never be able to lose this baby weight."

Under the free-flowing lacy white peasant shirt Katie wore over black leggings, Rachel could barely tell that she'd recently had a six-pound baby inside of her.

"It's sweet that Daniel showered you with all these gifts," Rachel said.

"It is . . . and it makes me nervous. I keep wondering what it means?"

"I think it's obvious. As much as you hate to admit it, the guy likes you."

"Do you think he'd mind if I put his name on her birth certificate?" Katie asked facetiously. "Seriously, though, how long do you think he's going to stay around? I now have a crying baby and breasts that leak. Bye, bye, Daniel," Katie said, waving toward the door.

Rachel picked up a couple of pieces of candy and smelled them as though she could figure out what was inside each one. When she finally decided which piece she wanted, she popped it into her mouth. "Daniel could be different. He does have great taste in candy," Rachel said, but it came out garbled as she tried to swallow the caramel she was chewing.

Katie slowly walked over to the window and looked out. "I really like him, and in the past whenever I told a man I had feelings for them, they'd flee like a sprinter at the Olympics, although my guy runs faster."

Katie turned back around. "What if Daniel hurts me?" she asked.

"What if he doesn't?"

"When did you become an optimist?"

"When it comes to other people I am." Rachel paused so long that she saw Katie watching her. Rachel crinkled her eyes. "My life is a mess. I found out Brett's been in Los Angeles for work and didn't ask to see me or even call and say he was here. How am I supposed to take that?"

"He might not be ready to talk."

"It still hurts. He obviously doesn't want to be around me. And I get it, who'd want to be with someone whose whole life became about having a baby? I really screwed things up. And I'm embarrassed that I've been sitting around thinking if he loves me, he'll come home, and I just needed to be patient."

"Well, you know that patience killed the cat," Katie said.

"I think that's curiosity."

"Patience killed curiosity?" Katie said with a straight face.

Rachel crossed her eyes and stuck her tongue out at her.

"So, why haven't you asked him to come home? Is it an ego thing?"

"No, yes, maybe."

"How far is that getting you?"

Rachel shrugged. A nurse opened the door, startling them. She came in wheeling a plastic bassinet with Olivia asleep inside. Olivia was wearing a blue and pink striped beanie that covered her head.

Katie gazed at her daughter. "Every time I look at her, I can't believe I 'made' that teeny human being."

The nurse gently picked Olivia up out of the bassinet and, without waking her, laid her in the neonatal crib.

"Did she pass?" Katie asked.

"Completely," the nurse said. "She's healing fast, you have a strong daughter. I think Olivia's going to be able to go home tomorrow. Dr. Pine will come see you in a little while."

Katie thanked the nurse profusely for all her help. The nurse smiled brightly and moved on to other patients. When Katie leaned down and kissed Olivia on the forehead, Olivia woke with a start, her face turning red. What started out as a squeak turned into a whimper and then a wail which echoed throughout the room.

"Her lungs definitely work," Rachel yelled out over the crying. Katie picked Olivia up, threw a blanket over her shoulder, and tried to get Olivia to latch on. Olivia jerked her head away and continued to howl.

Katie pulled her shirt down, muttering, "What is it? If you're not hungry, what's wrong?" She held her and gently rocked the baby back and forth, sweat forming on her brow. Rachel wasn't sure if it was possible, but she thought Olivia was now crying even louder.

"What if she's figured out that I'm the only person she has, and I don't know anything about babies?" Katie's voice trembled.

"No one knows what to do when they have their first child." Rachel put her hands out. "Do you want me to try?"

Katie nodded and handed Olivia over to her as if she was a hot potato. Rachel rubbed Olivia's back and patted her lightly until she let out a loud burp and then immediately stopped crying.

"You're so much better at this than I am. You stay calm," Katie said and plopped back down on the chair.

"She's not going home with me." Rachel put a happier Olivia back in Katie's arms. "She recently had surgery and your hormones are all over the place. It'll just take some time."

Katie stroked Olivia's cheek. "I heard that after you have a baby you're even more emotional than when you were pregnant. I had a hard time believing that, but now I go from happy to insane in under a minute. I feel like Beetlejuice, except he was more stable." Daniel walked into the room holding Katie's tote bag.

"Hi, Rachel," he said and gave Katie a quick kiss. "Am I interrupting anything?"

"Nope, we were just talking," Rachel said.

"What a good baby, she's so relaxed," Daniel said. "She obviously got your temperament, Katie."

Katie rolled her eyes at Rachel.

Daniel looked down at Olivia as if she were one of the seven natural wonders of the world. He leaned in and gave her the sweetest kiss, then smiled at Katie with a look of admiration. As Rachel watched this tender moment between them, all she could think was how she and Brett would've been that happy. A nagging feeling in her stomach turned into a heavy pain and climbed up to her chest and toward her face.

If she stayed in the room much longer, she was afraid she'd lose it, which was the last thing Katie needed right now. Especially when Olivia was finally quiet.

"I have to go," Rachel said, standing up abruptly and moving toward the door.

Katie and Daniel looked at each other.

"You don't have to leave," Katie said.

"Yes, I do." Rachel was out the door and speed walking down the hall before Katie had a chance to say another word.

Chapter Twenty
Katie

Katie walked back and forth in her living room, gently patting Olivia on the back the way Rachel had done in the hospital. Sandra finished putting dirty dishes in the dishwasher, then poured a cup of coffee, put it on the dining room table, and took Olivia out of Katie's hands.

"You need to sit down and get some coffee in you, even if it's decaf," Sandra said, then kissed the top of Olivia's head. "Are you so tired that you don't smell that?" Sandra asked, scrunching up her nose in disgust.

"I was just about to change her," Katie said. "You distracted me with coffee."

"I don't know how even coffee could distract you from that smell."

"I'll change her." Katie held her arms out for Olivia. "Unless you'd like to do it?"

"Sure, why not. Who wouldn't be thrilled to start their day with a dirty diaper and a friend who stopped washing her hair?"

"Nice, kick me when I can barely keep my eyes open," Katie said. "I'm joking about the dirty diaper, but I wouldn't be your friend if I didn't tell you that you need to do something about that hair." Sandra took Olivia into the other room to change her.

Katie put her hands on her head and tried to pat her hair down, but it seemed to have a mind of its own. When she went to get a brush in the bathroom and caught her reflection in the mirror, she giggled so hard she snorted. She looked like she'd spent the night doing handstands during a rainstorm. "Okay, hair, work with me here," she said, trying to brush it, which was only adding static.

Mr. Morrison walked on top of the bathroom counter, sticking his tongue in the sink, licking the faucet that was dripping.

"Messy hair and motherhood must go hand in hand," she said, giving up and carrying Mr. Morrison out of the bathroom.

She took a long swig of her coffee, then Sandra came back with a happier Olivia and handed her back to Katie.

"You're an angel coming over here every morning," Katie said, "but you should be sleeping in on a Saturday."

"I'm happy to help, but now I do have to go. I have tons of errands I need to get done before the work week. I don't get to lounge around with a newborn."

"Yes, I do plan on doing lots of lounging, in between changing diapers, feedings, and trying to sleep." Sandra picked up her purse.

"Are you sure you want to leave me alone with a person who

doesn't know how to tell me what she's feeling?" Katie said, mostly in jest.

"You'll be fine, I'm sure Daniel would love to help."

Olivia's tiny head bobbed and then she fell asleep. "Have you told him you love him yet?"

"I'm waiting until he says it first." Katie laid Olivia down in the bassinet, placing a light quilt on top of her.

Sandra opened the door to find Daniel with his hand up about to knock. "Or . . . you can say it first." Sandra gave Katie a knowing nod, then greeted Daniel. She held the door for him and then left.

"Hey, beautiful," Daniel said.

Does he not see my hair? Katie thought, realizing she hadn't showered in a couple of days. *I'm pushing this guy to the limit.* When Daniel bent down to look at Olivia, Katie casually stuck her nose in her armpit, then made a slight choking noise in her throat.

"Do you mind keeping an eye on Olivia while I take a quick shower?"

Ten minutes later, Katie came back wearing a maternity T-shirt dress that tied in the back. It said on the front, 'Mom, established 2023.' She'd also applied enough concealer to hide the circles under her eyes and a tiny bit of blush.

"Did you miss me?" she asked.

"Always," he pulled her into a hug. "You smell good," he said, sniffing. "Is that vanilla?"

"You have a good nose, which is why I'm glad you didn't get close to me fifteen minutes ago."

"You always smell good to me."

Katie patted him on his butt. "You're so sweet, which is why I love you," she said, then froze in place.

Daniel stared at her. "Did you just say you loved me?"

Katie couldn't look directly at him, "Uh, yeah, but it just slipped out, my mouth didn't think before it spoke."

"You love me," Daniel said again as if to convince himself.

"I think we established that."

"I love you, too."

Katie wondered if she heard him right. The blood rushed to her brain, making her dizzy. "Wait, you love me? You really love me?"

"Yes, I love you."

"Can you say it again?"

"I . . . Looove . . . Youuu . . ." Daniel pronounced this as slowly as he could, pausing between each word. Then he lifted her face up to his and gave her a long, slow kiss. "I've wanted to tell you, but I thought it best to wait until you weren't doubled over with labor pains. I was waiting for the right time."

"I think you were just waiting for me to shower." Katie's joy spilled out of her like a waterfall. "Other than the day Olivia was put in my arms, this is a close second to the best day of my life."

"I've never been so excited to come in second," Daniel said, and Katie kissed him again.

"Are you hungry?" Katie asked, heading to the kitchen. "Do you want some breakfast? I like to feed people I love."

"So do I. You sit, and I'll cook for you." Daniel walked into the kitchen. "Do you like scrambled eggs?"

"Yes, but I'd eat anything right now. Yesterday I had five slices of salami and a piece of cheese. At least I think it was cheese. And for dessert, I had three bites of an apple. Olivia wasn't in the best mood."

"Well, she's asleep now, so you can relax." Daniel pulled a chair out for her, and she folded her body into it. He made himself at home in her kitchen, pulling out a frying pan, eggs, cheese, butter, and milk. Katie couldn't take her eyes off him. She kept wondering who this wonderful man in her kitchen was.

Daniel put bread in the toaster and bacon in the microwave and kept up a steady conversation with her as he whisked the eggs.

"This is probably a dumb question, but have you had a chance to check your Ancestry.com account?" he asked.

"They sent me an email, but I haven't opened it. Olivia doesn't like to share me with a computer."

"I'm here, so if she wakes up, I'll entertain her."

Katie opened her laptop and signed into her email. She stared at the computer screen, feeling the blood drain from her face.

"What does it say?"

"The subject line says they found a match, but I can't open the email." Katie felt like she was going to be sick.

"Why not?"

"I'm scared," she said, closing her laptop and getting placemats for the table. "Besides, it's probably some cousin five times removed who'll ask me for money . . . . or my liver. Two things I don't have extra of."

Katie finished setting the table while Daniel plated their food and carried it to the table.

"That email's not going to go away," he said, opening the laptop back up. "You're going to hear it screaming in your sleep."

Katie looked at the email, then back at Daniel who gave her an encouraging smile. Finally, she agreed to sign into her Ancestry.com account.

Katie clicked the mouse a number of times, then stared at the screen with her head tilted, numb.

"What is it?" Daniel asked eagerly.

"This can't be right," Katie said, closing the computer.

"Wait, what did it say?"

"Nothing, it says nothing," Katie said.

"What do you mean, the email said there was a match."

"Well, there's been a mistake."

"I don't understand," Daniel said, reaching for the computer.

"Don't look!"

"What's going on?"

"It said my DNA is a fifty percent match with someone named Leah Kagen. That's Rachel's mom's name. Obviously, that's nuts."

"I'm sure there's more than one Leah Kagen in the United States," Daniel said, moving behind her to look at the computer. He wrapped his arms around her, and she leaned back into his embrace.

"What am I supposed to do with this information?"

"You could start by talking to Rachel's mom."

"Sure, because it's quite normal to ask your friend's mom if she's your biological mother."

"I guess that is kind of weird," Daniel said.

"Am I supposed to just walk up to her and say, 'Hi Leah, did you give birth to me and give me up thirty-two years ago?' Or do I stand near her and scream out 'Mom!' and see if she turns around? This is insane." She tapped her fingers on her forehead rhythmically, as if she were trying to get her brain to make sense of everything. "Right now I wish I hadn't sent in my DNA, then I wouldn't have to deal with any of this."

Olivia gurgled loudly, so Katie went to check on her. She'd kicked off her quilt, so Katie covered her back up, then went back to the table.

"You could ignore this information, but what if Rachel's mom is your biological mother?" he asked. "Wouldn't that be a good thing?"

"I guess. But what if she didn't want me to find her? Or she needs a liver?" Katie quipped.

"I get that after everything you've gone through, it's hard to believe there's a mother out there who'd want you."

"Exactly. My bio mom gave me away and my adoptive mom didn't want me, either."

"Well, whoever this Leah Kagan is, she wouldn't have put her DNA on the site if she wasn't looking for you."

"I guess."

"Why don't we take one thing at a time. First, you need to eat." He picked up a fork, handed it to her, and pointed at the plate in front of her. "After, you can figure out how you're going to talk to Leah."

"You are a godsend," Katie said.

"Considering we met at church, I would say that's pretty accurate."

Katie hadn't realized just how hungry she was until she started eating. "I just remembered that Leah gave me her phone number when I went to tea with her and Rachel," Katie said in between bites. "I hope the paper is still in my purse."

Katie ate quickly, so quickly that Daniel had barely eaten half his food before she was up and washing the frying pan.

When Daniel finished, he helped Katie clean up. "You know, if Leah is your mother, that makes Rachel your half-sister," he said, brushing Katie's hair off her face.

"I've always wanted a sister, but I don't know how I'm going to wrap my mind around all this. And what if I get excited, then find out it's a different Leah Kagan?"

"There's only one way to know for sure," Daniel said.

After calling Leah and seeing if she could stop by, Katie drove to Leah's house with Olivia in the backseat. She'd attached a mirror to the headrest, so she'd be able to see and talk to Olivia while they were in the car. Katie yammered on about everything from the color of the sky to apologizing for every bump in the road. She was trying to forget where she was going and why.

"Oh no we're almost there, Olivia," Katie exclaimed as they exited the 405 freeway. "What the hell am I going to say?" Katie put a hand up to her mouth. "Oh, sorry, I have to get used to not swearing in front of you. I better stop before you go to school and tell some kid to shove something up his ass."

Katie felt nauseous and the muscles in her back tightened up.

"I probably should've figured out what I was going to say before we left the house."

Olivia seemed to gurgle in agreement.

"Okay, so, should I say, 'Hi, I know this is going to sound weird, but are you my mother?'" Katie sat with that. "No, that sounds like the title of a sad children's book. Maybe I should say, 'This is the funniest thing, but is there a chance you could be my biological mother?'" Olivia grunted. "You're right, that might be too forward. I should ease into it. How about if I make small talk. I could say, 'How are you?' and when she says she's fine, I could ask, 'What were you doing thirty-two years ago on September 14th?'"

Katie glanced in her review mirror at Olivia who was rooting and arching her back.

"Yes, I know, she's going to think Mommy's crazy and she's going to stare at me the same way you're staring at me now." Katie was worried that a panic attack was starting, so she pulled over to the side of the road. She talked herself down until she felt more in control.

When she got to Leah's house, she sat in her car with the motor running. "As soon as I go inside, my whole life could change. I'm not sure I'm ready for this, Olivia. Maybe I should turn around and go home, pretend I never saw those results. Do you think I'm about to make a hugely embarrassing mistake?" Olivia hiccupped. "I'm not sure what that meant, but I'm here, so we're going in."

Katie turned off the car, got out, and reached into the back seat to take Olivia out with her car seat. "I've made a decision. I'm going to go with the straightforward approach. I think it's best." Olivia was incredibly quiet, her eyes wide open. "It's freaky that you're so calm. I hope you're not holding back until we get inside." Katie kissed her and thanked her for being such a good baby, then she carried the car seat to the front door and rang the doorbell.

Ezra opened the door and welcomed Katie inside. "Hi, you must be Rachel's father. I'm Katie." Katie wondered if this man could also be her father. She hoped he wouldn't think it was strange the way she was looking at him.

"It's nice to meet you," Ezra said.

Leah rushed to the foyer. Katie couldn't take her eyes off Leah. She studied her features, trying to see what about her could be similar to Katie. She noted that they had the same thick, blonde hair.

"Can I hold her?" Leah asked as she fawned over Olivia.

Katie nodded. Katie unbuckled Olivia from the car seat and handed her to Leah, who held her to her chest. "Rachel's here, we were about to go out to brunch," Leah said.

Katie's mouth got very dry, and she wanted to flee. She hadn't expected Rachel to be there, the thought of having this conversation with both of them made her even more nervous.

"I'm going to finish watching the baseball game, let me know when you want to go," Ezra said and went toward the back of the house.

"Is everything all right?" Rachel asked, giving Katie a hug. "My mom said you sounded funny on the phone."

Katie cleared her throat, then croaked out a few words. "Everything's fine, I just wanted to ask your mom something."

They all sat at the dining room table. Katie wasn't sure Leah was ever going to put Olivia down.

"Is Olivia okay? Is it her heart again?" Rachel asked.

"She's fine," Katie squirmed in her seat, everything she'd rehearsed on the way over seemed to have vanished from her memory. After a little small talk, she turned to Leah. "I don't know if Rachel told you about the conversation I had with my mother."

"She did," Leah said. "That's not the way a child should find out they were adopted. I'm so sorry she hurt you like that."

"Thanks," Katie said. She knew she was going to have to dive in and just spit the whole thing out, so she took a big breath. "Before Olivia was born, I sent my DNA to Ancestry.com, in hopes of finding my biological parents."

Katie looked at Leah to see if she had a reaction, but Leah didn't make eye contact, she was peering down at Olivia, who'd fallen asleep in her arms.

"I got an email from the site. There's a woman out there who was a fifty percent DNA match with me."

Leah looked up from Olivia, meeting Katie's eyes. The women didn't take their eyes off each other.

"Oh, wow, that's great! You found your birth mother!" Rachel exclaimed. "I'm so happy for you. It's exactly what you were hoping for!"

Leah looked away from Katie and began to cry.

"Mom," Rachel said. "Why are you upset?"

Leah didn't answer, she just kept crying. Rachel looked at Katie, whose body felt like jelly as she tried to center herself.

"What's going on?" Rachel asked.

"My biological mother's name is Leah Kagen."

"Wait, what?" Rachel said. "That's crazy." She let out an uncomfortable laugh. "Isn't that crazy, Mom?" Leah just stared at Rachel.

"Mom? What's going on?" Rachel asked in an octave higher than her usual voice.

"I found out this morning, too." Leah handed Olivia back to

Katie who held her close to her heart. "I wasn't planning on telling you any of this unless I had to," she said to Rachel.

"Telling me what?" Rachel stood so suddenly that her chair almost fell over.

Katie's heart was jackhammering in her chest.

"Sit, honey," Leah said to Rachel, who looked at Katie, then reluctantly sat back down. Leah's voice was almost a whisper as she addressed the two of them. "Two years before Rachel was born, I got pregnant, and I placed the baby for adoption."

Rachel looked like she'd been hit in the head with a shovel. Katie understood how she felt. Even though she'd known for the last few hours, she still felt like she was on a runaway merry-go-round. Her mind dizzy and whirling.

"I never stopped wondering what happened to that baby."

The air in the room seemed to be getting thin and Katie wasn't sure she was going to be able to continue breathing. "So, you are my biological mother?" she asked.

Leah cleared her throat. "Yes." Leah rubbed the back of her neck, her eyes darting between Rachel and Katie.

Katie didn't know how to react; she was face to face with a woman who gave her away. She scanned Leah's expression. *Is she happy I found her? Is she angry, wishing I'd never showed up? Will she hate me?*

"When I sent my DNA in, I didn't know if my daughter would ever want to find me, but I thought it was worth a try," Leah said. "I've thought about you constantly since the day you were born."

"This doesn't make sense, why wouldn't you tell me that you had a child before me?" Rachel said.

"When you got old enough to understand, I didn't know how to tell you that you had a sister, being raised by someone else. I thought you'd hate me, or try to find her yourself, and I didn't know if she'd want to be found." Leah looked at Katie. "Obviously, I was so wrong." Leah cried harder.

"Is Dad her father, too?" Rachel asked.

Katie's eyes grew wide.

"No," Leah said.

"Does Dad know you had another child?" Rachel wondered.

"Yes. He encouraged me to try to find her."

"I'm only two years older than Rachel, why did you decide to raise her?" Katie asked.

Leah took a big breath. "Give me a minute, I'll answer all of your questions," Leah said, looking as if she was in another world trying to find her way back.

Rachel and Katie looked at each other. Katie could now recognize the similarities between the two of them. They both made the same expressions with their mouth when they were emotional, they both could eat a lot and not gain weight, and all three of them snorted when they laughed. She wondered if Rachel was also sizing her up.

When Leah finally spoke, she looked deep into Katie's eyes and didn't blink. "It's important that you know that when I found out I was pregnant, I was incredibly excited. Your father was someone I met in college, and we fell madly in love. When we graduated, he went into the army and was sent overseas, but we stayed devoted to each other. The first year he was gone, he came home at Christmas, and proposed to me, and I couldn't say yes fast enough. We had a wonderful week, our friends and relatives were so happy for us, and then a month after he went back overseas, I found out I was pregnant. I was ecstatic and I knew your father was also going to be thrilled. He wanted to get married before you were born, but he didn't know if he'd get to come home in time." Leah paused for a minute and grimaced, then continued, "When I was seven months pregnant, his mother called to tell me that he was killed in Desert Storm. I couldn't stop crying the last two months of my pregnancy." Leah's chin trembled and she stopped talking.

Katie felt as if everything around her had come to a halt. An avalanche of disappointment crushed her, as the reality that she'd never get to meet her biological father seeped inside.

Leah continued, "I didn't think I could raise a baby on my own, and my mother thought every child should have a mother and a father. I couldn't have known that I would meet Ezra, and he would've been happy to take you as his." Leah cast her eyes down. "Right after I gave birth to you, I only got to see you for a couple of minutes before they took you away. You were such a beautiful baby."

Leah wiped her eyes with her fingers, then got up and left the room. Katie looked at her daughter sleeping in her arms.

I can't imagine only seeing you for a couple of minutes and then someone taking you away from me.

Rachel was staring at the ground.

"Are you okay?" Katie asked.

Rachel flinched but didn't look up or say anything. Katie had a knot forming, she could see that Rachel was reeling just as much as, if not more than, she was. She wouldn't have hurt Rachel for anything.

The remorse Katie saw in Leah's face when she got back brought tears to her own eyes. She'd been trying to stay strong to get through this, but one drop escaped and landed on Olivia, who stirred. *Please don't freak out, Olivia. We can't both freak out at the same time.* Olivia squirmed for another second, then went back to sleep. Katie sighed.

"I was told you were being placed with a mom and dad who'd adore you and give you a great life," Leah said.

Katie shook her head, and more tears fell. She was flooded with memories from her childhood. "You couldn't have known that the people who adopted me would end up being terrible parents."

"No, but that's not the life I wanted for you." Katie could see Leah getting smaller, as if she was going inside herself. Katie would've thought she'd feel so much anger, but she was surprised that she felt sorry for Leah. Now that she was a mom, she realized how hard that must've been for her.

"It's okay," Katie said, not knowing if she was talking to Leah or herself.

Leah looked as if Katie had given her a small gift. Then Katie realized Rachel hadn't said anything for a long time.

"Rachel, are you okay?" Katie asked again.

"No, I'm so confused," Rachel's voice displayed both anger and hurt.

Leah put her hand on top of Rachel's hand, but Rachel pulled away.

"Was I just a replacement for the daughter you gave away?" Rachel asked, her face tight, as if she were holding in a wave that might take her out to sea.

"Never!" Leah looked at Rachel with love in her eyes. "Six months after I put Katie up for adoption, I met your father." Leah smiled as if a memory took her over. "I knew immediately he was a good guy, so I told him the whole story on our first date, and he was incredibly supportive. He was there for me as I was still grieving my daughter and he helped me get through my deep depression." She put her hand over her heart. "We fell in love and got married and I got pregnant with Rachel on our honeymoon."

Leah looked as if she was reliving it. "I couldn't have been happier when I gave birth to another little girl," Leah said. "And every day I'm grateful that I got to raise a wonderful, caring, beautiful daughter." Rachel grabbed her purse and headed to the door.

"Rachel . . ." Leah called out after her.

The front door slammed, waking Olivia, who began to wail.

The weight of everything overwhelmed Katie. "I think I should go." Katie stood up.

"Please stay. At least until you calm the baby."

"Olivia needs to eat."

"Then stay until you finish feeding Olivia. It's kind of hard to drive with a kid on your breast," Leah said.

"It can't be harder than my mom driving with me after three quarters of a bottle of vodka."

"I hope you'll find a way to forgive me and let me a part of your and Olivia's life in whatever way you feel comfortable. I'd love the chance to make up for all the years I missed," Leah said. Katie pondered that, and saw the sincerity written all over Leah's face. This woman was her mom, a mom who might actually care about her.

Katie got a blanket, put it over her shoulder and unbuttoned her shirt. She moved Olivia around until she'd finally latched on. Then it was quiet except for the sound of suckling.

"I would never have wanted to upset Rachel," Katie said.

"Me either. I've been praying that someday you'd come looking for me, I had no idea you'd find Rachel first." Leah gave Katie a half-smile. "Rachel will eventually understand, but I should've told her before this. I convinced myself that she didn't really need to know. Or I was a coward. Probably both."

"I get it, some things you wish you could forget." With a slow, disbelieving shake of her head, Kate said, "I didn't wake up this morning thinking that I was going to get a new mother . . . and a sister."

"And I didn't wake up thinking I was going to get my daughter back . . . and become a grandmother," Leah said. "Oh, my goodness, Olivia's my granddaughter."

Leah began to cry again, but this time, she was smiling through her tears.

Chapter Twenty-One
Rachel

When the doorbell rang, the dogs jumped out of their beds and scampered to the front door. Molasses' deep Great Dane bark reverberated throughout the house. Rachel wasn't completely awake and prayed that whoever it was would leave.

Who shows up on a Sunday morning at eight? Burglars wouldn't ring the bell . . . unless they were checking to see if anyone was at home. If I don't answer, they may try to break in. And if I do answer, they'd see I'm here alone. I wish Brett were here.

When the doorbell rang for a second time, Rachel got down low and crept to the door. She looked through the peephole at her mom, who had dark circles under her eyes and appeared crumpled, as if she were a car that had been in an accident.

Rachel opened the door and Leah stretched out her arms for a hug, but Rachel took a step backward. She wasn't ready to act like everything was fine.

"Do you want coffee?" Rachel asked.

"Sure," Leah said. "If you're making yourself some."

Well, I wasn't going to for a few more hours because I would've still been sleeping if you hadn't rang the doorbell, Rachel thought.

There was a heavy silence between them as Rachel got out the coffee maker.

"I was upset about the way you left yesterday," Leah said.

"It was all too much, I had to get out of there."

Leah sat at the kitchen table; Rachel joined her while they waited for the coffee to brew.

"I know it's a shock," Leah said. "That wasn't the way I wanted you to find out."

Rachel folded her arms over her chest. "Did you want me to find out? It didn't seem like you were ever planning on telling me," she said brusquely.

"I understand your anger."

"I'm not angry, I'm hurt. Actually, I'm both. Most people I know avoid their mothers as much as possible. I always thought we were close."

"We are."

"'Close' means we both share things from our lives. I shared with you that Brett and I had discussed possibly adopting if we could never have a child of our own. How did it never occur to you to tell me that you put a child up for adoption?"

"I didn't like to think about it, so I put it out of my mind; as if it happened to someone else." Leah looked sheepish.

"That's bullshit!" Rachel surprised herself; she'd never gotten so angry at her mother before. She needed to get her emotions in check, so she got up and slowly poured the coffee, then brought the mugs to the table.

Leah's eyes were fixed on the steam rising from her mug.

Rachel wondered if her mother was going to say anything else.

"You're right," Leah said, as if in resolve. "I was worried that if I told you, you'd look at me differently."

"Why would I do that?"

"Because you're going through hell to have a baby, and I had placed my first born with another family," Leah said.

"You didn't give me enough credit," Rachel said definitively. "If you explained it like you did yesterday, I would've definitely understood."

"I see that now. I was wrong to keep it from you."

Rachel nodded in agreement, but the hurt stirring inside her was still holding on. "When I was sitting there yesterday, it hit me that Olivia is your first grandchild. I wanted to be the one to give you that." Rachel pushed her coffee away; the aroma was starting to make her sick. "Now it doesn't matter if and when I have a baby."

"That's not true."

"It is, and now I just feel left out."

"Katie and Olivia don't take anything away from how I feel about you. You've been my life since the day I laid eyes on you. I need you."

"Not anymore."

Leah got up and came around to hug Rachel, but Rachel turned away. Leah's head dropped down and she moved back to her seat.

Rachel continued, "You have a new daughter and granddaughter now."

"It's not a competition, your father and I have enough love to go around."

Rachel thought about her mother's words for a few minutes. "I've always wondered why you and Dad didn't have any more kids after me."

"We wanted more, but I could never get pregnant again. I used to think I was being punished, but now I know sometimes things happen that we can't control."

Rachel felt her defenses dropping as she realized that her mom was right. There were things that happened that she couldn't control.

"You're an amazing young woman, who I'm so proud of. You will have your own kids; I can feel it." Rachel had tears in her eyes. "Honey, would it be okay if I hugged you now?" Leah asked.

Rachel nodded.

Leah walked back around the table and enveloped Rachel, holding her as tight as she could. Rachel hadn't realized how much she needed to be in her mother's arms until that moment.

When Leah let go, Rachel felt as if the air in the room had been cleansed. "I thought it was strange that I felt so close to Katie," Rachel said. "We were drawn to each other the first time we met. Maybe we had a sixth sense."

"When you were growing up, every December, you begged for a sister for the holidays. Happy Hanukkah, you finally got that one present I couldn't give you," Leah said, her voice laced with irony.

"Only I feel awkward around her, now that . . . we're . . . related."

"I have faith that you two will be as close or closer than you were." Rachel nodded, but all she could think was, Katie is my sister . . . Katie is my sister. She said it a few times in her head. Rachel had been so busy being upset that Olivia was the first grandchild, she hadn't let anything else sink in.

Rachel could see Leah looked more at peace than when she'd come in.

"I have two daughters, how crazy is that?" Leah said.

"Crazier than when you told me the police would arrest you if I didn't go to my piano recital? God was I stupid." Rachel and Leah laughed until they both snorted.

"When we all got together at the Polo Lounge, I did think it was strange that we all snorted," Leah said. "Up until that moment, you and I were the only ones I knew who did that."

"You're right, that should've been a dead giveaway."

"Can I ask you something?" Leah said, putting her mug in the dishwasher.

Rachel nodded.

"What's going on with you and Brett?" she asked. "He's been gone a long time."

Rachel twisted her wedding ring around her finger; it felt heavy on her hand. "I know. I may have pushed him away for good, and he's the most important person in my life."

"Have you told him that?"

Rachel's throat felt as dry as a mirage in the Mojave Desert.

"No. Since yesterday I've been consumed by how angry I am

that you kept something so important from me. I felt like you didn't trust me enough to let me in. And now I realize that's exactly what I did to Brett." Rachel said as if someone took a light bulb and cracked it over her head. "He kept saying I was shutting him out. Why didn't I listen?"

"Sometimes it's hard to hear what someone is saying when we're drowning in our own pain."

"I was so selfish, Brett lost our daughter, too, and I didn't want to see how sad he was. Or I didn't look beyond myself to see it."

"Well, you see it now, that's what's important."

Rachel shrugged her shoulders and grimaced. "If it isn't too late. I need to make it right with him."

After Leah left, Rachel took a quick shower, then changed into a sundress. It was September, but Los Angeles had been having a heat wave, so it was over a hundred degrees. She brushed her hair, put on eyeliner and mascara, then grabbed her keys and ran out the door. She figured on a Sunday the traffic to San Diego wouldn't be bad, and she was right. She drove the 5 freeway, changing lanes often to get around all the trucks. For a while, she listened to a podcast with a guest psychologist on until she couldn't hear any more about someone else's messed up life. She jabbed the pause icon on the screen and drove in silence and for the first time in a while, she wasn't thinking about the daughter she'd lost. She was thinking about the husband that she didn't want to lose.

Rachel thought back to the time when she and Brett started dating. She recalled how they shared stories about their past relationships. They would spend time analyzing why those relationships didn't work out. The one thing they agreed on was that their previous partners weren't good communicators. Rachel couldn't believe that she'd become just like her old boyfriend who would shut down whenever things got hard.

No wonder Brett didn't want to be around me, she thought.

Rachel's foot pushed harder on the accelerator as she realized she'd made having a baby the only thing that mattered. She had been behaving as if being married to him was secondary to having a child. How could she have let that happen? She loved Brett no matter what. She tried not to drive above eighty, but a few times she found herself going ninety. She kept her eyes open for cops, but she needed to get to Brett as quickly as possible.

She was determined to find a way to work things out.

An hour and a half later, she pulled up in front of Brett's parents' house. Five years ago, she and Brett had gotten married in their backyard. Seventy-five of their closest friends and family watched them say their vows under an arch of purple wisteria and white roses. She could still recall the lilac scent and how the backyard had reminded her of an English country estate.

She couldn't think of a time when she'd been happier, and marrying Brett was the only thing on her mind.

Rachel turned off the car, and even though the air conditioning was on in force, her back was sweaty. She peeled her clammy thighs off her leather seats and got out.

I'm actually nervous to talk to my own husband, she thought.

Brett's truck wasn't in the driveway. *It would be just my luck that I drove over one hundred and twenty miles, and he's gone back to Los Angeles.* As she stood next to her car, looking at her in-laws' house and thinking about knocking on their door, something flashed in her head. *Oh wow, I know exactly where he is.*

Twenty minutes later, Rachel turned into the driveway of her in-laws' second home, a contemporary tri-level beige and white house at the end of a cul-de-sac at Lake Miramar.

Brett's white truck was in the driveway, and she parked behind him. She felt a cool breeze coming off the canyon, the fresh air soothed her. She rubbed the tension out of her neck as she walked to the front door; she felt like there was a hummingbird flitting around inside her. It was as if she was meeting Brett for the first time.

Before Rachel knocked, she raised her hand up to her nose and mouth to check her breath. She couldn't really smell anything, but just in case, she grabbed a couple of Tic Tacs out of her purse and popped them in her mouth. *It's now or never.*

She rang the doorbell, then waited for what seemed like forever. No answer. She rang the doorbell again, but after a few more minutes, realized that Brett wasn't there.

As she walked as fast as she could along the familiar path toward the reservoir, she thought about the first time she'd been there. She and Brett had been dating for four months when he invited her to come fishing, and he casually mentioned that she'd be meeting his parents. Rachel took two days to find just the right outfit. She wore boot-legged jeans paired with a tank top, an oversized blazer, and Dr. Martens. She didn't want his parents to think she was too straight-laced or too slutty; the balance had to be perfect.

The whole time Brett was driving to the lake house that day, Rachel couldn't stop drumming her fingers on her purse. She could've taken over for Ringo Starr by the time they arrived. When they pulled into the driveway, Brett's parents had rushed outside and hugged her as if she were already family. She found out later that she was the first girl Brett had brought home to meet them. The memory warmed her.

As Rachel neared the end of the path, she saw Brett sitting on a low beach chair near the edge of the water. The water was glistening, like the sapphire promise ring Brett had given her after they'd been dating for six months. It had been his grandmother's and Rachel had worn it on her right hand since the day he proposed.

Brett held his fishing pole but appeared to be staring off in the distance.

Rachel admired his profile. He'd barely aged since they met eight years ago; he had the same boyish face. His strong leg muscles were evident in the running shorts he wore, giving her goosebumps.

She was about to approach him when she saw his fishing pole jerk in his hand, and Brett jumped up to reel his line in. When he saw a trout on the end of the line, he radiated the pure joy of a six-year-old in line at the ice cream truck.

It felt like twenty years since the first time Brett taught her how to fish. She flashed back to the time she thought she'd caught something; she began waving her arms and dancing on her tiptoes, like a ballerina in her first point shoes. Brett instructed her exactly how to reel in the line without losing the fish, but Rachel had gotten so excited she almost fell in the water. He quickly grabbed her around the waist and helped her pull in what turned out to be something smaller than her childhood goldfish. The two of them couldn't stop laughing. Rachel was determined to be that couple again.

Brett had finished taking the trout off the line when Rachel called out to him. He turned toward her voice, his eyes fixed on her as if he didn't believe she was actually there. "Rachel?"

"Hi," she smiled, almost shyly.

"What are you doing here?" he asked, seeming surprised or thrown, or both, which wasn't the hello Rachel had hoped for.

"I wanted to see you. Nice catch, by the way," she pointed at the trout. He thanked her with a smile, but Rachel knew him well enough to see the sadness in his eyes.

He held the fishing pole out.

"You want to try?" he asked, and she nodded. He put a worm on the line for her, cast it into the lake, and handed her the pole. "I have a feeling you didn't drive all this way to come fishing."

"I've missed you so much," she said and paused hoping he'd say it back, but he didn't. "Do you miss me at all?"

"I do, but I don't miss the way we've been around each other."

"I know, and that's my fault." She looked at him, hoping he could see in her eyes how deeply sorry she was.

"I just wanted to be there for you." His face softened. "But you kept pushing me away."

"I know, I couldn't see beyond my own pain, so I couldn't think about what you were going through." She watched him carefully as she reached for his hand. She sighed inside when he didn't pull away.

"I was starting to resent you," he said, resigned. "I knew I had to leave before it got worse."

"I get why you felt that way. I started resenting you, too, for not wanting to get pregnant right away. I thought it was the solution for making this nightmare stop for both of us."

"It doesn't work that way."

"I get that now. I also know we need each other, not just as two people who want a baby, but as two people who love each other no matter what." Rachel wedged the fishing pole into the arm of the beach chair, then locked eyes with Brett.

Brett seemed to be staring deep into her soul. "Do you really mean that?"

"I can't live without you. If we never have a baby, I'll deal with it because losing you would kill me."

"All I ask is that you trust me enough to talk to me about anything." "I do . . . I will."

Brett's face relaxed into a huge smile. "Oh my god, I love you so much!" he said.

"I bet I love you more!" She leapt into his arms, and they held each other and kissed, then hugged, then kissed again.

"I do want to try to have a baby," he said. "And if that doesn't work out, then we can adopt. I think we'll make great parents."

Rachel felt like her cheeks were going to hurt from the biggest smile she'd ever felt. She took Brett's face in her hands and gave him a hard, passionate, kiss. She felt his mouth, his soft lips and luxurious tongue as he responded so fervidly. Every worry and negative thought disappeared.

"We'll wait to try again until we're *both* ready," Rachel said when they took a break. "Please come home." Before Brett could answer, a fish hit the line and Brett lunged for the fishing pole as it was being yanked toward the water. As he grabbed it, he fell into the lake.

When he stepped back on the shore, the fish had gotten away, and his clothes and shoes were dripping wet.

Rachel exploded in laughter. Brett grabbed her, picked her up, and held her over his shoulder as if he were going to throw her in. Rachel began joyfully screaming. She wasn't scared, she trusted that Brett would never do it. When he put her down, he shook the water from his hair and body onto her as if he were a dog, and she whacked him playfully.

"You have to come home now. After getting me all wet, you owe me," Rachel said.

"Fine, if I have to." He pretended to pout. Brett picked up the beach chair and Rachel grabbed the fishing pole, and they walked back to the house.

They decided to spend the night and go back home in the morning. Rachel called her mom, who was happy to go and feed the dogs. As Rachel was searching through the refrigerator, trying to decide what she could make for dinner with two hotdogs, yogurt and a carrot, Brett swept her up and carried her to the bedroom. The two of them made love as if it were the first time they were together. Afterwards, they lay in contented silence in bed, Brett on his back, Rachel with her head on his chest.

After a while, Rachel raised her head. "Oh, there's a huge life changing moment I forgot to tell you about. Something big," she said.

"Big, huh?" Brett said. "Let me guess, Molasses finally figured out that Honey stole her shark toy and hid it behind the rose bush." He smirked.

"A little more interesting. Remember Katie?"

"Yeah, did she have her baby?"

"She did."

"Cool," he said.

"And I found out that my mom is her biological mom."

Brett sat up quickly, accidentally knocking Rachel off him, "Wait, what? Is this a joke?"

"Does that beat a hidden shark toy?"

Brett stared at her. "Your mom is also Katie's mom?" He paused. "Is this for real?"

"Hard to believe, isn't it?"

Brett positioned himself over Rachel and looked into her eyes. "How are you doing with this?" he asked so gently and with so much love, that Rachel wished she could bottle up the way she was feeling.

"I couldn't sleep the night I found out," she said. "This morning my mom came over and we talked, and I get why she never told me. It's the same reason I may not tell anyone that we were going to abort our daughter. Some things are too painful to talk about."

Brett laid back down. "So, Katie's your half-sister." Brett said this as if he was trying to wrap his head around it.

"Uh huh." Rachel said. "And her baby is my niece . . . and yours."

"Wow." Brett sat with this for a moment. "It makes sense now why you and Katie got so close so fast. You usually take longer to get to know someone, but I just chalked it up to you both were going through a similar situation."

"I guess there's no fighting biology."

"I need to spend some time getting to know my new sister-in-law and niece."

"I'm sure that can be arranged."

"I would say a lot has happened in the last six weeks," he said.

"It did, so don't ever leave again." Rachel got on top of Brett and began kissing his neck.

"I don't think that's going to be an issue," he said, flipping her over, and making love to her again.

Chapter Twenty-Two
Katie

Three months postpartum

Katie felt like she should set up a tent and sleeping bag and camp out in both the pediatrician and the cardiologist's office since Olivia had surgery. Every time she stepped through their doors, she was racked with worry that she'd be told Olivia wasn't healing correctly, or that her heart was in trouble again.

"Thank you for coming with me to today," Katie said to Daniel. "I'm hoping this will be the last appointment until she can drive herself."

"I'd go anywhere with you two."

"I appreciate that, it can get lonely sitting here. Olivia doesn't exactly keep up her share of the conversation." Katie gestured to Olivia, whose eyes were as wide as saucers as she focused on the

Looney Tunes cartoon wallpaper. "I keep asking myself how I got lucky enough to find you."

"You're one blessed woman," Daniel said and bowed to her. "Make that two blessed women." He gently patted the top of Olivia's head.

"This one's just in training."

"I feel like I'm the one in training," Katie said.

"You're doing great in my book." Daniel walked around the room, picking up all the equipment. He examined the otoscope and the tongue depressor, and he used the reflex hammer on both knees. An infant scale at the end of the exam table had a plastic tub on top of a digital readout. Daniel placed his hand on it and checked out what it weighed.

"This is like a bigger version of my food scale," Daniel said. "Do you think Olivia is as heavy as a small turkey?" Olivia fussed in Katie's arms.

"Like any woman, she doesn't like comments on her weight," Katie said.

As Olivia continued to get antsy, Daniel made goofy faces at her. He crossed his eyes and stuck out his tongue and did a raspberry on her belly. Olivia stopped fussing and looked at him intently, then let out a tiny hiccup.

"That's so cute," Daniel said.

Katie patted Daniel on the shoulder. "Keep acting like a nut, she's loving it," Katie said and handed Olivia to him.

"Did you ever hear back from the text you sent to Rachel?" Daniel asked in between the silly faces. Olivia continued to hiccup happily.

"No. It's been two days and I'm worried that I ruined everything with my friend."

"You mean your sister," Daniel corrected.

"I'm still trying to get used to saying that."

"Give Rachel time, she just found out not only that her mother had another daughter, but that now she has a sister and niece."

"It may be a blessing for me, but it must be weird for her to have a sibling come out of the woodwork."

"I guess, but she'll realize how much she misses you."

"I hope so." Katie joined Daniel and made her own goofy faces at Olivia, who started fussing again. Katie took Olivia from Daniel and they decided to change tactics.

They began singing the children's song, "Where is Thumbkin" to keep her entertained. "Where is Thumbkin? Where is Thumbkin? Here I am! Here I am!" Katie and Daniel sang loudly and made their thumbs dance. "How are you today, sir? Very well, I thank you . . ."

As they continued, Katie was startled by Dr. Pine, who suddenly opened the door. She stopped singing, her face turning red.

"Don't worry, I've come upon much more embarrassing situations," Dr. Pine said. "I've walked in on couples yelling at each other, and one time a couple was trying to make another baby on the exam table. You guys singing a silly song to your baby is refreshing. Besides, I love that song," the doctor said and made his thumb dance for a beat.

Katie brought Olivia to the exam table, and Dr. Pine examined her. Katie watched every move the doctor made to see if she could detect any signs that indicated that something was wrong.

"You have one strong little girl here. She's healing perfectly," Dr. Pine said as Olivia grabbed his stethoscope and pulled the doctor closer, trying to put it in her mouth.

"Thank God," Katie said, trying to pry Olivia's grip open before she choked the doctor.

Dr. Pine handed Olivia back to Katie. "Keep doing whatever you're doing."

Daniel came up beside Katie, and Olivia gurgled happily as she reached out for Daniel.

"She sure loves her daddy," the doctor said, then wished them a nice day and left.

"He thought I was your father," Daniel said, gazing down at Olivia. "That's because we're both so adorable, although you drool a little more than I do."

I only wish you were her father, Katie thought, then picked up the diaper bag and headed toward the door.

"Wait, shouldn't we make out on the exam table?" Daniel asked.

"No, but maybe in the waiting room. We could give all those other tired parents something to talk about."

"That would be mean; they'd all be jealous of how much I love you," he said.

* * *

Just before two-thirty, Katie pulled into the elementary school parking lot. Rachel still hadn't texted Katie back, so Katie decided to take things into her own hands. She watched moms and dads greet their kids as the children ran joyfully into their open arms.

Katie couldn't believe that someday Olivia would be one of those kids and she'd be the one with her arms outstretched.

Olivia is going to be five, then ten, then seventeen, and then she'll be drinking underage, and I'll have to pick her up from a party and ground her, Katie thought. *Damnit, Olivia, I can't believe you'd put me through all that. Oh, Katie, get yourself under control, she's not even teething yet.*

Katie got out of her car when she saw Rachel walking toward her, totally focused on juggling her laptop, purse, and her keys.

"Hi, Rachel," Katie said.

Rachel looked up and stumbled, then recovered and mumbled "What're you doing here?"

"You never answered my texts."

"I wasn't sure what to say." Rachel looked around. "Where's Olivia?"

"With your mom."

"You mean our mom." Rachel hit the button on her key fob and her car chirped as it unlocked.

"Are you mad at me?" Katie asked gently.

"I'm not sure what I am." Rachel reached across the driver's seat and put her computer and purse in her car.

"I get that you're thrown, but I'm the one who got screwed. You had two parents who loved you and took care of you, and I spent my childhood cleaning up my mother's vomit. I'm sorry I intruded on your life and screwed everything up for you," Katie said, a little harshly.

Rachel paused. "You're right, I shouldn't have taken anything out on you. None of this is your fault. I've never had to share my mom, so you're going to have to give me a break while I get used to all this."

"We both have to get used to it. I just found out I was adopted. The people who raised me weren't the best parents, but they were the only ones I knew. Now I don't feel like I belong anywhere."

Rachel sighed. "I admit, I hadn't thought about how you must feel, she said, and she sounded sincere.

"If you need me to stay away from you and your mom right now, I will," Katie said.

"That wouldn't be fair to you or her." Rachel's voice was softer.

"Before all this happened, we were really good friends. Why don't we just concentrate on that for now?"

"I think I can do that."

Katie's jaw relaxed; she and Rachel exhaled at the same time. "We have to get one thing clear, though," Katie said seriously.

"What's that?

"You may be my sister, but I'm not going to be sharing my clothes with you." Katie winked.

"If I have to share my mom, you have to share anything I find in your closet."

"You're a pushy thing," Katie said.

"Get used to it. This is what happens when you have a little sister." They both laughed hard, then snorted.

Katie suggested they go get a cup of coffee.

"If we can substitute ice cream for coffee, I'm in," Rachel said. They agreed to meet at the Baskin Robbins a few blocks away.

Katie got there first and sighed with pleasure at the big pink and blue B and R on the sign. Baskin Robbins brought back good memories of when she was seven and her mother only drank at night.

Katie was sitting at a table, still thinking about her mother, when Rachel came in.

"You okay?" Rachel asked.

"Yeah, I was just remembering something about my early childhood. There were some days after school, my mom would take me to 31 Flavors, and as I ate my favorite kind of ice cream, she'd ask tons of questions about my day. She seemed so interested and I loved the attention, but on the drive home I'd get really sad. I knew that in a few hours, she would be a different person. I don't think I realized why at the time, I just knew on good nights, she'd ignore me and fall asleep early on the couch, but on the bad nights she'd berate me endlessly."

"Oh wow, that's awful," Rachel said.

"I realize now it was like living with my own Mr. Hyde. I would sit in my room and pray for her to turn back into the nice mom, but now I can see that she was Dr. Jekyll far more."

They got in line to order. Katie said, "Ice cream is on me."

"Is that what older sisters do?"

"Sure."

Rachel thanked her. "Then next time it's on me," she said.

They were waiting behind a couple in their teens. The boy was arguing with the girl about wanting to pay for her ice cream, but the girl wanted to pay her way.

"In a minute, I'm going to pay for both their ice creams," Katie said.

Finally, the couple got their cones and moved on. While Rachel ordered, Katie carefully scanned every tub and considered every flavor.

Rachel took her cone from the cashier and licked it.

"What did you get?" Katie asked.

"My favorite, pralines and cream. Don't tell me that you're going to order that too."

"Nope."

"Finally, something we don't have in common," Rachel said.

Katie ordered mint chip and they went back to their table. They both ate the bottom of their waffle cone first. "I have a confession to make," Katie said.

"Oh no, pralines and cream is your favorite, too, isn't it?" Rachel said.

Katie raised her eyebrows and shrugged her shoulders.

"Seriously?" Rachel said.

"No, I'm just screwing with you."

Rachel swatted her lightly and they went back to eating.

"Do you think it will be hard for you to get used to me being your half-sister?" Katie asked.

Rachel didn't say anything.

Katie's heart sped up, and even though the ice cream was chilling her insides, she felt her underarms start to perspire. "Why aren't you saying anything?" she asked. "Don't you think you can do that?"

"Now I'm screwing with you," Rachel said.

Katie playfully swatted her back. "Has anything happened with you and Brett?" she asked.

"Yes. He's home and we're working things out."

"Yeah?"

"Yeah. In the shower . . . on the kitchen counter . . . in the backyard," Rachel said, blushing.

"I'm glad, but I didn't need to know where."

"And in spite of all the terrible things I said about you, he still really wants to spend some time with my new half-sister." Rachel stuck her tongue out at Katie.

Katie pretended to try to grab Rachel's tongue, and Rachel screamed in laughter.

"And I want to get to know Daniel," Rachel said, then suggested the four of them go out one night.

"That would be fun," Katie said, "but I need a little more time to get to know him myself before I spring my new family on him."

"Good idea. We are a scary bunch," Rachel said.

"I also have to find childcare, although fortunately, we both know an older lady who'd make a great babysitter," Katie said.

Rachel chuckled. "Don't use her up before I need her to babysit for my kid someday."

"When Leah realizes that Olivia has perfected the art of an exploding diaper, she'll never babysit again."

"You don't know our mom," Rachel said, "she'll be bragging about it to all her friends."

* * *

A few months later, Daniel and Katie walked up Hollywood Blvd holding hands. They approached a dark building, except for the neon sign that read 'Lucky Strike' in bright red letters, with a giant blue bowling pin.

"I haven't bowled in years," Daniel said.

"Me either, but Rachel and Brett thought it would be a fun place to meet."

Daniel and Katie were stuck at the door behind four obvious high schoolers who were trying to convince the bouncer that they were twenty-one. Finally, the bouncer waved Daniel and Katie in.

"I hope Brett likes me because now I'm his sister-in-law," Katie said.

"He's going to love you as much as I do."

"I hope not as much, I wouldn't want to piss Rachel off." Katie winked at him.

"Okay, then he can love you half as much as I do," Daniel said.

They got bowling shoes then picked out their bowling balls and headed over to the lane Rachel and Brett were on, which was lit up by navy blue neon lights.

"Hi Rachel," Katie said, hugging her. Then she turned to Brett.

"Hi, Brett."

"Hey, sis," Brett said.

Katie couldn't contain her happiness at his warm greeting.

"Is it okay if I give you a hug?" he asked.

"Absolutely!" As she hugged him, she looked at Rachel over her shoulder, "I guess you didn't tell him horrible things about me."

"Oh, she did," Brett said, laughing. "I'm just incredibly forgiving."

"Brett, this is the famous Daniel," Rachel said.

"Famous, huh? That's a lot to live up to," Daniel said, shaking Brett's hand.

"Yep, Katie never stops talking about you," Rachel said.

Daniel leaned into Rachel. "Later you'll have to tell me everything she said."

"She can't, there's a super-secret sister code that I just made up," Katie said.

The background music consisted of old rock and roll hits, mixed in with some new ones. Two lanes over from them a bachelorette party with eight women wearing sashes and tiaras were chattering.

Brett listed all their names on the electronic board. He asked if they wanted to play in teams to make it more interesting, and Rachel suggested they play as couples. Katie sidled up to Rachel and whispered in her ear.

"I think the first game should be boys against girls," Rachel said.

"Should we give them a nice handicap?" Brett asked Daniel.

"No, we're fine," Katie said.

Daniel was up first, followed by Rachel, then Brett, and Katie. Rachel knocked down more pins than Brett and Daniel added together. When it was Katie's turn, she put her hands over the blower on the ball return like a professional. She scrunched up her forehead as she concentrated intensely, then threw the ball down the lane. The pins ricocheted off each other as the ball crashed into them. The video screen at the end of the lane lit up with a dancing bowling pin with the word STRIKE written across it.

Rachel and Katie high-fived.

Neither Daniel nor Brett knocked down many pins on their next few turns, while Katie got spares, another strike, and Rachel got no less than nine pins on each turn.

"Are we being hustled?" Brett asked Daniel.

Rachel winked at Katie, and Katie admitted that in high school she had been in a bowling league that won the championship for her school district.

"And you didn't think to mention that?" Daniel asked.

"There are so many things you don't know about me," Katie flirted.

"I look forward to finding out all of them." Daniel kissed her.

When they'd finished their second game, Rachel and Brett sat to switch from their bowling shoes to their street shoes. Katie sat across from them to do the same.

Daniel got down on a knee as if he were taking off his shoes, but instead, he took Katie's hand and pulled out a ring box. "Katie, I . . ."

"Oh my god, are you really proposing in a bowling alley?" Katie exclaimed.

"Yes, now be quiet so I can finish."

Rachel nudged Brett and watched as if it were a reality TV show.

Daniel continued, "Since my mother passed away, I haven't felt like I belonged anywhere. Until I met you. Over these last seven months, you've become the most important person in my life, and I love you more than I ever thought I'd love anyone. Watching you go through everything to find your family; I realized that I wanted you to be my family. I adore Olivia, and I want to be the father in her life that you and I never had. So, Katie Marie Doherty, will you honor me for the rest of my life by marrying me?"

"Yes, yes, yes! I want nothing more than to be your wife."

Rachel and Brett cheered as Katie grabbed Daniel and laid a big kiss on him. The women at the bachelorette party screamed and cheered for them.

"Yay, another bride!" one of the women yelled over. "Congrats!"

Katie gave them a thumbs up, then turned to Daniel. "Now let me see that ring." She held out her hand as Daniel pulled the ring out of the box and placed it on Katie's finger.

Katie held out her hand to show Rachel and Brett. "I'm engaged!" she screamed, then started crying.

"I hope that's a happy cry," Daniel said.

"It's an ecstatic one," Katie said.

Rachel took Katie's hand and admired the ring, then she hugged them both.

Brett shook Daniel's hand. "Welcome to the family."

Epilogue
Seven Months Later
Katie

Rachel and Sandra peeked out of the French doors that led from Rachel's parents' bedroom to their backyard. Katie twirled in an ivory lace strapless gown with a long veil draping down her back.

Leah knocked on the bedroom door, then came in with Olivia in her arms. Olivia wore a pink and gold lace dress with goldfish crumbs decorating her face and neck. When she saw Katie, she smiled from ear to ear and reached out to her.

"Mommy doesn't need your special brand of orange drool on her wedding dress," Leah said, Olivia squirming in her arms. Leah set her down and turned to Katie. "You look amazing."

"Doesn't she?" Sandra said.

"Thanks, I'm nervous," Katie said, "What happens if I trip on my dress, or have to pee during the ceremony?"

"If you trip, then we'll catch you, but if you have to pee, you're on your own," Rachel said. "Besides, if anyone is going to have to pee, it's me." Rachel said, pulling the maternity panel of her silver bridesmaid's dress away from her burgeoning belly. "I can't wait for when my son and Olivia can play together."

Olivia used the nightstand to pull herself up to standing, wobbling as she tried to reach for Katie's bouquet. Katie grabbed her bouquet. Olivia howled in frustration.

"Just don't blame me if Olivia teaches him some bad habits," Katie said as Leah tried to soothe Olivia by giving her one of her purses to hold.

Sandra looked at the time. "Are you ready?" she asked Katie.

"I've never been more ready."

Rachel opened the door to the hallway and gestured to Brett, and he came over to get Olivia, who was still holding onto Leah's purse. Sandra took her cue and was about to open the double doors to the backyard when she suddenly stopped. "Wait, do you have something borrowed or something blue?"

Leah gasped. "I knew I was forgetting something!" She moved quickly to her dresser. After rummaging through her drawer, dropping lingerie all over the floor, she pulled out a blue garter. "This was my mother's, and I wore it at my wedding, and Rachel wore it at hers. It's something borrowed and something blue. I hope you'll wear it, too."

Katie nodded, and with tears in her eyes, she let her friend and sister slip it up her leg.

"My dear friend," Sandra said to Katie. "You deserve this happiness more than anyone I know." She gave Katie a hug and an air kiss toward her cheek. "I'll see you on the other side," Sandra said, opening one of the doors and stepping out.

Katie could hear "Bless the Broken Road" by Rascal Flatts playing outside.

Katie watched through the window as Sandra made her way down the aisle, the ruffle at the bottom of her chiffon dress waltzing to the music.

"Your turn," Rachel said.

Katie took a deep breath.

"Let's get this show on the road," Leah said.

Rachel opened the doors, and she and Leah each took one of Katie's arms. Stepping out together, they headed across the grass toward the white runner that ran along the middle of the backyard. There were folding chairs on each side of the aisle and sixty-five of Katie's and Daniel's loved ones were chatting with each other.

At the end of the aisle, Father George was talking to Daniel, who was fidgeting nervously.

Father George looked at Katie, then asked everyone to stand up, and the wedding march began. All heads turned toward Katie, Rachel, and Leah as they walked slowly down the runner toward the arch decorated with white and pink lilies.

Daniel locked his eyes on Katie. His face brightened with a joyous expression. Katie's eyes got misty. *Thank god for waterproof mascara,* she thought. As she got closer to Daniel, she noticed he had tears in his eyes, too.

When Katie, Leah, and Rachel arrived at the end of the aisle, Father George asked, "Who gives this woman away?"

Leah and Rachel answered, "We do."

Leah took her seat in the front row next to Ezra, Brett, and

Olivia. Rachel moved alongside Sandra as Katie handed Sandra her bouquet.

Daniel took Katie's hands. "You're the most beautiful woman I've ever seen," he said quietly.

Katie felt all lit up. "I'm so grateful you came into my life. I'm also grateful you didn't tell me I had something in my teeth."

"I'd still marry you even if you had no teeth at all," Daniel said.

"What if I had only one right in the front?" Katie said.

"Now, that would be sexy," Daniel said.

"Would you two like me to marry you before I'm so old *I* have no teeth?" Father George asked jokingly.

Katie and Daniel turned toward the priest, and Father George began, "Dearly beloved, we are gathered here today to join this man and this woman . . ."

ACKNOWLEDGMENTS

There are a number of individuals, who contributed to this book through their support, their love, and their loyalty. I am grateful they're in my life, and I hope I've given back to them, as much as they've given to me.

I want to acknowledge my sons, Hunter, and Jake. Above everything else I've done in my life, I'm the proudest of helping raise both of you. You're talented, creative, and loving young men, and the world is a better place with you both in it. And the best part is you actually like being around your dad and me.

Bruce, words can't describe how much I appreciate you. We've been through a lot together, and there's no one else I'd want beside me as I get old . . . although I'm not planning on getting old. I can't wait to have many more adventures together.

I want to thank TouchPoint Press, especially Sheri Williams, Ashley Carlson, Kimberly Coghlan and Gina Denny for believing in this novel, and helping it come to life. I'm thrilled to be working with all of you. I'd also like to give a shout out to David Ter-Avanesyan. The book cover you designed was exactly on point. Your artistic talent doesn't go unappreciated.

I want to acknowledge pr machine's team of Mike Liotta, Rachel Hosseini and Grace Topalian for believing in me and the novel. I'm exciting to work with all of you and have you shine a light on my book.

To Annie Tucker, an incredibly talented developmental editor. Your help from beginning to end on this novel made it possible for me not to give up. I also looked forward to talking to you on the phone every other week, I consider you more than an editor, you're also my friend.

Melissa Gelineau, I wouldn't trust anyone else with my first draft. You're unbelievably generous with your time and you give the most insightful notes. Your experience and wisdom, and your help have been priceless.

To Suzanne Simonetti and Meg Nocero. I couldn't have made it through a day, let alone this whole journey without your friendship, your wisdom, your texts, and all the laughter. I adore both of you and plan to keep you around forever . . . if you'll have me and I'm not giving you a choice about that.

To Lori Wilson, you've been part of my life for more years than I want to count. And remember, we aren't old, we're still the same giggly teenagers we were when we met, just a few more lines around our eyes. I adore you, and I couldn't ask for a better friend, or confidant.

Jill Campbell, I never could've known that having a baby would also bring about a friendship that has been so special. We've watched our children grow up together and your calm, warm, loving demeaner has comforted me, especially when things were tough. Words can't come close to expressing my gratitude and how much you mean to me.

To Debi Pomerantz—Thank you for your friendship and support with my writing. You're always there to talk about a story or give me your opinion on a scene. I can't tell you how much that means to me.

A shoutout to my dear friends, Cayla Schneider, Erin Semper, Susan Nathanson, and Cindy Baron, and Lee Bukowski. You've all been a shining light in my life, and I'm honored to call each one of you my close friends.

To Liani Kotcher and Valerie Taylor for your insight and marketing talents. You've taught me so much and your kindness and support have been a gift to me.

A shoutout to Libby Jordan. Your help and advice and expertise in everything marketing has been incredible. You go above and beyond for your clients, and I'm grateful to have you in my life.

I want to acknowledge Julie Chan. You've been a wonderful surprise in my life. Not only do I consider you a good friend but being interviewed by you has been a wonderful boost for my career. Thank you for all your help.

I have met so many wonderful, talented, and supportive authors along the way. I wish I could mention you all by name, but you've been kind enough to buy my books, share my posts on Facebook and Instagram, and whether we met in person or on zoom, I consider you all friends.

Words can't express how much I appreciate Katherine Rieder and her excitement and cheerleading skills for my book. Yes, she's my mother, but she has gotten so many people to buy it, whether they wanted to or not. I'm lucky to have such a supportive person in my corner. And to my father, Howard Rieder, who is no longer with us. I hope he knows what a big influence his life and writing played on me. I love you, Dad, you were a force in my life, I wish you had been alive when my first novel was published, but I know you're looking down and getting a kick out of it.

To my older sister, Dee O'Reilly, and my younger sister, Linda Gardner, I wouldn't want to go through life without both of you. When the three of us are together, we're always laughing and sharing stories. I'm grateful that mom and dad blessed me with both of you.

Lastly, I want to send love to all the women I know, and the ones I don't that have fallen in love with the baby they were carrying only to have to go through the trauma of terminating that pregnancy. You're my heroes. You've battled so much in life and come out on the other end. Don't ever let anyone shame you for the difficult choices you had to make.

Thank you so much for reading The Stories We Cannot Tell. If you've enjoyed the book, we would be grateful if you would post a review on the bookseller's website. Just a few words is all it takes!

Leslie loves visiting book clubs either virtually or in person if you are in the Los Angeles area. Reach out on her website: https://www.lesliearasmussen.com

If you'd like to read another book by Leslie A. Rasmussen, her award-winning novel After Happily Ever After is available anywhere books are sold.

9 781956 851601